The History Maker

By

Eamonn Hickson

THE HISTORY MAKER
ISBN-13:
978-1478260899
ISBN-10:
1478260890

Paperback version originally published 2012

Acknowledgements

I would like to extend my thanks to a number of people:

Firstly, I would like to thank my sister Rose Hickson, editor-in–chief. Since she first read The History Maker, she has given such excellent advice on each and every draft. Her editing, proofreading and opinions were literally invaluable since I began writing this book in January 2010. I may have gotten sick of seeing the same story throughout each draft and edit, but Rose found new energy every time I asked her to re-read the novel, an energy I simply did not have. Also, I'd like to thank her for giving me the confidence to continue writing and finish this story with her words of praise, I really appreciate it. Her enthusiasm has been contagious, more especially in the weeks leading up to the final draft. It is likely that this book would not be published without Rose's input.

I would also like to thank Carmel Dixon, a woman who I only know a matter of months, but who brought a wonderful understanding to the characters and storyline. After reading a previous draft, Carmel spoke about the characters as if they were her best friends. I benefitted massively from her advice, as she threw such an educated and insightful eye on the cast of the book. Her words of encouragement were particularly appreciated, considering her experience and knowledge of books and novels.

To Kerry Williams, the first person, aside from me, to set eyes on the characters Adam and Britney, and the first person I told that I like to write. Her reaction helped me immeasurably, giving me the confidence to continue writing, which eventually led to this publication.

To everyone who read previous drafts of the book, especially Pat and Nora McKenna. I owe them an apology - I think I ruined a weekend break away for them, as they had to lug an A4 copy of my book around. I really appreciate you taking the time to read it and your feedback. To Paddy Hickson, who read the book and strangely did not ask too many questions about it, which was encouraging in itself. To Michelle O Connor, who has given me such support over the last few months, and urged me to keep pressing on with getting it self-published. Her advice and input to the cover, Facebook profile, website and launch night is unbelievably appreciated, and of course needed. Thank you so much.

To my family, friends and everyone who been really encouraging since they heard about this novel, I will not forget it. To the members of absolutewrite.com/watercooler, who helped me over the years with great advice and picky critiques on my writing, your expertise has been welcomed and appreciated. To all the shops and bookstores who stock copies of this book.

To you, the reader.

History has demonstrated that the most notable winners usually encountered heartbreaking obstacles before they triumphed. They won because they refused to become discouraged by their defeats.
- B.C. Forbes

The History Maker

Chapter 1

Madison pressed his face against the blacked out window pane. Even in the dimly lit room, the glass returned a frail reflection. Grey hairs, wrinkled skin, a frown. Pain etched itself on Madison's features, adding an evident torture to the ghostly image that stared back at him. Over the years, his relative seclusion meant he bothered little with personal upkeep. He shaved just to keep the greying beard from his face. He ignored the permanent bags that found residence under his eyes. It did not matter anyway, it was all for her, and she was gone.

Memories circled inside Madison, finding his heart with ease. Where there existed a dazzling, beautiful image of his lost wife, there also lived an opposite. Light and dark, life and death. The memories of that day never let Madison rest, replaying like an advert, until he woke every morning with the soundtrack in his ears and the images in his mind.

Madison stepped back from the window pane and opened his palm. Sweat glimmered on a tiny black box as Madison raised it to his lips and kissed it. A life without her is not a life, he told himself. She was gone, the man responsible for her death lived a happy life. Madison lowered the black box to the ground and whispered, "See you soon my angel."

<u>Boston, Massachusetts</u>
<u>Present day</u>

A man lay in bed, his eyes flickered open for an instant. *Where am I?* Reaching for a memory, he found a throbbing. He tried to move but pain shot through his body, forcing him to stop. Blinding whiteness from the surrounds stung at his fragile eyes as low murmurs found his ears.

A faint voice called, "Adam?"

He struggled to put a name and face to the voice, it was like trying to climb a slide with the water rushing downwards. A warm hand held his fingers.

"It's ok, don't worry! Can you open your eyes?" said the gentle voice. He opened his eyes fully, adjusting to the irritation.

"How are you feeling?" the voice asked. The man turned towards the woman next to his bed and saw a homely smile on her face. His vision cleared enough to show the woman's uniform, a nurse.

"Adam? Are you ok?" Facing the nurse, he asked, "Why do you keep calling me Adam?"

***

Britney sat in the long hospital corridor. Stroking the petals of her gift, lifeless sunflowers which were gathered in a hurry, her trembling hands failed to hide a growing fear. A dull scent drifted up from the flowers, asking Britney what she meant to accomplish with such a trivial gift. Passing trolleys with Boston's newest accident and emergency guests did little to take Britney's mind from Adam. Her eyes were too sore to cry anymore. She had never cried so much, her body knew that, her memories knew that. Worry circulated like a poison in her blood, she needed to know how Adam was, no other way to wash out the toxin.

Adam's father stepped out into the hallway from a ward, his gaze found Britney. She turned towards him, waiting for an expression to let her know Adam was ok. A relieved smile crept onto his face, feeling like a surge of painkillers flowing through Britney. She glanced upwards quickly and then stepped towards Adam's father. His embrace let Britney relax, but only for the slightest moment, as reality doubled back and snapped Britney out of her false security.

"Barry, I..." Britney stuttered as she leaned away from Adam's father.

"Adam is awake," Adam's father interrupted. His eyes danced awkwardly.

"What are you not telling me?" she asked, searching his face for answers, a now familiar pang of worry pulsing through her body again.

"Adam has suffered memory loss."

"...Amnesia?" Britney asked, shaking her head and lowering the bunch of flowers.

"He doesn't even remember us." Adam's father leaned closer and hugged her gently. Unsure of how to act, Britney let her arms tighten around him.

"Can I see him?"

As Adam lay in bed, he had seen a beautiful young woman speaking to the man who claimed to be his father, in the doorway. He had watched them embrace, seen the distress etched on their faces, apparently sorrow poured out for him and his current predicament.

Nothing registered.

The young woman stepped into the ward and walked towards Adam, struggling to keep her eyes on him. Flowers were clenched tightly in her grasp, slender fingers curled around the ribbon-tied stems. Her small but defined frame moved delicately past the other patients in the ICU, as if careful not to upset anyone. A nurse at the window drew across the curtain, dimming the dazzling sun that bounded off the tiled floor. A sympathetic smile sneaked onto her face as she approached Adam's bedside.

"Hi Adam," she said delicately. Her face changed, her forehead creased as she leaned closer.

"You can't remember me?"

Silent, Adam knew his face told the whole story. She placed the yellow flowers on a nearby locker and sat on the bed.

Adam did not feel a need to explain himself, he was the injured party. His eyes scanned the young woman's face, his brain worked overtime to make a link with the past. He studied her white skin, her blue eyes and her blonde curly hair which draped over her black t-shirt. Knowing it was far from a one-way exam, Adam watched his guest staring at his forehead, there must be something there. Her inquisitive eyes darted over him and to the tubes connected to his arms.

Reaching for Adam's hand, she whispered, "Britney, my name is Britney." Adam tried to recognise her hand, tried to make a connection between her soft skin and his.

Again, there was nothing.

He lay back in the bed and stared at the ceiling. He drew his hands close to his face, looked at the drips connected to his veins, and took a deep breath.

"How did I get here?" he whispered to Britney.

Britney hesitated for a moment before shaking her head.

"I don't think it's my place to tell you that."

"Are you not my friend?" Adam asked.

"Oh yes, yes I am. But I think I should wait for your parents to tell you."

"What will it matter if, you, claiming to be my friend, tell me, or some people, claiming to be my parents, tell me?" he sighed,

"Either way, I don't know any of you."

Britney eased herself off the bed and sat in a nearby chair. Combing her hair back with her hand, she turned towards Adam.

"You were in a car accident."

He nodded, trying to put it together in his head.

"Was I driving? Was anyone else hurt?"

Britney sat upright in her chair, "No, you were not driving. We don't know who was driving!"

Adam rubbed his head as if searching for answers in his hair. He tried to put the words together in his mind, but they came out in bits.

5

"So...I wasn't driving, and I got hurt, but there was no one else in the car?"

"Yeah, we don't know who was driving."

"Did they flee?"

Britney seemed to take a moment to align the words, and nodded.

A silence developed in the room as Adam tried to come to terms with his situation. He could see Britney was trying to console her *friend* in his dilemma. Her soft hands travelled along the bed sheet and held Adam's cold fingers. A squeeze injected a brief shot of comfort into Adam. Britney leaned in and placed a lingering kiss on Adam's forehead.

"I can understand how tough this is, I'll let you get some rest," Britney said.

"Thanks," Adam said, unsure of what else to say to this unknown woman. As he stared at the flowers on the nearby locker, words jumped around in his head. *I want to remember you, yet I can't.*

Adam decided to say the only thing that seemed to make sense, "I'm sorry for not remembering."

"You will remember in time Adam, don't worry. For now, you need to rest."

Adam lay back in the bed.

"See you soon," Britney whispered.

Adam watched her leave, for a moment the pain disappeared. He wondered was she a good friend? Was she always just a friend? Was there ever something more? He shook his head, ridding himself of such thoughts, for now.

In the hospital corridor, Britney exhaled a deep breath, letting relief in and stress out. Extra lights along the hallway flickered on as night time approached. A nearby door alarm rang, followed by a chill passing through the hallway, possibly some patient who failed to drive away a nicotine urge. As Britney reached into her pocket for her phone, a quick glance around ensured she was not being watched. Her fingers darted on the illuminated buttons, numbers popped up on screen, *call*. Britney swallowed hard as she heard the buzzing ring.

A voice answered on the other side, coarse and tough, "Yeah?"

"He doesn't remember," Britney whispered into the phone, her hand cupped around the mouthpiece.

"Did he say anything about me?" the voice asked.

"No, not a thing, he doesn't even remember me."

"Good." The line went dead. Britney watched the phone for a moment, and then lowered it into her pocket.

Chapter 2

Adam stared at the white bread sandwich on his plate, pressing on the crumbs to pick them up. The simple ham and cheese resembled the basic decorations in Boston's City Hospital. A nurse had earlier said that the curtains must remain drawn, so as not to cause discomfort to the other patients in the room. Just a glimpse of sunlight may have lifted Adam's mood, but he did not have the energy to explain. Anyway, he figured there were people far worse off than him in the room.

The old man directly across from him had not moved since Adam woke up. Maybe he was dead, Adam pondered. The next bed was a different story. That woman was definitely alive, her screams during the night kept Adam awake. He did not hear what happened, but as she was taken out of the ward for two operations in the last twelve hours, something serious must have occurred. The sedatives were doing their job for the last few hours, a random moan the only sound. A man, presumably her husband, had kept a bedside vigil since Adam regained consciousness, eighteen hours and counting. On Adam's right hand side, a man lay motionless, his body almost covered in casts. A cable held his leg up, swaying whenever the man spoke to relatives.

The man and woman who claimed to be Adam's parents, Barry and Erin, came into the ward and sat by the bed. Despite having no recollection of either of them, Adam felt sorry for them as his *mother* crouched close. She rubbed Adam's cast-covered legs, "The doctors say it will take time for you to remember us."

Erin's face trembled for an instant, until she forced her lips together and suppressed what Adam assumed was a tear. He tried to grasp how big the situation really was, but he still felt no connection to the woman kneeling next to his bed. He waited for a director to shout *CUT!* Then these *actors* can return to their real lives, a life without him.

Barry had brought a photo album into the ward. He placed it on Adam's lap, opening the first page. Pulling it closer, Adam's eyes focused on a recent family portrait. Instantaneously, he built the first bridge in his mind,

"This is me, isn't it?"

A smile came to his parents face, their first time smiling since Adam woke up. He stared at the picture of himself, a sense of what seemed like Déjà Vu rushed through him. *A memory?*

"This is a recent picture?"

Erin nodded, "Two years ago, your 23rd birthday."

The next two hours were spent going through the photo album, every picture explained in detail to Adam. Every few pages, he flicked back to a particular photo; one of himself and Britney laughing together on the couch. Adam craved to remember that moment, seeing Britney's slender fingers intertwined with his, her blue eyes looking nowhere else but at him.

A doctor entered the ward. He nodded to Adam's parents and then turned his attention to Adam.

"Hello Adam, how are you feeling today?" his tone was quick and sharp. Adam read *Dr. Gardenia* on the doctor's name badge, which was clipped onto an unusually casual brown-striped jumper and chords, all of which didn't quite fit the stereotype of a doctor.

"Sore, my legs are still numb."

The words had just left Adam's mouth when the doctor spoke again, making it clear the first question was routine. Even if he claimed he was dying there and then, Adam felt it would not have registered with Dr. Gardenia.

"Now that the initial swelling has gone down, I have scheduled a scan for later today, which will show the full extent of your injuries," he said plainly. Erin's nod sufficed, as Dr. Gardenia gave the smallest wave goodbye and turned to leave again.

"He must be getting paid per patient," Adam remarked, as a smile broke out on his face.

***

The next morning was different. The curtains were open, the grey sky stared in the window and droplets of rain sped down the glass like tiny ants. Adam wondered why they shielded the patients from the sun, yet gave them a front row ticket to the rain-show. Some kind of mental toughening the only reason that seemed to make sense to him. Even the nurses were in on the act, failing to greet

Adam with the same enthusiasm as the previous mornings, just a smile as they wheeled his bed towards the elevator.

Dr. Gardenia's office was a light blue, but being on the west side of the building coloured the room in a darker shade. The nurses rolled Adam in on his bed, raising the back so he could see Dr. Gardenia. Barry and Erin walked in and stood on either side of Adam's bed. The doctor seemed more professional this morning, wearing a black shirt, covered with a long white coat and black pants underneath.

Sitting behind his desk, Dr. Gardenia opened the MRI scan results. Rain trickling down the window pane caught Adam's attention as it took other droplets on its journey. Adam searched the doctor's eyes for a telltale sign, a silent precursor to the results, only to find nothing.

Dr. Gardenia held the results in his left hand.

"The stitches will be removed in a few days time Adam..." he began. Adam nodded, stitches were the least of his worries. *What about my memory?*

Dr. Gardenia lowered his head, he tried to hide his hard swallow, but to no avail. Erin stepped forward, "Please Doctor, when will Adam get his memory back?"

"It will take time, weeks, months. It really is difficult to tell with such neurological damage," he said solemnly.

Adam perked up a little, "That ain't so bad really?" He turned to his parents, either side of his bed.

"That's not all!" Dr. Gardenia interrupted.

The office went quiet, only the beating rain was heard. The bedside rail seemed colder than before.

11

"The scan revealed major damage to the base of your spine; your motor neurons were severed, almost completely destroyed. It is likely you will never walk again."

The bomb hit.

"I am sorry."

Dr. Gardenia stood up and excused himself from the room. Adam sank into the bed, feeling like he was in a grave; everyone was above him, looking down disheartened. Adam's chest tightened, an invisible force fell upon him, trying its best to suffocate him. He attempted to ignore the sensation of shock growing inside, it was to no avail. It travelled up his body and into his throat, ensuring he could not cry for help. To Adam, he had only lived for two days. Two days of memories were now the blueprint for the rest of his life, confinement.

He drew breath sharply as Erin pulled him close. Her heat did little to thaw the developing cold as Adam looked along casts that were keeping him hostage. He knew that inside the cold shell lay his legs, consigned to be forever useless and wasted. Erin squeezed Adam tighter and tighter. He watched the drops move swiftly along the glass, he longed for such freedom.

"We will get through this," Erin said. Barry moved to the other side of the bed and wrapped his arms around his wife and Adam. Surveying the ruins of the bomb, Adam came to his own conclusion, *this can't be real.*

***

Britney stared at the space where Adam's bed should be. She never learned to relax in these environs, despite her

12

familiarity with them. When she first came to visit Adam, Britney did not need to ask for directions to the intensive care unit. Although it had been over seven years since her father passed away, the reminders of that difficult period in her life had not disappeared. The pain chiselled itself deeply in the then 17 year old girl, but Britney moulded a mask to shade herself from the world.

Some people let it all out. Others store all the pain and act as if nothing has happened. Britney claimed the latter way was the right way, even more so when her mother broke down, turning her taste for alcohol into an addiction.

Britney rubbed her right ring finger and wished she had brought her father's wedding ring today. Unknown to her mother, Britney took the ring off just as the coffin closed for the last time. Since then, anytime Britney felt stressed or worried, the rounded golden ring had never been far away.

In the corner of her eye, Britney saw two nurses roll Adam's bed into the ward, her eyes finding their way to Adam's. His were lost, cold and flat. Nothing seemed to register in his mind now. The nurses rotated the bed into position until Adam was next to Britney, yet he still did not move. The nurses jumped ship as soon as they could. Britney's heart beat a little faster underneath her blouse. A silence spread throughout the room, as if the other patients knew what happened, a blanket of peace that did little to comfort Britney. She reached onto the bed and made contact with Adam. He did not move a muscle, he was stuck, and his eyes looked straight ahead, at nothing. Britney leaned closer to Adam, but the young man remained motionless.

"What did he say?" whispered Britney, her voice trembling as she asked. Adam turned towards her and let a sigh escape from his mouth. He shook his head and the pain from his eyes flowed into Britney, she knew better not to ask any more for now. Adam squeezed his lips tightly and took a deep breath. Tears trickled onto his white skin and down his face, where a tissue collected them. Britney traced the tears back to the source, lonely blue eyes. Erin and Barry appeared in the doorway and motioned to Britney. With that, she kissed Adam on the cheek and whispered,

"I'll be back in a moment."

She did not come back, she couldn't. Erin's words were like shards of metal, each one slicing their way through Britney's fragments of hope until all that remained was a nauseating reality. The thought of going back into the ward and talking to Adam drove Britney in the opposite direction. Making her way to the white ford at the back of the hospital parking lot, her vision blurred with tears as a familiar stinging came to her eyes. Imagining her now red-eyed gaze, Britney lowered her head to passers-by. She was sick of hearing the familiar *how are you?* Sick of getting stranger's pity handed to her, just sick. It took a third press of the key to unlock the car, as Britney tossed her hair back from in front of her face and quickly jumped into the driver's seat. She fumbled her phone as she took it out of her handbag, sniffling to stop her nose from running. The beep from every digit pressed upset her even more and her lips trembled when she put the phone to her ear. The call made a connection, Britney squinted. Her right hand ran over her face.

That cold voice answered, "Yeah?"

Britney stalled for a moment, sniffling again.

"I am at the hospital..."

"So? What's up now?"

"Adam got the results of the MRI scan today!"

"Oh, and what did they show?"

Britney lowered the phone and rubbed her eyes. The coarse voice still emitted up to her from the earpiece, "Britney? What were the results?" he demanded.

"Adam..."

Britney lowered her head into her lap, crouching up like a child.

"Adam is paralysed!"

Chapter 3

Six weeks of hospital confinement came to an end. It can't be worse outside, Adam told himself. Erin pushed Adam in his wheelchair along the hospital corridor towards the exit, while gazing eyes seemed to hover over him, their silent faces screaming questions. Each morning he had woken up, hoping his condition was just a dream, each morning he was disappointed. Crossing the metal threshold of the hospital entrance, Adam hoped for a change. He sighed when he realised it was even more frustrating to be outside; the vastness of the parking lot teased him, visitors to the hospital walked briskly by.

Erin pulled the seat belt across Adam in the back seat of the family SUV. The giant shadow cast by Boston City Hospital disguised the fact it was a bright October morning. Each scene was new to Adam, from the large glass covered building dominating the skyline as they left Boston city, to the intertwining I-93 highway twisting its way from the city shore to the lower Boston area. While Adam took in as much as he could, he tried to make connections in his head, but signals kept misfiring. The area called Dorchester teased the most; in every park people were active, children swinging on playground bars, throwing baseballs and smiles everywhere. The SUV drove over the Neponset river bridge and into Quincy.

Erin turned around to her son, "Recognise anything darling?" Adam shook his head, eyes still fixed on his new surroundings.

Erin's stories of Quincy over the previous weeks created an image in Adam's mind, yet all imagined visions missed. Despite being known all over the United States for being the hometown of two American Presidents, a fact that Erin was particularly proud of it seemed, Quincy sat firmly in the middle ground between stunning and standard. The roads were laid out in the *American-style* squares, block by block. Trees lined the neighbourhood streets, wooden-framed dwellings the norm, surrounded by green gardens. Barry and Erin's home was on Louver Street, located at the end of a cul-de-sac. A tall wooden fence separated them from the opposite neighbourhood, as kids played in the wide turning area at the entrance to their home. Adam peered between the two front seats as the SUV pulled onto the driveway.

"We're home Adam!" Barry said. Adam gazed at the white bungalow. All the way home, he hoped something positive would happen when he seen his *home*, but nothing.

Some of the children waved at Adam, he nodded back just to be polite. As Barry readied the wheelchair, Erin spoke about a time, not so long ago when Adam played soccer in the turning area with them. A flock of eight-year olds tackled Adam in an effort to take the ball from him, their laughs filling the neighbourhood. Through the talk of their parents, the children knew what happened to Adam. They may not have understood the severity of the situation, but their manners kept them from inquiring any further. To them, Adam Fletcher hurt his legs, but he will be back playing soccer with them soon.

Erin pushed open Adam's room door, "This way son."

Entering, Adam felt the heat of the evening sun coming in his window. A fresh scent wafted gently around. For an instant, it seemed Erin was preparing to give Adam a guided tour of his own room. After she closed the curtains to shield away the sunlight, she let Adam alone to take it all in.

He waited until the door had closed, then he set about examining the room. There was a Boston Revolution soccer poster on the wall and a large Red Sox flag was stapled to the ceiling. A desk in the corner was covered with books; Adam picked up one on construction and brushed off the dust onto the cream carpeted floor. A quick peek at the titles of the rest of the books was enough for Adam, more construction related scribes. He opened the laptop on his desk, letting it boot up while he investigated the remainder of the room. The white walls reflected what light seeped in through the curtains as the dazzle from a metal object caught his eye.

Adam approached the row of shelves near his bedside, and immediately recognised his name emblazoned on a miniature statue of a man.

Adam Fletcher – Player of the Year 2008

He held the award on his lap. Wiping the metal plating with his sleeve, his name sparkled as he placed it back on the shelf. Adam wondered how he won such an award, as he slid his hands along the cold metal frame of his wheelchair. In the corner of the room were two large suitcases, clothes nearly hiding them from view. The tags from the last flight were still attached, Logan airport in Boston to Buffalo, NY. The laptop screen lit up as the homepage loaded. There it was again, the picture of Adam and Britney on the couch. He stared for a moment at the screen until a knock on the door startled him. His mother entered just as Adam closed down the laptop cover,

"Dinner is ready."

***

The Banshee bar on Dorchester Avenue was busy as Britney pushed her way in through the dark doorway. Inside, the establishment's sporting side was evident, with the Red Sox and New England Patriots jerseys illuminating an otherwise dark bar. Britney went briskly up the stairs to the games room on the first floor.

Lights over the pool table were the only illumination. Most of the young men in the room used the darker corners as their perch. Britney's eyes strained as she adjusted to the darkness. The two men playing pool didn't even look twice at her.

"Shaun?" she called out. Unintentionally, the pool players glanced into the far corner of the room. Britney did not wait, she stepped into the darkness. A silhouette turned into a face, the face turned into Shaun McCoy.

"Yeah?" he asked, in that cold and harsh tone she was used to. The darkness threatened, suffocating Britney.

"Can we speak, alone?"

Shaun stood up, towering over Britney as he stepped out of the darkness.

"Okay, come with me."

**

Adam failed to hide the feeling growing inside. Sitting at the table with his *parents*, he wondered was he really part of this family? Or did these two people just offer to take care of him? Despite photos claiming otherwise, Adam felt like an intruder at dinner. Erin and Barry acted like parents, or so Adam thought, but he struggled to *act* like a son. Erin placed his dinner in front of him, a well-done steak with pepper sauce. The table conversation was limited and tense, as if they all were afraid to interrupt each other, should someone speak. Elvis sang quietly in the background, gently buffering out the scrape of the cutlery against the plates.

"Do you remember anything in your room?" Barry asked, breaking the silence. Adam shook his head, the picture of him and Britney flashed in his mind. Of all the reminders placed along his path since the accident, none stood out like the picture. His memories were gone, so what was this? A damaged mind creating little moments of relief, or was it a trace of his actual life? No emotional connection to Erin and Barry existed, yet a sense of normality flowed through Adam whenever he thought of Britney. He was sure about her. As for the two people eating dinner with him, the jury was still out.

Chapter 4

Midnight swept over Louver Street, yet Erin did not sleep. The pain inside was winning the battle so far, doing its best to keep her awake in an attempt to prolong the agony and watch the reaction. She could not control what whirled into her mind, as images of Adam down the hall in his bed came through. Erin pictured her son sitting motionless, alone and bewildered in his unfamiliar surroundings, yet she failed to muster the courage to comfort him.

Erin sniffled again, wiping her eyes on Barry's t-shirt. The dampness pressed against her face, its warmth rapidly diminished by Erin's numb skin. She questioned her reality. Had she slipped into some dream, some nightmare and this was the unfortunate climax of it all? Erin shook her head, praying to wake up, wishing things went back to the way they were.

It only hit Erin when Adam arrived home. The hospital shielded her from the pain she reckoned, as most nights Erin and Barry slept, and despite the pain they felt for their son, closed eyes brought a certain degree of relief. But when Adam finally came home, he inadvertently brought a lot more than just the crash injuries and a wheelchair.

Erin remembered many moments in her life. The good were easy to recollect; meeting Barry, her wedding day and most of all the day Adam was born. As with most people, Erin hated the unease that accompanied the bad moments. Just like everyone else, the bad moments are seemingly etched a lot easier into the mind's catalogue. That afternoon a new entry inscribed itself in Erin's life, possibly the toughest one to take. Adam, her son, wheelchair bound and lost, entering what was an alien home to him.

She began to curse whatever Creator done this, but it took too much energy. Instead she quivered in her husband's arms for hours, shaking even more when his tears slipped onto her hair and made her skin tingle.

Six weeks ago life had a structure, *bad things never happened to regular families.* The only thing that remained now was purpose. The details changed, but Erin still had a job to do. Life turned right back on itself, placing Erin in the mother's role again.

***

The gentle hum of a David Gray CD wafted through Adam's bedroom like a sedative, taking him off into a deep sleep. He had not slept soundly since the accident, mainly because of being on medication and also the rigid form of hospital beds. That night, Adam fell asleep like someone knocked him unconscious.

Adam did not savour his first dream since the accident. A dull sound of people screaming replaced the fading music. In the land created in his mind, the shrieking continued, diminishing as it moved further away. Yet, the quieter it got, the more alone Adam felt. Though he saw his hands open and close, he did not control them, like observing someone else's body function through their eyes. A flow of paralysis ignited in his fingers as they stopped moving, numbness tightening its grip on his body, he tried to scream for help but it hurt too much. Despite the pain, the cold leather backseat of a car underneath his palms came into view. The black interior faded in and out of view as Adam tried to focus, only for the paralysis to climb further up his body until he finally got wind into his lungs and shouted.

Adam clambered free of his dream to wake in his dark bedroom. Gasping, he tried to control his breathing, motioning with his hands, in and out. He stared at the dark ceiling, into a comforting blackness, compared to the dream. Adam wiped traces of sweat from his forehead and relaxed when the soothing music caught his attention once more. Closing his eyes again, a spark ignited in Adam's brain, *was that my first crash memory?*

***

The moon peered over the eastern horizon as Madison stepped onto his front garden. Midnight had passed over the street, taking any sign of life and enabling Madison to prowl freely. He walked toward Adam's house and stopped at the small timber fence separating the two plots. Motionless, he gazed at the white Fletcher residence reflecting in the moonlight, straining to make out what hummed from a ground floor bedroom. Taking

23

a deep breath he turned back towards home, letting out a small chuckle as air escaped his lungs and sailed into the sky.

In Madison's front room, he popped open his laptop. It was obvious this was not any normal device, immediately numbers and letters flew across the screen, the computer loaded in mille-seconds. He typed a password and unlocked the main home page. Reaching to the top of the monitor, he adjusted the webcam lens to direct it towards himself.

Madison clapped his hands, the room lit up. What began as a living room now resembled a tool shed, empty boxes of new computers and parts filled most of the room. A laptop was transformed into a *super-computer*, over three feet wide and two feet high, tucked in under a flimsy desk. Lights flashed and blinked along the computers edges as the mutated device awaited instructions. Sitting upright in his chair, Madison pressed some buttons and looked into the webcam. The same phrase kept blinking on the screen:

Connecting, Connecting, Connecting....

Madison rubbed the unlit LED on the side of the monitor, urging it to work.

Transmitting, Transmitting, Transmitting....

The LED flashed in a bright green.

"October 17th, broadcasting transmission 1.1; step completed; Adam Fletcher has returned home."

Chapter 5

Britney climbed the front porch and stepped inside. She did not have to ask Erin if Adam was awake, she knew his habits, good and bad. Early to rise was one of the good ones.

"How is he?"

Erin shrugged, "He hasn't spoken since he came home Britney." The two women whispered in the hallway, careful Adam could not hear. Britney's searched for somewhere to look, something to take her gaze off Erin's watery eyes.

"I'll talk to him, I'll try," she whispered.

Britney stepped into the kitchen. Adam turned his head towards her, the slightest smile acknowledged her presence.

"Hi!" she murmured, flicking her hair back from in front of her eyes. Adam pushed a bowl away from himself into the middle of the table. Seeing this young man, her best friend, trapped in a wheelchair sent a surge of guilt through Britney, but, she knew breaking down in front of him would be of no benefit. She dragged a chair up close to Adam and sat down.

"How are you feeling?" was the only question Britney could think of, regretting it as soon as the words left her mouth. Adam sighed and glanced down at the wheelchair.

"Britney..." he couldn't finish what he wanted to say, and she didn't need to hear it.

Britney leaned towards Adam and held his hands tightly, this time she thought before she spoke, "We are gonna help you every step of the way, don't you worry Adam."

Adam gripped her hands tighter for a second.

"Can you take me to where I crashed?"

***

Britney's white ford turned off shortly after Canton town, towards the sloping hills of southern Massachusetts. Within minutes of leaving the main road, they were surrounded by thick forests, which spread south as far as the state line. The roadway twisted and weaved uphill, where banks of earth sloped higher on either side. Britney remained silent, seeing that Adam could not take his eyes off the trees that whizzed by.

"The trees, I think I can remember them!" Adam whispered. They stopped at a dangerous corner in the road, where Britney carefully pulled into a forest pathway, across from the scene of the accident.

Adam sat motionless in the car, his eyes locked on the huge wall that had left him paralysed. The luminous police tape hung lifeless in front of the stone structure. White scrapes and black paint marks were etched along

26

the twelve feet high barricade; its intention in years gone by was to keep out intruders from the large estate that stretched out behind it. No need for such fortification nowadays.

"Where in the car was I sitting?" Adam asked, gaze still fixed on the wall.

"Back left I think!"

Adam nodded, "Did the car have a black leather interior?"

"Amm, I don't know, something coming back to you?"

He shook his head, "Nah, just a strange dream. It's nothing!"

A lifetime of friendship did not go to waste, Britney read Adam in an instant. Information, knowledge, no matter how small, existed behind those eyes. However, now was not the time to pull it out. A cold autumn breeze ruffled through the trees, causing the luminous tape to jump, breaking Adam's fix on the wall.

"Thanks for this Britney. I have seen what I needed to see."

Instead of turning for home, Britney kept driving towards the summit of the hill, where a large viewing bay spread out before them. The trees were not planted near the top in an effort to maintain this place as a tourist attraction, but a lack of advertising meant it was deserted most of the year. Britney stopped near the edge of the viewing bay, facing south-eastwards. In the distance the Atlantic Ocean sparkled like a tray of diamonds as the sun reflected off it. To the north, the Boston skyline perked above the trees and to the south the land sloped gently down into Providence and Rhode Island.

"I really like it here," Britney sighed, dreaming of times past when her father would bring her up here on a long summer's day.

"The three of us would have a picnic here, and then cycle down the trail to the east. It was...perfect."

"Do I know your parents?" Adam asked.

Britney's mind flooded with memories of her father's last days, where Adam skipped school just to be with her in hospital. Even though he was a teenager, the compassion he possessed astounded Britney and her mother. After her father passed, Adam became the man in Britney's life. He was never thanked for simple chores like cutting the grass, taking out the trash and preparing dinners, but Britney appreciated it. Adam was her best friend, and at times her only friend.

"You know my mother, you knew my father."

"Knew?" Adam asked, "Oh Britney I'm sorry, I didn't-"

"It's okay Adam, it's okay. It was a long time ago."

Britney rubbed Adam's hand, knowing he saved her years ago. Now, the chance to save him appeared, she hid.

"Adam, I have something to tell you."

He turned gently towards her, "Yeah?"

"You saved me back then."

***

The neurology wing of the Boston City Hospital was a different world. Dim lights illuminated the long corridors, the damp smelling hallway added to the sombre tone and even the staff seemed to trudge from office to office, ward to ward. Erin knew the dimmed lighting aided patients with various types of epilepsy, yet decided to keep such information from Adam.

In a letter she received from the neurologist soon after the accident, Erin was given specific guidelines to follow, in order to give Adam the best chance of regaining his memory. The first one almost seemed like a contradiction; *Feed Adam info, but when he reacts, or catches a 'grip' on some thought/idea, let him go.* Adam glanced upwards when they passed the overhead lighting. While Erin considered telling Adam the reason for the faint lighting, she refrained, hoping it would spark some memory about the accident.

For the next thirty minutes, Adam and Erin sat through a verbal re-hash of the original letter from the neurologist, albeit with more extravagant terminology. Erin tried to take it all in, but some words just whizzed over her head, *Lacunar, retrograde amnesia, damaged hippocampus.*

"Doctor," Erin interrupted, "in plain English please."

The Doctor sighed. Obviously, rarely had someone cut in while he was in full flow. But Erin knew that listening to a medically-worded report would do no good, except maybe feed the neurologist's ego.

"Okay, basically what has happened is that your brain has reset as a result of the accident. We call it post-traumatic amnesia." Adam nodded at the first non-medical statement to come from the neurologist.

"There are two mains types of amnesia, anterograde and retrograde. You have the latter."

Erin sat forward, "So, what is retrograde?"

"This is where Adam's pre-existing memories are lost to conscious recollection." Turning to Adam, he added,

"But, you will be able to memorise events since the accident, as if nothing happened."

Adam looked out the window. Erin heard Adam's next question in her mind, she wanted to ask the same.

"So, is it permanent?"

"We cannot know for sure at this point. It could take months or years to regain your memory. Or it may never happen."

Erin, while shocked at the bluntness of the neurologist's statement, appreciated the honesty. Adam did not.

"It's better to have no hope, than false hope eh?" He said. Erin reached around her son, wanting to pull the negativity from his very bones.

"Adam," the neurologist spoke, "is it not better to have something to aim for, than living a life with no direction."

Adam did not answer. He spun around in the wheel-chair and left the office, despite Erin's outstretched arms.

"Do not worry Mrs. Fletcher, I have seen patients react a lot worse than that."

***

Watching the children play soccer in the turning area was strangely comforting for Adam, as if they were a connection to his past. Britney walked down the driveway and sat on the pavement next to him.

"I remember the laughter," Adam said gently, as if not wanting to blow the memory away by speaking about it. Britney smiled, "See, you'll be back to normal in no time."

"You're a very bad liar Britney."

She froze momentarily and looked at the pavement.

"What do you mean?" she asked.

"You're not confident that I'll regain my memory?" Britney raised her head and looked Adam square in the eyes.

"I know you'll be fine. You're memory is already coming back, and I know that the physiotherapist's sessions will bring you on."

"Ahh, the physio!" Adam sighed. Britney leaned closer to Adam and laughed.

"You can't remember what being treated by a physio feels like, so why are you sighing already? The first smile Adam's face had shown in weeks crept out, "Yeah, you got me there I guess!"

The sudden buzz of Britney's phone startled her as she got to her feet and reached into her pocket.

"My mother!" she sighed, waving the phone, "should have been home two hours ago!" She rubbed Adam's shoulder and flicked the phone onto silent. Adam nodded as his eyes followed Britney to her car.

"Thank you for today," he shouted as Britney opened the door of her car and waved.

The soft swishing of grass alerted Adam to someone's presence.

"Hello!" A man said, walking across his garden towards Adam.

"Hi?"

"My name is Madison, I am your new neighbour. I moved in a few weeks ago," the man said, pointing to his house. Adam relaxed a little in his chair, relieved it was someone new and not a forgotten friend.

"I'm Adam. I live here with my parents. I'm only here a few weeks as well."

"Oh? Where did you live before that?" Madison asked.

Adam bit his lip, regretting his previous statement,

"Long story."

Hoping to stop further questions coming his way, Adam threw a question at Madison.

"Why have you moved here?"

"That's a long story too!" Madison said, smiling as he sat down on the pavement. Up close, Adam saw the greyness sprinkled over Madison's hair. His black t-shirt and pants suggested mid-fifties, but the wrinkles that etched themselves on Madison's face shouted considerably older.

"I am an inventor," he said.

"What have you invented?"

"Nothing good so far I'm afraid."

Adam racked his brain, why would someone move here? As far as he had seen, there was nothing exceptional about Quincy.

"A new start..." Adam began, feeding off the uncertainty on Madison's face, "will do wonders for you."

"Well, more like making up for lost time," Madison said, rising to his feet. "Nice to meet you Adam, I'll introduce myself to your parents in the coming days."

Adam gave a small wave to Madison as they parted, pondering if he upset his new neighbour already.

Chapter 6

Adam sat at his desk and stared blankly at the laptop screen, erratically tapping buttons, but sliding over to delete them immediately. Erin entered with a tap on the bedroom door, snapping him out of his trance. He rubbed his forehead insistently and lowered the screen.

"The Detective is here Adam," she whispered.

"Ask him to come in please."

Moments later, a large African-American man greeted Adam, standing in the doorway to his bedroom.

"I'm Detective David Murray, nice to meet you Adam."

Murray's large hand dwarfed Adam's and his arm shook with an authority all of its own. Adam assumed a solid handshake was part of being in law enforcement, a form of intimidation. But Murray's strong arms were ably supported by his dominating shoulders, his big frame enhanced by deep breaths and a concrete stare. The black tie and suit jacket blended with his dark skin, a short military-style haircut added to Adam's sudden nerves. The detective's eyes scanned the room, maybe an automatic reflex.

"Rev's fan eh?" he asked, glancing at the soccer poster over Adam's bed. He did not want to seem cheeky by telling a detective the obvious, he lost his memory. Instead he nodded, "Yeah!"

Murray reached inside his coat pocket for a notepad and dictaphone and placed them on the bedside table. For the first time in weeks, Adam felt his heart beating through his chest. Sweat formed under his arms, thankfully hidden from Murray's view. The detective sat on the bed, forcing Adam to turn around in his chair and face him. Adam did not cause the accident, as far as he knew, but was Murray here to prove otherwise?

"Adam, can you tell me what you remember about the accident," Murray asked, in a soft tone while he pressed the record button on the dictaphone.

"I am struggling to remember anything, except a black leather interior of a car. I am assuming that was the car I was found in?"

"Yes," Murray sighed, un-approving of Adam's way of answering a question with a question.

"And dull screams, faint and muffled," Adam continued, quietening to a whisper, fixing his eyes on the digital timer on the dictaphone. Murray sat silently, letting Adam's words swish around inside, nit-picking for clues. His eyes never budged, each second causing more sweat to trickle down Adam's armpits and sides.

"Anything else?" Murray asked.

"No, that is all I can remember."

"I don't mean to be insensitive Adam, but it is vital we get to the bottom of this. You may be an innocent victim, so let us work together to find out who is responsible."

34

May?

Adam's gaze darted, yet he still managed to nod at Murray. Adam assumed he was innocent all along, but Murray planted a seed. *What if I caused it? What if I'm the bad guy?* The unerring stare was feeding the seed, causing Adam's doubt to grow exponentially with each second the detective stalled. Sliding his hand over, Murray stopped the recording.

"I do not want to put too much pressure on you at this time Adam. Would a visit in a few weeks be ok?"

"Sure," Adam replied, feeling another trail of sweat slide down his side.

***

Shaun McCoy entered his bedroom on the top floor of a Dorchester apartment. He slammed the door shut and locked it with a home depot dead bolt. Sure of his security, he knelt on the floor and pulled a large suitcase out from under his bed. He rubbed his hair in excitement as he flicked open the case and glanced back at the door. Shaun removed a large dark cloth that covered the interior of the case. He dropped the cloth by his side, always sure to have it within reach. Leaning down into the suitcase, a tinge of cold ran into his fingers, or maybe it was the excitement he figured. Shaun tightened his grip around the metal, slowing his breathing until –

Bang! Bang! Bang!

His father pounded the door, causing Shaun to quickly throw the cloth into the case, close the lid and slide the case under the bed.

"What? What do you want now?" Shaun said.

"They were here again today Shaun, why haven't you returned their calls boy?" came his father's distinct Boston accent. Shaun raised his middle finger to the door.

"People like them don't come looking for people like us too often boy," his father urged, in an easing tone. Shaun pulled at his hair, shaking his head.

"Do you wanna be like me? Stuck here like me?"

Shaun leaned his back against the door and slouched down. He was sick of his father, he was sick of them, *why can't they just let me be*. The corner of a white envelope underneath the door caught Shaun's attention. Pulling it through, he sighed when he read the sender: Boston Community College.

"Stop annoying me," he whispered to the letter and tossed it into the bin.

Chapter 7

Michael Lenard sat at his desk in the rehabilitation wing of the Boston City Hospital. It was early morning, a time he dreads. The appointments for the day arrive on his desk at eight o clock, teeming with pages and pages of bad news.

As the day moved on, Michael remembered why he does what he does. The feeling of anticipation, knowing someone under his care will be able to get on with their lives brings him right back. Michael's aim is simple; just to see people walk out of his office healed, when months earlier, they arrived on crutches or even in a wheelchair.

Reading Adam Fletcher's file that morning, the sense of anticipation was absent. Patients with paralysis generally have one major thing going for them, their mind. Michael was a firm believer in the power of thought - what you think, you get. He even had a plaque inscribed with one of Buddha's quotations:

All that we are is the result of what we have thought. The mind is everything. What we think, we become.

So, by infusing the patients' heads with positive thinking, he hoped it would add to the physical therapy he provided. Sadly, the note at the base of the report, titled 'other' did not inspire confidence.

There is post-traumatic Amnesia (Retrograde) present in the patient.

***

Even being outside the Boston City Hospital intimidated Adam. The afternoon sun hid behind the cellular block structure of the building, which in turn guided a crisp early winter wind through the streets. Erin pushed Adam up the access ramp into the main reception as he glanced around to see what other misfortunate graced this place. He felt eyes immediately being set upon him, silenced thoughts more than likely asking what happened to this young man. Adam slid his hands out of his pockets and grabbed the wheels.

A whiff of pine fragrance greeted Adam when Erin opened the door to Michael Lenard's waiting room. The secretary threw them a routine smile and asked, "Adam Fletcher?"

"Yes," Erin interrupted, and turned to Adam.

"Whatever happens today, remember this is only the beginning," Erin said, rubbing Adam's shoulder. He responded with the slightest of nods, just as Michael Lenard opened the door to his treatment room. Adam was surprised by Michael's appearance. He imagined the physiotherapist as an older man, dressed in white clothes similar to the other staff at the hospital. This was not what emerged.

Michael Lenard was young, thirty, thirty-five max. Dressed in dark jeans and a blue t-shirt, his forearms were well defined as a result of his occupation. His muscular image was complimented by his tight dark hair and dark features.

"Hello Adam, how are you?" Michael said, reaching out to shake hands.

Adam nodded, knowing it was easier than opening his mouth and speaking.

"Would you like to go into the treatment room?" Michael said, pointing the way, yet motioning for Erin to stay outside for a moment. Adam crossed the threshold into the room, yet his ears remained pricked as Michael sat down with Erin.

"I must apologise..." Erin started.

Michael interjected, "No, please don't Mrs. Fletcher, I see this with almost every patient that comes in here. If Adam was all smiles and laughs, I'd be worried. It shows he is human. Mrs. Fletcher, I have something to ask," Michael's tone changed.

"Yes?"

"Would it be okay if you did not come into the treatment room, mentally, for Adam it might not be the best?"

"Yes, that is no problem."

"I have found that one of the biggest inhibitors to a person's recovery is pressure. I feel at this stage, Adam needs to concentrate solely on recovery, but recovery for himself."

Michael then followed Adam in and closed the door.

"Now Adam, let's begin."

The treatment room wall was decorated with physiotherapists' qualifications; a degree in physiotherapy, PhD in spinal rehabilitation and member of the Chartered Physiotherapists of America. Dotted all over the room were plaques with motivational quotes from famous figures throughout history. Adam sensed Michael's personality just by looking at the sayings.

"Do you like them, the quotes?" Michael asked.

"They're different I guess."

Michael followed Adam's gaze and began to read one.

"The only way of finding the limits of the possible is by going beyond them into the impossible. That is one of my favourites."

Adam wondered if he inadvertently met a monk instead of a physiotherapist.

"Okay Adam, let's do this."

***

Street lights spread out on the pavement, illuminating the darkening Boston evening. A cold breeze travelled down Louver Street and blew against Adam's face. Since the accident, over two months ago, Adam read the consultant's report almost daily. Until now, words caused the pain, like he was under oath to stay in the wheelchair. But today, the constraints of being partially paralysed came through in another way. His heart grew heavy when he remembered how Michael Lenard lifted him onto the table. He struggled to shake the feeling of embarrassment from his body, assuming being confined to a wheelchair did not help either. If reading reports about his disability were crushing, the physical reminder appeared unbearable in comparison.

A man approached in the distance, Adam struggled to see a face as the man walked into the dark areas between lampposts. He glanced at his neighbour Madison's house. Even in the dusk, it was clear to see this man was organised and clear. The scent of the newly painted fence drifted with the cool air, as the white timber traced a guard around Madison's home. The porch and inside hallway light were on, attracting the last of the autumn flies.

"Adam?" a man's voice called.

"Hey."

"Are you okay?" Madison asked, stopping next to Adam.

He tapped the chair in response, "Too many reminders."

"What happened today?"

"My first visit to the physiotherapist...did not go well."

"I'm sorry to hear that. But, I know you'll get out of this."

Faking a smile, Adam retorted, "Yeah, how do you know that?"

"I can see something in you, a kind of inner strength you don't even see yet."

Adam shuffled in his chair, slightly fazed by such a statement from a man whom he met a matter of days ago. *Either this man is certifiably crazy, or else he actually believes that I'll get out of this.*

"Thank you for that," Adam said.

"I would not say it if I did not believe it," Madison added.

Madison looked around for something to sit on and noticing a small waste bin for recycling, he dragged it over next to Adam. In the silence, Adam looked at Madison, unable to shake the statement from his mind. *I have inner strength? What is this guy on?*
Nonetheless, Adam appreciated Madison's help and being rude is no way to repay him.

"Tell me about you? Where are you from?"

"Me," Madison said, "I'm not an interesting guy."

"Everyone is, it's just that some have a lot of boring wrapped around them," Adam said, causing Madison to break into laughter.

"I guess that's true. I'm from the city and have lived there until now."

"What on earth made you move to Quincy?"

Madison failed to hide the facade of discomfort imprinted on his face. Adam thought about taking back his question, but decided against. After all, he wanted to get to know his new neighbour.

"I lost a part of my life; I need to get it back."

"We have something in common so! Have you succeeded yet?"

"Not yet," Madison said, "but I'll keep trying."

Adam looked at his new neighbour sitting next to him on a cool November evening. Madison sat on the waste bin, gazing down towards the pavement, unintentionally showing Adam the remains of a broken life underneath those eyes. What did Madison lose that made him turn into this Adam wondered.

"I need to *start* trying," Adam whispered.

"Don't worry, this is temporary confinement!" Madison said, shaking the metal bars of the wheelchair.

42

Chapter 8

Detective Murray crossed the bridge over the Charles river so many times over the years he could count all the cracks in the concrete paving from his home to his office. While the jog to work benefitted Murray, it also told him when the winter ice was coming close. This year, November 14th signalled the change. With each deep breath, the cold air stung his throat and lungs, making the run to work seem more like a trek. A pain erupted in his chest, causing Murray to moan quietly to himself, hiding his *weakness* from fellow runners. There was snow in the air, Murray sensed it. Within days, he knew Boston would become a blanket of white and his runs to work would become walks.

After showering in the police station, Murray sat at his desk and rummaged through a pile of letters.

"About time!" he said, reaching for a brown envelope marked *Confidential*. Murray glanced out from his office as he opened the envelope. Murray used to abide by the rules. But he is well aware of how close he came to dying, just because he listened to what the rule book said.

He was lucky the previous summer. While investigating a number of small bank thefts in Charlestown, he did what most other detectives would do. Follow the rules, obey people's rights, and wait for warrants to be issued. Laying in hospital for two months with numerous gunshot wounds opened Murray's eyes. A little research would have revealed what his suspects were up to; gun-running, robbery, extortion and even dipping into the drug trade. Scratching the surface did not reveal this, however a few methods that bent the rules, or even broke them, may have helped. The bullets that lodged in his hip and chest reminded Murray there are many sides to a story and the side he had seen was coloured. If he had the information, the facade would have been shown in its true colours, and maybe he would not be working alone now. His job to him was more than good versus evil, through the medium of a civilised society. No, it was good versus evil by any means necessary. The letter marked *confidential* was one of Murray's new found methods.

Murray tried to get the idea of first impressions out of his system. Adam Fletcher seemed harmless. *Was he the innocent victim in all of this?* He shook his head. Murray unfolded the letter to give a different side of Adam Fletcher. *Guilty until proven innocent!*

***

Stepping out of *Dunkin Donuts* on a wintry Dorchester Avenue, Britney pulled her coat closer and wrapped both hands around the steaming coffee. Her nose had already gone red when the first flakes of snow descended on Boston.

Britney liked the snow. It reminded her of better times, like when she was truly part of a family. Tip-toeing out on the white pavement every morning, screaming when the snow plough roared through her street, building mounds along the sidewalk. She remembers her little mitten-covered hands, dwarfed by her father's as he walked her to school. Even as a young girl, Britney longed for that secure feeling of her father's attention. Attaching her school paintings to the fridge, only one character seemed reasonably life-like, that of her father.

When Britney was seventeen, her father suffered two stress-related heart attacks. The admittance she *could see it coming* from Britney's mother made matters worse. Within weeks, her father was dead.

Over the following months, her mother became the reluctant reservoir from which Britney took strength. Unfortunately that well ran dry, her mother found other ways to distract from their loss. People who were so sympathetic on the day of the funeral soon returned to their normal selves and with it the offers of a helping hand stopped. It was just Britney and her alcoholic mother now. Boyfriends were a short-lived pleasure for the teenager, because as soon as Britney started to care for a man, her mind drew inevitable comparisons. And the spotty-faced teenagers always lost out.

Britney recognised a disturbing pattern as she walked along Dorchester Avenue; the leading lights in her life were all taken away. The only man who came close to her father is in a wheelchair and he cannot even remember who she is. Adam Fletcher was there from the start. He was the Constant in Britney's life.

Britney's breath floated high in the cold hallway of her Quincy home.

"Mom?" she shouted, hearing her echo bounce around the empty house. She knelt down in front of the open grate and lit the fire, one she had prepared earlier just in case her mother decided to come home. The fire lit immediately, throwing shadows on the pale yellow walls. Britney sat on the couch with her dinner; a microwavable pasta dish. The TV was on, yet she paid no attention to it. Instead, the orange fire drew her into a trance. Jumping flames danced like a hypnotist trying to induce sleep, Britney's eyes got heavier.

Like a gunshot, someone pounded on the door, causing Britney to fall back into the couch. Taking gentle steps into the hallway, she noticed a large dark figure through the frosty front door glass. They banged on the door again, even louder this time. Who is it, she asked silently, too afraid to transfer the question to her mouth.

"Britney, open up!" came a loud, deep voice.

Shaun rushed past Britney as she opened the door and jumped onto the couch, immediately helping himself to some pasta.

"What do you want Shaun?" Britney quizzed, standing in the living room doorway.

"Relax, come sit down," Shaun said, while rubbing the couch.

"I'm good here!"

A creepy smile came to Shaun's face, turning Britney's stomach. His fingers in her pasta ended any thoughts of finishing her dinner. Folding her arms, she leaned against the doorway, urging Shaun to speak.

"Looks like you haven't been telling me the whole story!"

Britney squinted, "What do you mean?"

"Did you think that I wouldn't need to know about the pig's visit? Slip your mind or something?"

"I...I...didn't even think-"

Shaun stood up, "Are you stupid?" he barked.

"Everything that happens with Adam, I need to know," Shaun said as he stepped closer to Britney. His sheer size dwarfed Britney and the fire behind him cast a bigger shadow onto the walls.

"Adam will never remember what happened!" Britney tried to remain calm as she lied. Shaun laughed, raising his hand to her throat and pressing her back against the wall. Britney felt his grip tightening, pasta sauce slithered from his hands and down her neck. The warm scent hit her nostrils, doing its best to find her stomach and turn it, aided by Shaun's acidic breath on her face. Maybe it was the shadows she thought, but Shaun's eyes had turned black as he leaned closer to her.

"He won't remember," she whimpered.

"For *his* sake, you better hope he doesn't!"

Chapter 9

Three new books sat on Adam's bedside locker, each recommended by Michael Lenard. Reaching for one, Adam studied the title, *The Science of Amnesia.* He flicked open the contents, slid his finger down until he reached the section entitled, *Post-Traumatic Amnesia (retrograde).*

Over the following hour, the book confirmed everything the consultant had said;

Amnesia caused by physical injury is one of the harder forms to treat. With many other forms of amnesia, a suitable environment and surrounding oneself with familiar objects and people can help kick-start connections in the brain. The main problem with physical injury-related amnesia is that synaptic connections in the brain may be temporarily or permanently severed.

"I'm gonna pretend I didn't see the word permanently," Adam sighed, closing the book and placing it back on the shelf. A voice in the hallway caught his attention, "Britney?"

She stepped gently into Adam's room, scanning it quickly.

"Hey, figured you'd be up," she said, "what have you been doing?"

"Reading."

"Oh! Anything good?"

Adam shook his head and patted the books, "Research into depression."

Motioning for her to sit, Adam did not take his eyes off Britney's face. Maybe it was the supposed comfort of being home for the previous four weeks, but to Adam, Britney looked more beautiful each time he saw her.

"Can you remember anything?" she asked, her gaze fixed on the book.

"No."

"In time, you will, you have to hope."

Adam pushed his wheelchair towards the door and gently closed it, leaving a smile escape.

"My only hope is that, some morning, I will wake up and everything will be clear. All my memories, good and bad will come at once. That day, I will be living in colour, and not in this prison of grey."

A smile crept onto Britney's face, she tried to stifle it, yet she relented.

"That almost sounds poetic," she laughed.

"Yeah," Adam said, feeling warmth grow on his cheeks, "didn't mean for it to come out like that!"

Britney stepped closer to Adam and knelt down level with him. Leaning in she hugged him. Unsure of where to place his arms, Adam let them dangle by his side.

"You will be okay Adam, I promise," Britney whispered. Adam raised his arms up and around Britney, changing his mind each second as to what he should do. Questions raced around inside, were we close before? Does she want me to hug back? It was too late, Britney sat back and smiled. *I have to ask her, was there anything between us?*

"Britney, can I ask you something?"

Her delicate blue eyes were drawn to the door, as a knocking found Adam's ears.

"Adam, Detective Murray is here to see you," Erin said from outside. Adam stalled, eager to find the beauty that existed in front of him again. But, Britney had stood up and turned away.

"Amm, yeah, show him in."

He turned to Britney, "I'm sorry about this, I'd better see him..."

Britney smiled, "I understand. I'll wait outside."

Murray opened the door, standing aside to let Britney out. From such a harmless woman, to a giant of a man, the contrast could not have been more obvious Adam thought. Murray closed the door and then placed some sheets of paper over Adam's books on the bedside table. Refusing Adam's motion to sit down, Murray sighed loudly. There it was again, the sweat growing on Adam's skin.

"Is everything okay Detective?"

"I have discovered startling information about you Adam."

Adam pushed himself up straighter in his wheelchair and looked at the sheets of paper on the bedside table. He assumed there was no information printed on them; Murray was merely using them as a form of intimidation. Paper or not, Adam was intimidated. He coughed to relieve his drying throat and took a breath.

"I can guarantee this will be news to me. I can't remember anything more from the crash."

"You must realise Adam, you had a life before the accident."

"Of course, but I know nothing about it. Not a thing!" Adam sensed a heat developing inside, growing like a furnace in his chest. His face trembled for an instant, was he going to cry? The armrests of the wheelchair were wet, plastic glistened in the light. Murray reached down for the sheets of paper and handed one to Adam.

"Explain this."

Adam read the contents of the letter once, twice, three times. *This can't be right?* He wiped the sweat from his eyebrows, unintentionally rubbing his fingers into his eyes. Blurry vision only made the information appear more fictional.

"Are you sure this is mine?"

"I'm sure," Murray said, his voice scratched like rough sandpaper in Adam's ears.

"How is this possible?"

"You tell me!"

Adam turned the sheet over, the content looked real. *But was it*?

"Is this a test?" Adam asked, immediately regretting the question as Murray squinted his eyes, focusing his stare back at him.

"I am a Detective in the Boston police force, we don't do jokes."

Shaking his head, Adam looked at the paper once more, "Maybe in time I may be able to answer it, but now, I don't have a clue."

Murray folded the other pages into his jacket and turned towards the door.

"I'll leave that with you Adam, it may help re-focus your memory."

Reaching to open the door, Murray flicked his jacket backwards, revealing his gun. Adam swallowed, "The moment I remember anything, I will contact you."

Murray nodded, "Have a nice day Adam."

***

Madison shovelled traces of snow off the walkway running though his garden. In the corner of his eye he saw a plain clothes detective walking out of Adam's house. When the detective's car went out of sight, Madison quickly ran into his house. He turned on six switches in the front room, causing a line of green and red dots to light up on the super-computer. Madison sat down in front of the monitor, waiting for the screen to load. He glanced at his watch, "November 15th?"

Something was wrong. He tapped the keyboard, fixed his eyes on the screen. He quickly picked up the headset lying on the ground, and waited for a line of red dots to change.

"Come on, transmit!" he beckoned.

Signal connection - Offline

Madison sighed and threw off the headset as he stood up. Outside on the front decking, two mini-satellite dishes were placed on either side of the house. The dishes, which were four inches in diameter, faced each other. He examined them, finding that snow lodged on one of the dishes and melted, causing the system to short-circuit. Forcefully, Madison pulled the wiring from the dish and followed it to the next connection point. After attaching a new section, he stood directly outside his front door.

A beeping noise started in his pocket. He glanced left and right at the two dishes, he was now standing midway between both. He took the beeping device from his pocket. It was the size of a cell phone. Madison tapped the touch screen and it lit up. A symbol resembling a pulse appeared on the three-inch screen. Within seconds, the pulse changed from red to green. With that, Madison walked back into the house.

Returning to his computer, Madison lay back in his chair, the line of previously red dots turned green.

Transmitting, Transmitting, Transmitting...

"November 15th; broadcasting transmission 1.2, query; Detective David Murray arrived at the subject's home today, reason; unknown."

From the darkness of his front living room, Madison noticed Britney driving past his house. She looked up at the front decking, pulling her blonde hair back to disguise her intentions. She must have seen him fixing the mini dishes from her car, Madison thought. Within seconds, she was out of sight. Britney was a beautiful woman Madison knew, yet he must be close to thirty years older than her. Shaking his head Madison laughed,

"Get that idea out!"

***

The *Banshee bar* on Dorchester Avenue was busy for a Monday night in November. The crowd puller- New England Patriots, were displayed on three large TV screens. Britney sat in the back with two friends. Her mind raced, trying to decipher the day's events. What did the detective show Adam to leave him speechless? And what was Madison's reaction about?

"How is your friend, the guy who was in the car accident?"

"He is doing good, considering," Britney replied, her tone more obvious than intended, as the girls changed the subject.

Out from the crowd of alcohol-fuelled supporters stepped Shaun McCoy. Britney did not even try to hide her disappointment, she sighed in full view of him. He nodded for her to follow him as he passed. Reluctantly, she got up and stepped out into the smoking area.

There were only a few people in the smoking area, the cold chill of winter too much for most sober smokers. Shaun opened a pack of cigarettes and offered one to Britney. She refused.

"So," Shaun inhaled, "what is he telling that Detective?"

Britney swallowed hard, she imagined Shaun's reaction before she spoke.

"He is telling him nothing, because he remembers nothing."

"Ha, you expect me to believe that?" said the young man, stepping closer to Britney. His thick jacket made what was already a big man, even bigger. Britney took a step back, under the outdoor heater.

"Yes, I do. That is the truth." Shaun laughed as he exhaled the cigarette smoke.

"You think that those pretty little blue eyes will work on every guy eh? No, I ain't buying that."

Britney's phone rang, *phew!* She reached into her pocket. She focused on the caller. Shaun grabbed the phone as they looked at each other for what seemed like minutes, until he broke out with a smile, "Adam."

With that, he grabbed Britney and bundled her into the nearby male toilets. Locking the cubicle door, he handed the ringing phone back to Britney.

"Loudspeaker!"

She answered.

"Hey Adam, how're you?" trying her best to hide the nerves which caused her body to tremble. The sheer ease with which Shaun shoved her into the toilets repeated in her mind, Britney was powerless.

"Hi, you free to talk?" Adam's distinct voice came through the phone.

"Sure, what about Adam.....you ok...?"

Shaun's eyes fixed on Britney, his two arms her held against the wall, she was certain that Adam would hear his breathing.

"This might sound weird Britney, but..."

Adam took a breath on the other side. Britney tried to crouch up before the words left Adam's mouth, but Shaun's arms held her upright.

"Have I ever been involved in something illegal?"

"Illegal?" Britney replied, relieved to a certain extent.

"Yea, like anything illegal from which I could have made money from," Adam answered. Shaun's grip loosened, allowing Britney to slouch a little against the wall.

"I don't think so Adam. Why do you ask?" Britney countered. Shaun nodded his approval.

Sheets shuffled on Adam's side, a few moments later he responded, "No reason, just wondering."

Shaun pressed a little harder on Britney's shoulders to get her attention, and even though he was just looking at her, she understood. Her skin became trapped underneath Shaun's hands, pinching her to react. At first she shook her head, he pressed harder.

Reluctantly, she asked, "Adam, what did the detective want today?"

"He wanted to show me something, see if it would help reignite my memory."

"Oh! Did it help you?"

Shaun held his breath and leaned closer to the phone. Adam was busy on the other side, paper shuffled again.

"Sorry Britney gotta go, just seen something that may help me!" With that, the line went dead.

Shaun released his grip. A knock on the door unsettled them, until Shaun shouted, "two minutes!" at the man outside. The knocking stopped immediately. Shaun looked her up and down, his arms still on her shoulder. She tried to shuffle a little, he was too strong.

"He is gone, let me get outa here," Britney whispered. She pulled her arms up to her chest and pushed herself back against the wall. Shaun leaned closer and kissed her neck. Britney tried to extend her arms to push him away but it was useless.

"We both feel the same for each other," Shaun whispered as he kissed further and further up Britney's neck. His right arm slid off her shoulder, down along her side and grabbed her hip.

The faintest, "No," emitted from Britney's mouth. This did not stop Shaun and he pulled her hips closer.

"No Shaun!" Britney exclaimed louder, extending her arms to push him away. Unlocking the door, he just laughed and walked out. Britney slammed the door shut and sat down. A stinging came to life in her eyes. Men waited outside the toilet door to come in, Britney did not care. They could wait.

Chapter 10

The couch was soft. It was inviting. Adam threw himself onto the cushions, he felt different. The giddiness was unusual for him. Even though he was alone, he felt like he was surrounded. He decided to put a name to the new found feeling, anticipation. He steadied on the couch, tried to act calmer until the door opened and his heart beat a little faster. He did not take his eyes off the woman who was standing there, Britney. Suddenly, he looked at what she was wearing. It was all making sense now, it was prom night.

Adam stood up and hugged Britney. She looked amazing, *she was amazing.* Her blonde hair curled, draped over a black dress, sliding off the side of her breast. Blue eyes looked so innocent and pure. Every time their eyes made contact, it sent a tingle throughout his body. He wanted to kiss her, but something said stop. Britney sat down on the couch just as Erin walked in. Taking a camera from its pouch, she told Adam to sit down. He put his arms around his date. He could see himself with Britney on the couch. He assumed this feeling was happiness because it had been so long since he felt it. They froze momentarily for the snap of the camera; there was the picture on his laptop screen, the same one from the family album, taken right before his eyes.

He tried to get up but his legs would not let him. Surprised, he tried again. Adam looked at Britney for help, she still seemed happy. He called for his mother to help him up, but she took the same picture again and again. Legs transformed into pillars of concrete, rooting themselves to the ground. Adam shouted and screamed, but no one paid attention to him. Pain tingled in his feet and crawled into his hips and stomach. It was climbing higher and higher until it held his whole body, suffocating him. Screams were drowned out by the pain. He was paralysed.

Adam shouted in the darkness. His hand reached to the bedside table, flicking on the light. Wiping the sweat from his forehead, his breathing relaxed. The wheelchair near his bed reminded him it was all a dream. But a tiny fragment of optimism remained in his body shouted differently, Adam had found another memory. In the darkness, Adam debated the one major question he wanted answered, was he in love with Britney before the accident?

***

The physiotherapist's secretary's office was warm. Adam noticed it was an attempt to take his mind off the pain that lay beyond the next door. It did not work for Adam, it only succeeded in making the contrast clearer.

Relaxing, warm and easy, compared with hard, painful and real.

Adam hated the feeling of the leather table. Even though it was only his second session, it seemed like he was coming here for months. As he lay in his t-shirt and shorts, he looked down at his white legs. He imagined how they looked the previous summer, judging by the award on his shelf, he assumed he was one of the fitter players. But now, those two *things* joined to his hips were more of a nuisance, skinny and fragile.

"We're gonna keep these muscles loose Adam," Michael said, as he ran his hands down Adam's legs, "remind the muscles that we'll need them soon!"

Adam nodded and laid back. He questioned Michael Lenard's philosophy. Was this positive thinking an act? Or did this man really believe in the power of the mind?

"Do you think I'll walk again?" Adam said, bluntly. Michael stopped. He stared into space for a moment and then turned to Adam.

"I cut the tendons in my arm when I was fifteen." Raising his arm up to Adam's chest, he twisted so Adam could see the scars.

"*Partial movement and limited power* were their exact words."

Michael's eyes focused, his cheeks tensed as he gritted his teeth underneath. Adam knew this man believed when others did not, and he was determined to pass his mentality on to his patients. Michael tensed his arm; his biceps were huge, veins pressed against the skin, the detail in his forearm was astonishing. Adam was amazed how this man had been hiding such a physique under the loose, grey shirt.

60

"Guess they were wrong," Michael whispered, running his hands down Adam's legs again.

***

Britney poured two cups of coffee and placed them on the table. Erin smiled and reached for the milk. The last few months had taken its toll on Adam's mother. Up until recently, she was praised for her appearance, considering she celebrated her 45th birthday the previous summer. But the last three months were decades to her. She was lucky to still have her son with her, Erin knew, but the shock of the accident was still dwelt inside.

Every night since the accident, Erin asked why. Why Adam? Why cripple this young man who had done nothing to deserve it? Nights were spent crying in silence, cursing the fact that drug dealers, rapists and thieves roamed around the city with ease. Yet, her son was paralysed in bed after an accident no-one could explain.

Some days she woke up happy, until the thought of Adam crossed her mind, dragging her spirits down again. Seeing his lonely face every day made her want to give up her life, just so that God might reward her, and let Adam walk again. Britney visiting was one of the few things that helped lift Erin out of her rut.

Erin had seen the way Adam was around Britney before the accident, life-long friends that may develop into something more. Adam used to laugh off suggestions he liked Britney, but the way he turned into a different person when Britney was with him, showed otherwise.

The two women spoke quietly in the kitchen, careful not to let Adam hear. Erin handed Britney a white envelope.

"What is this?" the young woman asked.

"Detective Murray gave it to Adam, he can't explain it."

Britney reached inside for the letter. Moments after reading the letter, Britney asked, "Is this a joke?" Erin shook her head, and wrapped her hands around the warm cup of coffee. Britney re-read the letter. She blinked, as if trying to remove any trace of fiction from the contents.

"Adam was in hospital during this period, no?"

"September 2nd to October 17th, meaning that Adam could not have done this himself."

"So, Adam was a millionaire for two weeks?" she asked. Britney lowered the letter onto the table as she tried to comprehend its contents;

6th September:
Lodgement $1,000,000
Balance $1,000,956

20th September:
Withdrawal: $1,000,000
Balance $956

"Yeah, I suppose so," Erin answered, reaching for her cup.

"Adam has no idea where the money came from?"

"No," Erin whispered. "If this is a surprise to us, imagine what it feels like for Adam."

Britney stood up and placed her cup in the sink. Her expression was just as lost as Adam's, Erin thought.

"What will happen now?" Britney asked.

"Detective Murray said that finding the source of the money may become a federal investigation, but he wants to keep it from them, for now anyway."

"Is he awake, Adam?"

"No. He went to sleep after he called you earlier."

"Tell him I'll be back soon."

Britney stepped out, leaving Erin alone to question the deposits and withdrawals again. How could Adam lodge $1 million when he was in hospital, and withdraw it two weeks later? The only conclusion she could come to was that this was an elaborate plan by the Detective Murray, a plan she did not comprehend, maybe a new-age technique by the police force. Erin stared into space, trying to relive the detective's visit. He did not stay for long, almost as if he knew Adam would know nothing about it.

Chapter 11

Britney stood in the hallway of Shaun's apartment block, steadying herself before she knocked on the door. She took a deep breath, fuelling herself. Knocking on the door, Britney begged it to open quickly; the smell of the hallway had started to play with her stomach.

Footsteps approached from inside the door. Straightening her stance, she pushed her hair behind her ears.

"We need to tell him!" she blurted out, as Shaun McCoy opened the door.

He smiled, "Hello to you too."

Again Britney exclaimed, "We have to tell Adam the truth!"

Shaun took a step back into the apartment and motioned for Britney to come in. She followed into the dark hallway. It smelt better in here, despite a dampness that lingered in the air. Shaun walked through the dimly lit hallway and into his bedroom.

The bedroom was a world away from what lay on the other side of the wall. It was warm, bright and the smell of men's deodorant took Britney's attention for a moment. A large television hung on the wall, over a large cabinet stocked with DVD's, games and a playstation console. Fitting to the stereotype of a young man, the bed was undressed. But Britney noticed this seemed to be the only item not in its place in Shaun's bedroom. His clothes were neatly tucked away in the ceiling-height wardrobe in the corner, with an array of shirts hanging on one side and a collection of winter coats on the other. Three suits hung in the corner of the wardrobe, two black and an unusual looking dark pink one.

Shaun jumped onto his bed and laid full length, crossing his arms behind his head.

"So," he said, "what seems to be the problem?"

Britney shuffled, until Shaun motioned for her to sit on the end of his bed.

"We cannot go on like this," Britney answered, sensing the energy which was so abundant just a few moments ago, beginning to fade.

"Britney, it's just keeping a little secret," Shaun spoke. He is doing it again, Britney thought. While Shaun was predominantly aggressive, he had the knack of toning it down when it suited him. Britney shook her head, trying again.

"You don't understand what this is doing to Adam, what it is doing to his family."

Shaun sniggered, "And you don't understand what will happen if you let our secret out."

He unfolded his arms and sat up in the bed, forsaking his relaxed demeanour. In her eyes, he grew to twice his normal size.

"You can't..." Britney tried to regain her composure, "you can't expect it to just blow over. If we come clean now, maybe we will be looked on favourably."

Shaun laughed and shook his head, "Are you serious? How can you expect to come out of this looking good when you have lied to wheelchair boy and his family every single day since the accident?"

Without laying a finger on her, Shaun winded Britney. It took the words of a man she hated to show her how heartless she had been. Remembering the day of the accident, Britney hated the thought of how Shaun used her shock of the event against her. And now, more than three months on, she was in an even worse position.

"We can admit to our mistake for starters!"

Shaun burst out laughing, and whispered to himself. Britney kept trying, "But it will help Adam get his memory back, let him get on with life."
Shaun threw his legs off the bed and jumped up close to Britney. His sniggering tone died, replaced by slow and coarse words.

"If Adam Fletcher's memory decides to come back, that will be a sad day for him. If you care about him and his wellbeing, you should not help him along his way."

"You are a cold, cold man."

"Be realistic for once. It's me that is saving you, saving all of us. Now get some common sense girl, we're on the same side."

Drenched in disappointment, Britney trudged down the five flights of stairs and into her ford. She hated what she had become. She hated the feeling of being held to ransom by Shaun. Failing to muster up the strength to slam her car door, Britney slumped on the steering wheel and sobbed.

Arriving on Louver Street over an hour later, Britney parked her car two houses before Adam's. Her courage deserted her, muttered promises of coming clean vanishing once Louver Street came into view. She knew the truth was not coming out today. Starting the car to turn for home, a tapping on her window startled Britney.

"Are you ok?" asked Madison, his voice dampened by the glass barrier.

Britney lowered the window and looked at the rake in Madison's hand.

"Yeah, I'm okay," she lied.

"I don't mean to intrude, but anything that I can help you with?"

Am I that obvious? she shrugged, "There is always something wrong, that is just the way my life is!"

Immediately, she regretted speaking, this man did not need to know her problems. Before Britney had a chance to reassure Madison that she was ok, he offered, "cup of coffee?"

A smell of curry drifted into the hallway when Madison opened the front door, beckoning Britney inside. She was surprised by how well Madison kept the kitchen, and indeed the house. A black marble-top island stood in the middle of the room, with a dark timber table butted against it. Drying dishes were stacked near the sink, along with one knife and fork, something Britney was used to. He raised a glass jar with Nescafé coffee for Britney to approve, she nodded.

Madison poured Britney a cup of coffee, "So, what is bothering you?"

He acted like he knew Britney, judging by the ease with which he asked. Usually, she was wary of this approach, but Britney saw this man meant her no harm. Maybe it was the fact they were making eye contact every few moments or how relaxed they seemed together. She thought back to before the accident, this was how she felt with Adam.

Sipping her coffee, Britney fixed her thoughts into meaningful sentences, without giving too much away.

"I see what I have to do, but there is something stopping me from doing it," she said while twirling her finger around the edge of the cup, "I guess I'm just a coward."

Considering she was opening herself up to him, Madison appeared very comfortable. He never looked away in awkwardness, always listened to Britney's words and took everything in.

"There are times when it's better to be a silent coward than a brave loudmouth."

Britney looked at Madison's aging face. For a man in his fifties, he was well worn. His distinctive blue eyes the only part of his face not ravaged by time. She guessed he had a hard life; the fact his tight grey shirt showed his considerable frame, reinforced this. Thoughts jumped around in her head as to what he could have been previous to this. His haircut shouted of an army-like life. But, when he spoke, Madison showed compassion and sincerity not normally associated with hardcore drill sergeants.

What the hell. Britney spoke, "What do you do? For a living I mean?"

Madison's face dropped a little, had she stepped on fragile ground?

"I used to work in construction. That all changed when my wife died."

Madison seemed to pause for the usual *sorry* but none came. Britney knew that when a close family member died, the word *sorry* does very little.

"What happened?" whispered Britney.

"A man burgled our home, he assumed it was empty...she got in the way."

"Oh my God, I'm so sorry!"

"It was a long time ago, thank you though. I changed jobs soon after, to what I am now, an Inventor," he said, lightening the mood.

"You're an Inventor?" Britney quizzed while sipping.

"Have you invented anything I could use?"

He smiled, "Well, what do you need?"

"I need so many things...maybe a time machine? Have they been invented yet?" she laughed briefly, but the pain of her reality came back to her mind, a flashback of Adam in his wheelchair. Madison stood up, opened a cupboard and grabbed a packet of biscuits.

"Not trying to pry, but what would you change?" he asked.

So many events rushed to Britney's mind, her father's death, her mother's fall into alcoholism, yet one stood out before all others. Maybe it was just the fact it was the most recent, but to Britney, it felt the most relevant.

"I would try to sort out Adam's life."

"Stop the accident from happening?"

Britney forced a gentle smile and tried to control her darting eyes. The silence grew rapidly until it began to smother Britney. She reached for a biscuit, the noisy foil packaging cut through the tension, allowing her time to think. *Speak!*

"Tell me about your wife, please."

"She was perfect," Madison whispered, as if being careful not to erase the memory of her. His eyes almost glazed over, no doubt picturing his lost wife, Britney figured.

"Her blue eyes were hypnotising, I could look at them all day and not get bored. They told me everything she was too afraid to say; when she was hurting, when she was lonely and when she loved me. A true passage to her soul I guess."

Britney leaned on the table when Madison spoke, her coffee finished, paying total attention to the woman he described.

"I can still feel her hair draped over me as we lay in bed, the smell alone was numbing. As I lay in her arms I felt so content, I cared about nothing else when she was with me. And I know she cared for nothing else but me."

Britney glimpsed a trickle of a tear escaping Madison's eyes. He squinted hard, eager to suppress any more.

"The pain is still here," Madison said, laying his hand on his chest.

A saddening silence developed, only the sound of Madison's deep breathing entering the vacuum. Britney rubbed her ring finger, images of her father's last breath flashed in her mind, "Unfortunately for us," she whispered, "history is made only once."

70

"Yet, even in that one roll of the dice, we still get to become somebody's hero."

Britney closed her eyes and took a deep breath. She could smell the scent of her father as if he was sitting right beside her.

"I don't think that I'll ever be anyone's hero."

"People destined to become heroes never accept it straight away. Fools prefer to think they are heroes from day one, whereas true heroes only see it when they need to see it."

Britney looked Madison in the eyes, slightly astonished at the possibility of what wisdom lay behind that aging exterior.

Chapter 12

Adam awoke with a start. A spark ignited inside. The puzzle of the $1 million played on his mind all night. Where did it come from? Who lodged and withdrew it? Why did they use his bank account? The laptop seemed to be running slower than ever Adam thought, as he waited for the screen to upload. Moments later, after quick taps on the keypad, a wide grin came to Adam's face as he stared at the information flashing on his monitor, a *Boston Globe* news story from early September.

All but one of the Massachusetts Megabucks winners showed up at Lottery headquarters yesterday, as six lucky people shared in September's $6 million first prize draw. Five winners, four from Boston and one from Springfield collected their winnings at 9.00 am, obviously all eager to get their hands on the large sum. Of the six who shared the jackpot, one ticket holder held off, possibly wary of the publicity that comes with such a win....

Adam tapped the buttons on his phone and placed it up to his ear. He glanced at the headline again, it lifted an invisible weight off his shoulders each time he read it.

"Hi Britney, can you come over? Thanks!" he said excitedly, and hung up just as quickly.

Within twenty minutes, a gentle knock accompanied Britney's arrival.

"Hey, is everything okay Adam?"

"Look at this!" Adam said, turning the laptop towards her. She sat on the bed next to him and read the online article. He saw a smile creep to her face, her eyes darted back and forth along the digitalised screen, taking in the good news.

"This is good Adam," she said, not fully seeing the cause for excitement. "But, what does this tell you?" Adam smiled, "Whoever collected the $1 million, regardless of privacy acts, will have submitted their name and a form of identification upon collection."

"The winner did not reveal their identity?" Britney stated.

"Yeah, but Detective Murray, I hope, can request that information."

He lay back in his bed, "It is a serious case, after all."

"So, what is the plan now?" she asked.

"I'm gonna ring Detective Murray and tell him about this, see if he can get a copy of the winner's details."

Britney nodded in approval, leaned in and hugged Adam tightly. Her hair rubbed his nose, the smell was intoxicating, Adam closed his eyes as he breathed it in. A sense of progress flowed through his body, a momentary thrill of relief when he imagined the secrets of his life unravelling. The hug lingered, causing Adam to wonder if he had grown up with Britney being so close. For all he knew he might have. Molecules of her scent travelled up his nose and into his brain. There, the brain broke the odour down and reassembled it again. Millions of electrical signals sparked in Adam's brain, he remembered this smell. *Just like the book said - surrounding oneself with familiar objects and people can help kick-start connections in the brain.*

Britney pulled away, he wanted to scream stay but decided against. That hint of her, that hint of memories invigorated Adam. He sensed thoughts and memories clambering to become visible, he pictured himself on a steep slope, one where the top just appeared from behind the clouds. Adam now understood how powerful the mind could be. On one hand it was the origin of his negativity and yet it still possessed the ability to give his life new meaning. A life before the accident existed and Britney was a major part of it, he was beyond sure.

"I'm so happy for you Adam."

"At last, I can see some hope," he said.

"It's still early, get some rest. I'll see you soon" Britney whispered softly.

Adam smiled goodbye, his eyes fixed to Britney's every move as she walked out. It had taken until now for him to realise how physically beautiful Britney was; her tight clothing revealed a toned physique, short slender arms matched her small frame perfectly as her breasts pushed at the pink t-shirt. Her blue eyes, he stuck in his mind. Her almost snow white skin so soft and striking-in his mind he traced it down her face to her neckline, where the tiniest protrusion of her collar bone showed when she stretched. Even though Adam cannot remember seeing it, he imagined her toned stomach, hidden from winter's breeze by layers of cloth. Britney closed the bedroom door, leaving his view. Adam glanced out the window at the falling snow, so pure and clean, such things reminded him of Britney. He may not remember what he felt for Britney before the accident, but Adam buzzed at the thought of what might re-emerge from his memories. And, he did not want to fight it.

***

"Maybe this kid ain't so bad," Murray said to himself, scribbling on a piece of paper. Adam had revealed his theory about the $1 million and Murray found it hard to argue against it. Certainly, if Adam was bullshitting, he was good at it. Not a trace of worry or nerves existed in his voice earlier. Murray lifted his handset and dialled again, *now, the hard part.*

Murray held the phone close to his ear.

"Hi, can I speak to O'Neill, it's Detective Murray."

Moments later, O' Neill answered.

"What?" he slammed.

"I have a request, I need a search warrant for the Bank of America branch on Regal Street."

"What for?" O' Neill said.

"I think that a lodgement and withdrawal may be connected to the car crash in Canton in September."

"The car crash with the young guy? I assumed you had that written off as a case of joy-riding gone wrong?"

Murray hesitated, "There is more to it than that...Sir."

75

"Plus, what could a lodgement and withdrawal tell you about a car crash Murray?"

"That's the thing-"

"It doesn't matter," O' Neill interjected, "the answer is no!"

"With all due respect Sir, this could provide a major breakthrough in this case."

"Murray, NO! Don't push me."

Murray took a deep breath, eager to push, but O' Neill was gone. He gripped the phone a little harder and placed it down. Murray silently cursed his superior, knowing that with one swish of a pen, a domino-effect would be initiated; who lodged and withdrew the money, what connections they have to Adam and hopefully, the other people in the car will be identified. With O' Neill's answer, Murray's chance of pushing the first domino was gone, for now.

Chapter 13

The faint boom of fireworks from the city reached Adam's ears, some four miles away. An evening spent with his parents, watching the nation's annual countdown on television proved too much. With midnight edging closer, Adam went to bed. In his dark room, the quiet murmur of music pushed him closer to sleep and into a new year.

Winter snow falls had crippled Boston. There was some comfort in this for Adam, who had been housebound for the last number of weeks, barring the twice weekly visits to Michael Lenard. Christmas dragged, each day filled with friends of the family and relatives who made a special effort to visit because of Adam's condition. While he appreciated their attempts, he hated the 'forced affection'.

His daily routine was set. Get up, eat breakfast, read online papers until twelve, and then an hour of massaging from his city hospital nurse. Michael Lenard had recommended this, even though it was not generally part of a patient's recovery. Adam grasped the negative side to this added treatment, assuming his situation was so bad he deserved special attention. But, Michael Lenard insisted his reasoning was different; constant massaging of Adam's legs helped prevent atrophy, where the muscles become smaller and weaker as a result of disuse. After his hour long session, Adam spent the rest of the day reading, playing computer games or online poker. Adam hated the routine he had fallen into, but he figured there was no way to break out of it. The only light in his daily schedule became apparent, Britney.

She always arrived with something, whether she knew it or not. She considered a magazine, a new pastry from Greenhill's cafe or gossip as something, but even the days she came empty handed, Adam felt like Britney had given even more, her very presence being enough.

That night, similar to every previous night, was spent alone. Just like the daylight, Britney brought a welcome break. It was no coincidence she disappeared with the darkness. She had a life to live as well Adam knew.

The music ended, and with it Adam's motivation to stay awake. What a way to spend your *first* New Year's celebration, he thought. Closing his eyes, he heard the front door open. At first he took no notice, until the footsteps travelled along the hallway to his bedroom door. Someone stood outside his door for a moment. Then a gentle knock, Adam realised it was not breathing, but sobbing.

The door opened, light from the hallway rushed in. He squinted to adjust to the black silhouette of Britney in the doorway.

"You still awake Adam?"

"Yeah, you okay Britney?"

She sniffled softly. Stumbling to the bed, she slipped out of her high heels and knelt next to Adam. He tried again,

"What's wrong?"

"I'd rather not talk about it," she sighed. With that, Britney pulled the covers down and lay next to Adam. He pulled the covers over Britney as she lay on his chest.

Adam decided against persisting with questions, he just kissed Britney's forehead and whispered, "Happy new year."

The morning brought no answers. Britney had crept out while Adam slept. He lay awake in the cold morning, none the wiser why she had abandoned her new year's celebrations and come to his home, crying and silent. His phone on the bedside table shouted at him to pick it up and call. He decided against, why bother a seemingly fragile woman even more.

***

Across Quincy, Britney unlocked her front door and stepped into the cold house. Her breath drifted in the hallway when she blew into her closed palms, a futile attempt to heat them up. She slumped onto the couch and sighed, "What am I doing!"

Thoughts of Adam lying in bed flashed to her mind, confused over the previous night's events. Britney reached for the phone and pressed the illuminated buttons. She held her breath as the phone rang, expecting a barrage of questions.

But there were none, just "Hi Britney, hope you're ok?"

She smiled.

"Yeah, I'm okay now. I'm so sorry about last night."

"It's ok, don't worry," was Adam's response.

Britney relaxed at Adam's thoughtfulness, one of his best traits, only asking the questions he knew she wanted to answer.

"Wanna do something later, I've an idea?" she asked, not needing to hear the answer.

***

Adam and Britney crossed the threshold, swapping cold for hot. She pushed the wheelchair, allowing Adam to take in what the Banshee offered. He turned to Britney as they moved along the front of the bar, "I know this may not be the greatest thing to say, but I think I remember this bar!"

"Don't worry Adam, you were not an alcoholic!" she laughed.

Britney put two bottles of Budweiser on the table and sat next to Adam. He was like a child in Disneyland; smiling at the surroundings, questioning everything and eager to know so much more. A strange feeling of familiarity stayed with Britney all evening as they drank bottle after bottle. She remembered nights, only a matter of months earlier when she and Adam used to spend the evening in the Banshee before going into the city, staggering out of taxis at three in the morning. The alcohol let her thoughts and memories seep to her mouth, all but one.

The front door opened, sending the winter breeze to the back of the bar. A sudden chill caused Britney to turn around, finding Shaun McCoy standing at the bar. She turned her back towards him, hoping Adam would not realise what she was doing.

"So," he rubbed her knee, bringing her back to the conversation at hand, "what else did Madison say?"

"Oh, he just spoke about his wife for a while. The poor man is still distraught over losing her," Britney answered, while looking for Shaun out of the corner of her eye. Her heart jumped as she seen his broad frame step away from the bar and approach her.

"He seems coo..." Adam stopped mid-sentence. Shaun passed, they made eye contact for a split second and Adam looked down at the table quickly. Britney felt a question building up behind those eyes. Adam used to, since she could remember, fall into a deep stare when contemplating something big.

"He seems kinda what?" Britney quizzed.

Loosely sipping his drink, Adam looked like he just swallowed a poisonous bug. He leaned back in his chair. Every beat in Britney's neck doubled, her mind scrambled at what Adam would say next.

"He...sees...seems?" she urged Adam to speak.

"Déjà Vu.....I think!" he said.

Adam's eyes fixed on Britney. Her heart punched the inside of her chest. Shock electrocuted her body, *he knows!* Adam titled forward and asked,

"Do *I* know him?"

In an instant, various scenarios played out in her mind, tell him yes or no, make up some story of a past friendship or war. She decided to go with one that meant minimal explanation, "No, I don't think so."

"Well, he knows me," Adam said. Britney shrugged,

"So, what were you saying about Madison?"

The tension lifted as Adam's eyes changed back to their normal state, fluid and at ease.

"I was saying he seems cool for an old guy."

Britney nodded, "Yeah, and kinda hot for an old guy!"

They both smiled as they tapped bottles, *Cheers* and drank.

***

Louver Street had long gone to sleep. Fresh snow erased the trails of footprints left by kids in the gardens. Britney stepped out on the Fletcher's front porch with two bottles of beer in hand and sat next to Adam. Pulling a blanket over them both, she leaned closer and rested her head on his shoulders. Snow fell like dust over the neighbourhood with the soundtrack of a hallway clock, chiming for midnight.

"I think that this is getting to me," Adam said as he raised the bottle. "But I like it."

Under the blanket, Britney squeezed Adam's fingers tightly. For an instant, the idea of telling him the truth appeared realistic, but the calmness of the moment kept her from doing so. Words that wanted to be spat out were swallowed once again, down deep into where she kept her darkest memories and secrets. The feeling that someday, somehow they might surface felt like a knife inside her, but for now, Britney laid all her weight on Adam's shoulder.

Above the glare of the streetlamps, Britney saw some stars sparkle.

"What are you thinking?" Adam asked.

"It's nothing really, something silly."

"I like silly."

"Okay, fine. Do you think there is something else after this? Something like an afterlife?" Britney replied. She looked around and connected the light flaky snow, the gentle breeze and the midnight chime, realising each one added to a sense of the spiritual and mystical.

"I don't think any other-worldly Gods care about us now," Adam said, putting a damper on Britney's hopes.

"I used to think there was someone, or something, looking out for us until we got *there*. But recently, my theory doesn't seem to be holding up," Adam continued.

Britney nodded and sipped. "Well, I like your theory, I believe in it."

"Your father?" Adam asked. Britney acknowledged by squeezing his fingers.

"I must visit his grave again, it's been too long."

"I will go with you, if you like?" Adam said. She smiled at Adam and rubbed his hands. Even in the dim light, Britney could see his genuine expression, his gentle, caring face. Leaning in, she lowered her head onto his shoulder and sipped again.

"Britney," Adam whispered, seemingly careful not upset the peaceful mood, "I have been dreaming a lot recently."

"Yeah?" she replied, "What about?"

"I thought it was just random, crazy dreams, but....I think I'm getting some memories back."

Britney rubbed Adam's hands again, "That's great to hear-" she whispered, the cold night appeared to cut her sentence short. Or maybe it was her nerves she guessed. Britney pulled her arms from underneath the blanket.

"Bed time I guess?"

"It's ok, I think I'm gonna stay out here for a while. Besides, I think you've done enough for me today." They hugged, Adam's warm breath broke through the winter's night and caressed Britney's neck.

"Goodnight Britney."

"Goodnight Adam, I had a great evening," she said while kissing him on the cheek. As their eyes met for an instant, Adam broke the developing tension.

"This is embarrassing, I may have lost my memory, but I'm pretty sure the guy should walk the girl home!" Britney laughed and turned towards the access ramp that snaked around the Fletcher porch.

"Someday soon, you can walk me home." She carefully treaded down the driveway, creating new prints in the snow.

Twinkling stars overhead caught Britney's attention just as Adam called, "He is still watching over you." Britney smiled, for once forgetting the treason she committed. Despite her unfaithfulness, her supportive Adam still existed.

Chapter 14

Adam tapped his nails on the steel rim, this was a big day and he knew it. Even the developing goose pimples on his arms failed to take his mind off the task in hand. Only now, months after lying on Michael Lenard's table for the first time, did Adam feel confident at the thought of the physiotherapy session. *I must walk her home* Adam repeatedly told himself. The night on the porch, six weeks previously, equipped Adam with a renewed drive, enabling him to see the positive in his rehabilitation.

The daily massages were beneficial, each week Adam felt more and more. He wondered if he was the only person on earth who wished for pain. The tingling he felt grew with each session, and though movement was minimal, he could at least imagine a day where his legs might be able to support him. Adam longed for when his nerves would fully fire again, and shoot signals along the electrical highways of his body.

The crunching of snow snapped Adam out of his day dream as Madison climbed over the white fence bordering the gardens.

"Hello Adam."

"Hey Madison, what's up?"

"Just saw you sitting here for the last few minutes, everything ok?" he enquired.

"Yeah, thinking about today?"

"Today?" Madison asked.

"I am trying to walk, well that is not really true – I will be able to use my hands to support myself."

Madison climbed the front steps, stopping one short of Adam.

"I hope it goes well for you. How have your sessions being going?"

"As good as can be expected I guess! Fingers crossed that today will show an improvement," Adam said.

"Remember Adam," Madison said, "today is not the defining day. So, even if it does not go perfectly, just know you will be given more chances to succeed."

Adam smiled as Erin interrupted, opening the front door and rubbing Adam's shoulder, "You all set?"

"Yeah, I am."

Madison patted Adam's legs and stepped away.

"Thank you for that Madison," Adam called out as his neighbour climbed back over the fence. Madison acknowledged with a raised hand. Adam turned to his mother, "Let's go!"

***

Michael Lenard's treatment room was different. The table had been stowed away next door, and the room was taken up with a set of parallel bars, standing three feet high.

"Adam, how are you feeling?" Michael asked.

"Pretty good," Adam answered.

"Great!" Michael exclaimed, as he pushed Adam to one side of the parallel bars.

"Now Adam, I think you know what you have to do here." Adam gazed along the bars, which were just wider than his shoulder width. As he sat in his chair, they were touching his upper arms on each side.

"I'll help you to get up to the bars, but from then on, it's you," Michael said. Erin stood inside the door, her hands placed over her mouth. Adam knew the score, should he fail.

"Sorry, but is it ok if...." Erin did not hesitate, "I understand Adam."

Adam knew failing here could hurt him, but the pain his mother would have to endure went beyond what he imagined. Even though he could not remember specific events with his *parents*, he knew the people who claimed to be so close to him at the hospital were indeed his parents. It felt so right over the last number of months, they smiled when he smiled, they were down when he was down, and they were always there for him. Today, should Adam fail, he wanted to save them further hurt.

The course was short, a mere ten feet. Adam reached up to the metal bars. They felt strangely warm. Michael put his hands underneath Adam's armpits and helped him to stand. He powered his arms and stood. His arms trembled, holding his entire body weight, bringing a smile to his face.

"Well done Adam, now put some weight on your legs."

The thought of putting weight on his un-used legs felt like pressing his skin onto broken glass. Looking down, Adam felt a tickling sensation in his legs more than ever. He bent his arms to let his feet touch the floor, the wobbling in his legs stopped when his feet planted themselves on the wood.

"Think about using your legs Adam," Michael whispered. Adam stared at his legs for what seemed like an eternity, willing them to move. His right knee lifted, carrying his foot forward a matter of inches and placing it down again abruptly. Pain hinted at its presence in his lower back.

"Well done Adam, your first step, now try another."

Adam's stare fell on his left knee, begging it to repeat the rights heroics. An intense pain developed in his arms, he intentionally placed more weight on his legs to ease the burn. His left knee moved. Left foot passed the right foot, Adam smiled.

"Excellent Adam, now more weight," Michael said. Adam concentrated again, relieving pressure on his arms a little more. A trickle of sweat gathered on his forehead and nestled in his eyebrow. Despair seeped into his thoughts when he looked at the distance remaining. Despite the pain of taking two steps, he was still less than a quarter of the way there.

"Come on, keep it going Adam!" Michael said, adding urgency to his voice.

Adam took a deep breath again and tried to move his right leg. His body shook, trembled. Pain crawled into his triceps. They had never, in Adam's mind, worked this hard. Every nerve in his body tried to move the right leg, even they knew he needed it, another step just to reinforce the appearance of improvement.

"Try harder Adam!" shouted Michael, clenching his fists. "You're on your own here, no-one is gonna catch you, keep going!" Adam squinted in pain as the nerves in his legs awoke. But the messages they relayed were not of joy, as Adam released some of the throbbing with a dull roar.

"I...I...can't..." he gasped, his body shouted stop and he fell to the floor. Michael leaned down to help him up but Adam managed to gasp, "Leave me here. I need to lie here."

Adam lay face down on the timber floor, sweat covered and gasping, he never knew such pain could exist. His eyes caught the glint of sunlight on the steel frame of his wheelchair, the thought of a life confined to it sent a shudder through his body until he turned his face away. Sweat poured into his eyes, stinging like acid, forcing him to squint. Adam did not know which part of his body to hold onto, the pain spread through every available cell.

Michael leaned down next to him, "It is supposed to feel like hell the first time. Just know that today does not define your progress."

Adam faced Michael, Madison's words earlier that morning had sounded strangely similar. Adam shook his head, not bothered about the weird coincidence for now. Michael helped him back into his wheelchair, while a soaking t-shirt and his vigorously beating heart reminded Adam he had failed today. It repeated the fact he was still no closer to walking again. No closer to walking Britney home after a night out.

The kid's laughs failed to conjure up imagined memories of better times anymore; instead they mixed with the clicking of the wheelchair when Adam pushed himself up the driveway, producing a cocktail of anger which he could not help but ingest. Everyone and everything seemed to tease with their mobility. The wheelchair was a prison that Adam clambered to get out of once he reached home.

"Can I get you anything?" his mother asked, standing at the bedroom door.

Shaking his head, Adam reached out and knocked the wheelchair over. The wheel seemed to get the last laugh as it spun freely, continuing its new found clicking. A gentle knock on the door snapped Adam from the torment, "I'm okay for now."

The door opened just enough for Adam to see Britney's fingers on the edge, "Britney?"

She paused momentarily, "Will I leave you rest?"

"No...Please come in."

Sitting on the end of the bed, Adam looked everywhere except at Britney. Even in the quiet bedroom, an invisible pain floated from his broken body, into his lungs and almost suffocated him. Britney rubbed her hands over the bed sheet that covered his legs.

"I failed," he said so quietly, painfully.

Britney squeezed his legs a little tighter as she rebuffed his claim.

"No, no you didn't."

She slid along the side of the bed up towards Adam, urging him to believe her words, "It's only the beginning. There is plenty of time to get through this."

"Yeah, that is the problem. This is the beginning, what if this is how things are gonna stay?"

Britney sat closer again, "No don't think like that Adam, I know you, I know what you are capable of."

He looked into her eyes, "But you don't know how it feels to be me right now."

"You're right Adam, I don't know what you are feeling," Britney said. "I have been down before, depressed even. But when I got over the loss of my father, I started to live again with your help. I wanna return the favour."

"But, you're not over the loss of your father."

Adam knew it, Britney's eyes confirmed it. She blinked incessantly and shuffled on the bed, like Adam had just poured dust down her back.

"You will get over this, you have to believe." She grabbed his hands.

"Believe? The only thing I believe is that I'm gonna be stuck in that *thing* for the rest of my life," he stared at the wheelchair in disgust, "and I don't know if I'll be able."

"What are you trying to say?"

"I cannot spend my life confined, restricted, tied up." Adam slid his hands away from Britney, fearful that his depression would travel to her. *One loser is enough.*

"I can never have a normal life, I can't even run away. No chance to just pack my bags and walk. Forever depending on someone else to help me live my life, needing support for every step. Never will I be able to go out and enjoy myself like everybody else. No freedom, no independence, no life."

"Stop!" Britney said, pulling Adam's hands close and laying a kiss on them. "You will have us next to you all the way."

"I am not going to let my problem ruin your life. I want you to be free, do all the things that you should be doing," Adam replied, struggling to look Britney in the eyes.

"I must accept that I'll never be free from this torture, might as well not be living."

"Stop talking like that. Losing someone is the worst feeling in the world, don't even think like that. We all love you!"

Hanging his head, he sobbed, "Different kind of love." Britney leaned closer to Adam and lifted his head up. Her eyes never left his, her small thumb wiped away his tears and she laid a kiss on his lips.

Adam raised his arms and pushed her away, "Don't do it out of pity."

Gently shaking her head, Britney smiled and kissed him again. This time Adam did not stop. He wrapped his arms around her and kissed her again. The tender feel of Britney's lips on his made Adam feel free, the thoughts of failure and despair which had been circling in his head for hours now suddenly vanished. A tinge of excitement ignited in his body as she leaned over him and sat on his lap. Adam rubbed his hands along her white t-shirt separating his skin from hers, finger tips pulled at the cloth sporadically, as if they had a mind of their own. Britney leaned back from Adam, her blonde hair fell down in front of her face and perfect blue eyes peered through. Slender fingers slid down his side, until they nestled underneath his t-shirt, feeling like silk on his skin. Adam's analytical mind shouted, *why is she doing this?* But Adam blocked them out; the feeling of being alive for once was too enticing to risk losing it all because of an internal, silent battle.

Chapter 15

The sun crept up in the east, sending long morning shadows along Louver Street. A cold crisp air ensured that the layer of frost and snow stayed intact, despite the glowing morning rays. Adam lay awake in his bed, staring at the ceiling. Britney had gone before he woke, at first he was saddened by this, but when he tried to recollect what he had dreamt during the night, he realised it was better to be alone with his thoughts. He knew his mind and memories were fragile, but something told him last night's dream, memory, was more than a random concoction of images.

Various health magazines stated it was easy for amnesia sufferers to piece different snippets of everyday life together and recognise them as actual memories. Adam knew this was real. He picked up the phone to dial Detective Murray's number, feeling he had just taken a step off the bottom rung of the ladder. *My recovery starts now* he thought, as the phone rang.

In the cold hallway of Shaun's apartment block, Britney crouched against the wall. Her mind was restless, every minute she read the text she received from Adam earlier:

Hi Brit, woke up this morn with gr8 feeling, I remember who was driving d car. Thinkin about ringing Dec Mur... So happy, come over when u can.

Britney looked left, down the hallway to the stairs, contemplating running back to Adam's house and admitting it all. *Does he know? Is this all a plan?* A rumbling began in her stomach, she wondered whether it was hunger, worry, or guilt. Imagining Adam's reaction, Britney squeezed her eyes closed and pushed her thumbs over her eyelids to the point of pain. Slouched against the wall, guilt pressed its invisible form onto her shoulders, reminding Britney how Adam pulled her through after the loss of her father. The compliments she received for being 'so strong and courageous' danced in her mind, when in truth Adam was the strength that hid behind the curtain all along.

Britney turned her head to the right and gazed upward at Shaun's door. The threats he made that day in September, while convincing her to stay silent, still loomed in her sights. It was possible that Shaun may be reeled in very shortly, Britney thought, yet some small part of her shouted she can slip through unimpaired, as long as Shaun kept his word. The tiny crack of light at the end of the tunnel was urging Britney to keep up the facade, to keep portraying herself as innocent in an effort to shield the truth from Adam.

Standing up, Britney turned towards the stairs. But before she could take a step, Shaun appeared at the end of the hallway.

"What now?" he sighed, walking toward her.

"Adam is starting to remember the accident. He knows it was you who was driving," She mumbled in reply, her gaze darted all over to avoid Shaun's stare.

"Did you tell him?"

"No, no, I swear I didn't."

"What's Adam gonna do about it?"

"He is thinking about ringing the detective," Britney said. Shaun brushed past Britney, unlocked his door and stepped into the dark apartment. An open door was enough of a sign for Britney, she followed. Shaun sat on his bed and stared at the floor for a moment. "What are you thinking?" Britney asked. Closing his eyes, he rubbed his hands all over his face. Britney realised this was the first time she had seen Shaun nervous, first time to see a weakness.

"We should come clean..." she said.

"No!" he interjected, "I have a plan."

***

The supercomputer in Madison's front room flickered on, sending red dots onto the walls. He drew the curtains even tighter and sat down and placed a headset into his right ear.

The absence of light in the room stirred memories which were hidden deep in his mind. Madison could hear his wife as if she were next to him. Time had passed so quickly since her death, yet every memory of her was so fresh in his mind, he assumed daily re-runs was the reason. In the weeks and months after her death, Madison looked for ways he could have saved her. Every theory he conjured up was shot down by friends and family, seemingly eager to rid his mind of such 'ludicrous' ideas.

Remembering the last conversation he had with his wife, Madison fell into a day-dream; breakfast turned into a friendly war of words just because of some man's view on a retiring politician, Sundays spent in bed, goodbye kisses at the front door. Madison froze the image of his wife at the door, her eyes looked so peaceful and loving, every part of him longed to run back and rub her face, to kiss those lips.

His heart sank when he stepped out of the dream, energy sapped by the realisation he was alone, and the only reminder of his wife he has is not even physical. A connection of signals and sparks in his brain were the only link to a time when his life spelt *perfection*.

Green dots illuminated his face, *transmitting;*

"13th February, broadcasting transmission 1.3..."

Madison leaned back in the chair and closed his eyes, hoping to re-ignite the feeling of being with his love again.

"You were right, this is harder than I expected." Leaning forward again, Madison traced his finger over the letters flashing on the screen.

"I have been here for months now, so close to my target yet unable to initiate the plan. I feel like a child with an unopened toy at Christmas, patience is not one of my virtues here. That surprises me, because before I got here, I was so focused, so determined and so patient."

Madison stood up as the headset lead unravelled and followed him from the computer in his slow trance around the darkened room.

"Don't get me wrong, I'm still on course. It's just that...so much planning, the result is so close I just want to reach out and grab it. I guess this is what happens when the mind has too much time for itself."

Turning the monitor off, Madison shook his head, "I'm talking to a computer screen!"

Chapter 16

Murray walked through the Bank of America branch on Regal Street, keeping his glare fixed on the path to the manager's office. The glass door was ajar as Murray knocked.

"Come in please," The bank manager stood up and shook Murray's hand,

"I'm Mr. Brownrigg, how are you?"

"I'm good. I appreciate you making time for me on such short notice."

"That was no problem Detective," he said, pointing to the seat, "please, sit." Murray sat in a leather chair and placed a large envelope on the desk.

"I assume your secretary has informed you of my query?"

"Yes, she has," Mr. Brownrigg said.

"Before I begin, I must remind you that all information discussed here is confidential, and is part of an ongoing investigation." Mr. Brownrigg nodded and sat up in his chair. Murray opened the envelope and took out the contents.

"Here I have a bank statement relating to a man named Adam Fletcher."

As the paper was slid across the desk, Mr. Brownrigg's eyes immediately found the important part, the $1 million deposit and withdrawal. He turned to his computer, shaking the mouse to restart the monitor. After a few quick taps, he checked his records against the statement.

"Yes, I remember this client, Mr. Fletcher."

Murray pulled a notepad out from inside his suit jacket, flicking it open he placed it on the desk.

"I stand open to correction, but I think Mr. Fletcher was a winner of the lottery. Although, I think that was supposed to be anonymous!" Mr. Brownrigg smiled.

"Yes, that's correct," Murray said. "Do you remember anything unusual about Mr. Fletcher?" Nodding, Mr. Brownrigg glanced upward and to the right, as if trying to recall specifics.

"Yes, the day he lodged the winnings, he immediately requested that when the cheque cleared, he wanted to withdraw the full amount in cash."

Murray squinted, unable to control his surprise, "And you did not think to report this?"

"Lottery winnings in Massachusetts hold back 5% tax, what Mr. Fletcher was given was all his. We have no obligation to disclose information about the withdrawal unless requested to do so," Mr. Brownrigg replied.

Murray scribbled a few lines in the notepad and turned to the manager again.

"You say that Mr. Fletcher was in your office on the day he lodged his winnings?"

"Yes."

"And you were sure of his identity?"

"It was the first thing we checked and double checked detective, his social security number and passport!"

Murray lay back in his chair and tapped his pen against his notepad.

"And just to clarify, he was here again two weeks later to withdraw it?"

Mr. Brownrigg nodded, "With such large withdrawals, I like to personally give the money to the clients. They are, after all, our biggest customers."

Murray ceased writing. He rubbed his stubble while gazing at a copy of the statement. As if doubting himself, he searched through his documents until he found a hospital print out of Adam's stay.

"Is everything okay detective?" Mr. Brownrigg asked.

Biting his lip, Murray muttered, "The two days that the young man was *here*, he was also laying in a hospital bed with a badly damaged spine."

Mr. Brownrigg sat back in his chair, seemingly replaying the detective's words again in his mind, until something sparked with him, "The young man?"

***

Murray followed Mr. Brownrigg into the surveillance room, where two security officers were positioned, constantly switching their gaze from one screen to the next. The wall was covered with monitors, each showing the bank from various angles; a partial street view outside, entrances, emergency exits, helpdesks and cash counters. In the middle of the array of screens was a larger monitor, which displayed a constant stream of footage from the central lobby.

101

"Would you excuse us for a moment please?" Mr. Brownrigg said. Without hesitation the guards stood up and quietly left the room. Murray was about to ask who will operate the monitors, but Mr. Brownrigg sat down, tapped at the keypad and typed in 06-Sept. The main screen went black for a moment, then rebooted with September's footage. Mr. Brownrigg turned to Murray,

"I assume you would like a copy of what we see?"

Murray remembered the phone conversation he had with his superior earlier in the week. When he suggested that getting bank footage may be useful to the case, Murray's request was shot down. And there he was, standing in the surveillance room of the bank, with the manager offering him a copy of the camera footage. He nodded to the Mr. Brownrigg, and thanked God he did not force the matter earlier by throwing his *warrant* on the manager's desk. To disobey a direct order was one thing, but to forge an official request for information was quite another. *So far so good,* Murray thought. Mr. Brownrigg flicked through various camera angles until he found the view looking directly at the exterior of his office. He fast-forwarded until he saw a man standing leaning against the door frame.

"I think this is Mr. Fletcher," Mr. Brownrigg said.

Murray shook his head. The man on the screen had long, afro-style hair, which covered his forehead and neck. His attire was not in keeping with a young man's outfit the detective thought, as he noticed a dark purple suit with high collars shielding his neck, should his hair fail in doing so.

"That is not the Mr. Fletcher I know. Are you sure this is him?"

Mr. Brownrigg nodded, "Yes, just to confirm, I will skip to the withdrawal date." Within moments, the same camera angle flashed up, with the date 20-Sept on the bottom right corner.

"There he is again, on the day he withdrew the money."

Murray concentrated on *Adam's* body language, looking for some distinguishing trait to confirm or deny his theories about this case. But there were none. Just the same stance, clothed with the same purple suit and the same hairstyle.

"Can I have a recording of both dates, two hours either side of Mr. Fletcher's arrival?"

Opening the door, Mr. Brownrigg motioned for one of the security officers to come in.

"Gabriel, I need you to do something for me."

Chapter 17

Muffled cries spilled out from under the pink duvet, which Britney had wrapped around her trembling body. The darkening Boston evening fell around the house, adding to the claustrophobia that swelled inside Britney, threatening to tighten around her throat. She peered over the covers every few minutes, hoping her mother would step through the front door. She never came.

Britney slid her hands over the couch, imagining there was someone to hold her. Her isolation just served as a reminder, taking her back to when she was a fragile, lonely and delicate girl. The pain she endured in her teenage years was akin to her being a decorated china cup on a shelf, and the owner, life, throwing open the doors to all sorts of rampaging livestock.

Adam had saved her. He changed her from a frail being, pulled her from the track she was destined to take and made her realise you decide your own direction in life through your thoughts and actions. Now, she pondered, how did she let herself get into this mess? She used the powers Adam had given her, and turned them around, into an evil, unnatural magic called deceit. How she longed to take the easy way out now. Claim her ignorance and lies were all a result of a troubled past, seeping upwards to the surface after years of forced hiding. *Lying was hard.* Last September, the easy way out disappeared, fading when Britney failed to act. In the frantic minutes after the accident, she turned away. The same actions still defined her life five months later.

Britney rubbed her cold and bare fingers. Her father's ring was upstairs in her bedroom, but the thought of leaving the relative security of the living room couch was too daunting.

"Mother?" she whispered from underneath the blanket.

"Mother?" she cried louder. Only a vacuum of silence answered, as a draft of cold air drifted in from the hallway, making Britney cower below the pink blanket again.

While hiding under the cover, the solution popped into Britney's head. *Will I run?* She immediately picked out all the positives of that plan. For a woman in her early twenties, she had very few connections with this place; an alcoholic mother whom she rarely sees, a college degree yet no employment, and her best friend who would be better off without her.

Even though she had tried hard to live like a *normal* teenager after her father died, Britney knew she was different. Her only connection to *normal* life was Adam, and even he was nowhere near normal. It seemed obvious to her now; jump out of this riddle that was written by Shaun, Detective Murray and Adam, and hope it all falls flat without her, like a missing link in a chain. Her mind looked for more reasons to back it all up, fabricating ideas of how it would help save Adam in the long run. He will get hurt regardless, Britney thought, but better this way than having to break the news to him. But, in the new plan, there were some rebellious signals, gathering together to make a giant 'HELP' sign in her conscience, yet she quashed them without notice. She threw the blanket to the floor and ran upstairs.

***

Despite the disappointment of the physiotherapist session, there were so many positives that kept sticking in Adam's mind. He replayed one image more than others, the look in Britney's eyes before she kissed him. He smiled, *such beauty, such perfection*. He questioned if it was Britney's intervention that sparked another, more significant memory that night. All of a sudden Michael Lenard's words leapt into his mind, as Adam made connections between the positive thinking, which was spurred on by Britney, and the recollection of the mystery driver.

***

Britney pushed down on the suitcase and slid the zips closed. In the corner of her eye the streetlight reflected on something shiny. She tried to ignore it as she heaved the suitcase off the bed and onto the floor. The thud vibrated throughout the entire house, deadening and blunt. She reached into a bedside drawer, facing away from the source of the shine, her father's ring.

106

Slouching down on the floor, Britney slid the gold ring along her finger, feeling an unusual cold sting off it. Thoughts of her father trickled into her mind. Pangs of embarrassment made her heart beat harder as she imagined her father watching her now.

He raised a good girl, Britney whispered in her mind, not this woman who was ready to run from all of her problems.

"I don't know if I can stay."

The empty house swallowed her words, in seconds it was still again. Britney contemplated looking upwards, but instead knelt on the floor and leaned over the bed, all the while twisting the ring on her finger.

"I need you here, I am falling." The loud buzzing of Britney's cell phone startled her. Glancing down at the caller, she sighed.

"Hello?"

***

Adam positioned his wheelchair between the counter top and the island in his kitchen. He reached forward to grab a walker frame and slid it closer. The front door opened, and within seconds Britney walked into the kitchen.

"Hi!" Adam smiled, as he concentrated on the walker. Britney crossed her arms and watched, letting a smile creep out. She threw her car keys on the central island.

"Tea?" she whispered to Adam. He nodded, leaned forward out over his lap and pushed himself out of the wheelchair. His legs touched the floor and his knees wobbled.

"Well done Adam," Britney said, stepping closer. Adam was now standing, with his arms supporting his entire body weight. A laugh escaped, causing his arms to shake, "Enough for now," he said, sitting back into the wheelchair.

He landed with a thud as Britney held the chair steady, rubbing his shoulder, "Well done Adam," she repeated.

The kettle clicked, taking Britney away from Adam. Even feeling her hand on his shoulder gave him tingles. He thought about reaching back and holding her hand, yet decided against. Adam relaxed and watched Britney preparing some tea. He considered it unusual for Britney to break from her routine of coffee, maybe she needed a change, and anyway, it afforded Adam a chance to gather his thoughts about the previous night.

"About last night-" Adam said, trying his best to suppress a smile, not wanting to seem too eager.

"Maybe it shouldn't have happened," Britney interrupted.

What? A sting started up in his chest, he could not describe what it was, but he knew he did not like it.

"What was it? Did you not want to?"

"No, I did!" Britney said, "Maybe the timing was a bit off." Adam digested the comment.

Timing a bit off? He wondered when would be a good time, considering he has been wheelchair bound for months now, and will be for the foreseeable future. Something inside urged him to argue this point, but he thought better of it.

"Oh, okay."

The pair stayed facing away from each other, Britney preparing what seemed like the slowest cup of tea ever, Adam rubbing the table while looking for words to say.

"You didn't have to-"

"I wanted to. I just think we should stay friends, not ruin everything."

Her words came out like blades. Britney placed the tea next to Adam on the table, leaned down and kissed him on the cheek.

"I'm sorry."

Adam had words to say, but they all ended with question marks. There it was again, the cold stinging in his chest. He took a deeper breath to fill his lungs, hoping it would cleanse his airways and provide some relief. But no, all it did for Adam was to reconfirm he was powerless. He looked around as Britney reached for her keys, he wanted to shout something that would change the whole situation, one word that would make them go back to normal, yet even to utter goodbye was impossible.

Chapter 18

Shaun had waited for Britney to call for hours. He lay on his bed and imagined her stepping through the door, with that sorrowful look she has worn for months. Britney's gaze would dart from wall to floor to ceiling, anywhere but in his eyes. Then, a deep breath as she puked out her true feelings, caring words tinged with guilt. Her act was getting old, well out of fashion at this stage. Shaun knew Britney feared him. *Everybody does.*

On the day of the accident, Britney stalled. The hurt caused by Adam's injuries opened her up, and Shaun crept in, controlling her from that moment on. He figured guilt can make a person crack and fall into control of the next person that comes along. Shaun played the guilt card every time without fear of negative reaction.

His ears perked up when he heard commotion in the hallway. Soft footsteps approached his door. The person outside took a moment to compose themselves, everybody seemed to do that around him, Shaun thought. The door opened.

"Hey?" Shaun said.

"I haven't seen you in days."

"Yeah, sorry Rach- was busy." Rachael lay on the bed next to Shaun and kissed him.

"Is everything ok between us?" she whispered, her voice cracked. Shaun kissed her on the lips and smiled,

"Perfect."

He curled his arms around Rachael, realising he had been dealt another card.

"I missed you. Did you miss me?" Rachael said, planting a kiss on Shaun's lips.

"Yeah, course I did. Babe," Rachael turned towards him, "can you do us a favour?" Shaun asked.

***

Bringing her car to a halt, Britney glanced at her home, still deserted. A surge of guilt passed through her body as she reached into her pocket and pulled out a key, avoiding looking directly at it, the key to Adam's home.

"It's not too late!" Britney whispered to herself, with her head pressed on the steering wheel of her car. The keys on the passenger seat seemed to come alive. Britney could hear them demanding to be taken home, back to safety. Glancing up at her dimly lit house, Britney decided she would rather spend the evening in darkness than with the keys, which seemed to speak louder with every passing second.

As she stepped into her home, a car turned up the street and parked next to Britney's white ford. She waited in the hallway, with the door slightly ajar, peering out into the unlit walkway leading up to the door. Britney's skin tingled, the person who stepped out

111

of the car looked like her mother. Opening the door further, she shouted, "Mother?"

No reply came. The black figure kept walking up the pathway, slowly and eerily. The beating in her chest became heavy and dull, coinciding with the onset of fear again.

"Who are you?" Britney shouted, straining her eyes to make out the dark figure.

"It's Rachael!" the figure replied, stepping into the light of the hallway. A fly buzzed around the tall lamp in the corner, drawing Rachael's attention away from Britney momentarily.

"Remember the last time that we were both here together?" Rachael said. It did not take Britney long to bring up that particular memory, the day of the accident.

"Yeah, I'm afraid I'll never get out of my mind," she said.

The lamp sprayed light on the teenager, showing just how young Rachael was. Her innocent looking eyes darted and gazed with such peace, no doubt in contrast to Britney's strained and agitated movements, she assumed. Her thin, narrow face showed her age to be nothing more than eighteen or nineteen and her slender frame reinforced the impression.

"Shaun told me about the keys," Rachael said.

"I didn't get them," Britney replied.

"You have to do what is right for all of us."

"Do what is right?" Britney said, stunned by Rachael's cheek.

"The right thing is to go to the cops, admit to what we've done, and hope they go easy on us!"

Rachael did not stir.

"Ok, let all five of us go to jail, or let Adam get over this, y'know, walk and stuff, and no need to tell him about our involvement?"

For a moment Britney wished she possessed the carefree attitude of the teenager, throwing off life's problems, like flicking over to another channel, a new picture, and a new scene.

"Which is worse; ruin all our lives, or one?" Rachael asked.

"Adam's life is already ruined, while we've stood by, too cowardly to own up."

"Well, if one life is already ruined, why make it another five?" Rachael replied. They must be Shaun's ideas, Britney guessed. *Keep the pressure on in case she tries to turn back.*

"Are you that insensitive, or is that Shaun talking?" Britney broke through the facade. In the momentary silence, Rachael was stripped down. Shaun's ideals no longer poured from her tongue, her carefree attitude seen to be anything but and her heart thawed right before Britney's eyes. Her teenage face shrugged *I'm sorry*, as she stood up.

"I know you love Adam and want to protect him, but, I feel even stronger for Shaun."

"Somehow, I doubt it," Britney said.

"Well, you fooled us," Rachael said, walking out and gently closing the door.

***

Murray spent the day examining the recordings from the bank. His eyes grew heavy from ingesting clip after clip of people, entering and leaving the premises, all on their

113

own little mission. When *Adam* entered, a few looks were thrown his way, due to his afro style haircut and purple suit, yet none of the glances seemed to be one of recognition. Inserting a different disc every hour only provided another viewpoint of the same scene. *Who is he?*

Murray broke the law, and all for nothing. He needed to have information that would identify Adam's imposter, or unlock something in Adam's memory. This unknown man, who went to the trouble of posing as Adam while the real Adam lay in bed crippled, must know him personally, Murray figured. While acknowledging that information about the accident could travel fast, Murray thought it was more than a mere coincidence Adam's identity was chosen as the one to imitate.

Two choices formed in front of Murray, find the fake Adam, and then work on the driver of the car, or vice versa. The chances that *Bank Adam* and the driver was the same person only added spice to Murray's quest, dragging him on in his search through heavy eyes.

He knew that a man, who imitates another's identity to cash $1 million, is unlikely to be a community care worker or a major philanthropist. Murray knew the possibilities were, unfortunately, endless.

It was 23.09 and Murray retraced every person's steps captured by the camera. It was of no use. Adam's afro-haired impersonator still did nothing unusual, he walked through the front door, asked for the manager at customer service, waited outside the office for a moment and then entered. *Hang on!* Murray rewound the footage. Had he finally found something about the man, something that can link an unknown face to a known identity?

Slowing the footage down, Murray examined the scene where the man waited outside Mr. Brownrigg's office for a moment before entering. A smile crept onto Murray's face when he saw a potential source of fingerprints flash before his eyes. Already in his mind, connections from the fingerprints to some bigger crime were being made. He could imagine one of Boston's better known criminals ending up behind bars as a result of fraud and theft, the excitement made the detective giggle loudly in the near deserted staff room.

He scribbled down a note for the forensic unit to read in the morning and dropped it into their pigeon hole on the lower level. Murray left the station feeling satisfied, such a feeling had been missing for some time now. Yet as he sat into his car, Murray felt his shirt rubbing off a scar on his chest, where he had been shot the previous summer. All of a sudden, thoughts of a high profile arrest evaporated. Flashbacks of what criminals can do sprang to mind, the earlier surge of excitement now drowned in a well of conservation. With his new found phrase, *guilty until proven innocent* floating into view, Murray sat in the car with conflicting thoughts circling inside.

Is Adam hiding something more? Was the lottery tip off only a throw in the wrong direction? Could the accident have been something more than a random joy-ride? Murray's first impressions tried to defend Adam, but the detective quashed them, deciding he must treat Adam as he would any other suspect, wheelchair bound or not.

Chapter 19

Britney never knew hours could last so long. The constant changing of her mind only unsettled her more. Knowing Rachael only visited for the keys, she was surprised her phone remained silent, considering Rachael returned empty handed. Relaxing, Britney assumed Shaun changed his mind. Drifting close to something resembling sleep, Britney was pulled back by her vibrating phone on the bedside table. Reaching out a blind hand, her fingers grabbed the phone and pulled it towards her ear.

"Hello?" she croaked.

"Thank you, I couldn't have done it without you," Shaun whispered.

The line went dead.

Her body dragged her weary mind back to sleep. It was about to go under when her mind grabbed on, throwing out a word to wake her up, "Keys!"

Britney grabbed a robe and ran down stairs and outside to her car. Reaching for the door, she slid her hand under the latch, squinted her body as she pulled.

Please be locked, please be locked. The latch popped, the door opened. Tired eyes glanced down at the empty passenger seat.

"Rachael!"

***

On Louver Street, a banged-up Mazda stopped three doors down from the Fletcher household. The moon, a natural spotlight, hid behind thick clouds. Darkness spread where the streetlights' influence ceased. One faulty lamppost at the end of the street kept the occupants of the car alert, unintentionally grabbing their gaze with random flickering.

Three men sat motionless in the car. Their collective breathing was the only sign of life, until Shaun leaned forward between the front seats and glanced at his two companions. Their white faces looked like they were floating, as the black attire covering the rest of their bodies blended in with the dark interiors.

"Ready?" Shaun whispered.

Shaun led the way, bouncing along the pavement, dressed head-to-toe in black. His two friends were clearly more agitated, dancing from dark spot to dark spot in an attempt to avoid the light. Shaun took out his phone and began dialling as they approached the house. While he awaited an answer, he motioned for the two men to check around either side for lights.

Standing in front of the Fletcher's porch, he whispered hoarsely into the phone, "Thank you, I couldn't have done it without you."

The two men ran around to the front again, signalling *thumbs up*. Shaun lowered the phone into his pocket and

117

pulled out a set of keys. The three men smiled as they approached the front door, slowly and silently. Shaun's carefulness was like a vacuum, sucking the sound from the Fletcher's hallway. The door opened, dark sneakers landed on the tiles. Shaun slid a small flashlight out from his pocket and aimed it at the floor. A ray of light travelled along the hallway, pointing to the door at the end. Shaun nodded his head towards the door and lead the way, tip-toeing in the dark.

He leaned his glove covered hand gently on the door knob, squeezing until it had sufficient grip to turn. The door squeaked loudly, sending echoes down the hallway, making his two companions shudder. Shaun shook his head at them, annoyed at their nervousness. He turned the knob a little further and the door opened.

Adam's room was even darker than the hallway. A quick flash around the room with the light helped Shaun gather his bearings. Straight ahead, Adam's bed was the destination. He handed the flashlight to one of the men. He reached into his jacket pocket as he approached the bed. Adam's breathing was soft. He was so still, motionless.

Pushing the wheelchair out of the way, Shaun leaned on the edge of the bed. His mates were invisible, bar the shaft of light that came from the torch and shone onto the carpeted floor. Shaun reached into his jacket, hearing deep breaths from his companions, as he leaned forward with the handgun.

His left hand slid around Adam's neck, getting tighter and tighter until he noticed a reaction. Adam shuffled, his breathing interrupted. Shaun released, Adam's eyes opened as he gasped for air. In a daze, Adam squinted as

118

the light was directed at his face. Shaun leaned in and pressed the gun against Adam's head.

"You have a visitor tomorrow. If you mention my name, it will be the last word you'll ever speak."

One of the men slapped Adam's face, demanding an answer to Shaun's threat. Adam nodded, with his eyes still half closed from the blinding light. Shaun tapped Adam's nose with the gun, reminding him of the consequences.

"And hey, it won't be just your life ending. This place can get very hot, very quickly," Shaun whispered as he stood up.

Within seconds, the men had left speedily and quietly. Shaun walked into the dark kitchen and stood in silence for a moment, observing the position of the table and the nearest window. The clock erupted, sending two loud chimes throughout the house, startling Shaun in the process. When his heart rested, Shaun opened a window and walked out the front door.

Outside, he locked the Fletcher's front door and proceeded to walk to the open window. One of the men ran up the driveway with a straightened length of industrial steel wire. Shaun placed the keys on the hook-like ending, and fed the wire in the window. The beam of light was focused on the keys making their way to the kitchen table. The steel wire bent slightly, as the keys landed on the edge of the table. Shaun twisted the wire until the keys slid off. Retracting the wire he smiled and pushed the window closed.

The three men sat back into the car.

"A job well done guys!" Shaun said. He took his phone out of his pocket and started typing a text

119

message. The Mazda turned quickly at the end of Louver Street and accelerated hard, speeding past a white ford coming in the opposite direction.

***

Britney ran inside and snatched her car keys from the living room. A quick glance at her phone read 02:01 as she started the engine. How she hoped Shaun had not reached Adam's home yet, she could still stop him from going in, she thought.

Tyres squealed as she took a hard left turning on to Louver Street, missing a parked car by inches. She pressed hard on the gas toward the end of the street, ignoring a *new message* beep from her phone. Reaching into her pocket, she slowed down as a car passed her by. At the end of Louver Street, there was no sign of Shaun, no parked cars on the street, nobody walking by. *Good, I'm here first.*

Britney turned off the engine and picked up the phone, waiting for the new text message to load. Britney read the message three times, each time her heart sank lower, illuminated words telling her the horrible truth,

Nothing to worry about, he will stay quiet.

Britney was too late. Shaun had come and gone. Her mind went crazy, was Adam ok? Did they hurt him? Does he need her help? The lights in the Fletcher house stayed off, Britney took that as a good sign. She buried her face in her hands when she imagined what the conversation tomorrow would be like, yet another day of lying to Adam. *Or was it finally time to come clean?*

***

Madison pulled the curtains closed in his front living room. He had seen the entire night's events; Shaun breaking in, putting the key back, and Britney arriving too late. He had seen her parked on the street for over twenty minutes now, her head buried in her hands. At first he assumed she was speaking to someone, he could make out her lips moving. But, on reflection, he realised it must have been a solitary conversation, or one with a higher force. Nonetheless, he had seen enough of this one woman battle. Tiredness held precedence in his mind now as he locked the living room door and went to bed.

"Do not worry Britney. It'll all be over soon," Madison said aloud, flicking off the light.

Chapter 20

The next morning on Louver Street was a world away from the events which took place only hours earlier. While all the parties involved lay in their beds, Madison sat on his front porch with a cup of coffee and a homemade flapjack. Madison had seen the events of the night unfold in front of his very eyes, but, the unusual situation was what had stuck in his mind. He could not get the image of Britney crying out of his head. Shaun and his gang entered the house and enacted their cover up of the break in by placing the key back in through the window, it mattered little to him. Instead, it was the arrival of Britney moments after that gained Madison's attention.

The fragile woman sitting in the car alone triggered recollections in the man. No matter how hard he tried to block them, memories of his wife and her last day on this planet repeated within Madison. A dull stinging grew in his chest, a familiar feeling over the years. His brain conjured up more images of his darling, dying alone in their home. Their love, lives, plans all trickled away with her blood. Madison remembered the feeling of her cold body, lying broken in his arms.

He had cursed his neighbours for months, asking how no one noticed the break in. Until his close friends drilled the 'truth' into his head; *Human's are greedy, they only live for themselves.*

Madison did not take this onboard. He insisted there is good in everybody and the trick is to press the right buttons to unlock it. Madison's life quickly disintegrated as he began a quest to get his love back, spiritually or otherwise.

Many mediums promised they would be able to reach her, but Madison found faults with all their so called connections. Every day he looked for some confirmation his wife was still alive, somewhere. He longed for a sign, anything to prove she still watched over him, knowing what he feels, knowing how much he still cares.

Nothing came.

One night while searching for his next medium, Madison stumbled upon a low key convention. He still remembers the night he read the words that changed his view on religion in one lecture; *if heaven existed, science would have found it.*

Listening to scientist after scientist, student after student, Madison changed. He threw his rosary bead into the bin on the way out, its punishment for leaving so many riddles unsolved. *How could they have fabricated this lie? All along, we have been told God loved us, yet he let my wife die? He let me live this torturous life since?* So many questions buzzed in Madison's mind, and religion failed to answer one. That night, Madison held the hand of science for the first time.

The light emitting diodes flashed red, red and then green. Madison was transmitting. He sat in front of this super computer for months now, armed with information that could change people's lives forever. It was growing inside of him, the longing to open the front door and run out into the street, shouting and yelling about what he knows.

He knew better. The hardest part was done, Madison told himself, reassuring his mind, should it break now. So much time was dedicated to this task, countless weeks and months of living like a hermit, cut off from the real world.

He remembers the first day that he spoke of his plan. While he claimed it was a new concept to him, in reality, it existed for years. Whatever judgemental eyes lay upon Madison, he knew such embarrassment paled into insignificance to what he felt over the loss of his wife. He never spoke publicly of his motivations, sometimes he did not even admit it to himself, but in his heart he knew his deceased wife was the energy, the spark within him.

The monitor was on standby, awaiting the simple push to light up. But the reflection was of more concern to Madison. The struggle of the last few years manifested itself on the screen, throwing back a dimly lit portrait of a lonely fighter. Grey hairs weaved into the man's hairline, spreading their fibres, shaping an older image than he expected. Waving wrinkles grew from his eyes and outward, forced from days of no rest. Madison had seen enough, as he pressed the power switch. The screen illuminated, covering the evidence of a weary man, getting old before his time. For a man in his fifties,

Madison felt double that. But, *it would all be worth it in the end*, he silently swore to himself.

***

The Bank of America branch on Regal Street did not open for another hour, but Murray and a forensic scientist stood outside the door. A call to Mr. Brownrigg earlier that morning did the trick, as the bank manager opened an emergency exit and let them in.

"Your phone call was very brief detective, what do you think you have found?" inquired Mr. Brownrigg.

They walked towards the bank manager's office, Murray, pointing to the forensic analyst in tow said,

"*Mr. Fletcher*, while he was waiting for you on the day of the deposit, touched a part of the door frame. My hope is no one else has done so, and then maybe we can get a set of fingerprints."

"Lights please," he told Mr. Brownrigg, while motioning for the analyst to hand him an ultra violet flashlight. The bank grew dark, as Mr. Brownrigg reassured the staff everything was ok. Murray hovered the light over the lower part of the door frame. Hundreds of prints showed up, evidence of years of different fingertips making contact, mostly those of Mr. Brownrigg no doubt.

As the light travelled up the door frame, the prints became more scattered, until the light reached over six feet. There, alone, was a print. Nearly a foot away from the nearest mark, *Adam's* impression stood out like a beacon. Murray smiled as he stepped down, handing the light back to the analyst.

"Stands out like a sore thumb!" he laughed.

125

Chapter 21

Adam awoke with a start.

"These dreams are getting more vivid."

He reached to his left and pulled one of the curtains open. Light dashed in, showing a trickle of illumination along the bed and wall. Adam lifted his left hand closer to his temple, questioning his *dream*. He imagined a gun barrel pressed against his skin. The feel of a man's hand on his neck lingered. Musk floated around his room, dirtied and different. All of Adam's senses screamed at him to accept the obvious. But, he needed more proof.

Adam rolled the wheelchair down the hallway, looking for the slightest hint of disruption. Upstairs, his parents lay asleep, oblivious to what new turmoil gushed around their son's head. The morning sun crept up peered through a pane of glass on the front door, covering Adam's face with dazzling rays. The floor showed no sign of intrusion, which only kick-started the doubts in Adam. He thought about retreating into his own world, where knowing nothing would keep him safe. His eyes stayed up, afraid to find clues of an intruder. His brain battled with them, *I'm in control* it screamed. He leaned forward, grabbed the door handle and pushed it down.

It was locked.

Adam cursed his creative mind, asking if this was the start of insanity. Had the moment arrived where he had to question what is fact and what is fiction? Were these the first signs that his physical illness was now spilling over, filling his fragile mind with even more problems?

While he sat at the table, Adam found it hard to remove the images from his mind. As was the case with every scene his mind remembered, or conjured up, the picture was tinged in black. The hours spent reading medical journals only helped to throw more obstacles in his way, *is this the start of memory distrust syndrome*, where the sufferer begins to question their own memories. In his mind, shadowy figures lurked in the darkness, tiny features revealed, but pulled away again just when the brain reacted. Recognition and reassurance left dangling for the slightest moment, only for the canvas to fall face flat to the ground, covering the picture for now, damning Adam's hopes for now. Only one small spec of light could be summoned in his mind, as he reached into his pocket for his phone.

***

Another tissue fell to the ground, wet with tears, laden with regret. A fresh one was dragged from the box, only to be drenched within moments. Britney's red eyes blinked incessantly, unable to control the flow. Her phone lay next to her on the bed, offering a way out of this mess, fighting the feeling she was powerless, the damage was done. Her still packed suitcase under the bed had screamed for hours now, begging to be flung into the back of the car and whisked away. The idea of a new start, away from all of the pain and guilt in Boston appealed to Britney. She clenched her hands tightly and closed her eyes. In her mind she muttered snippets of prayers; the room grew silent as her sniffling stopped, even the street outside seemed deserted as Britney knelt on the floor.

A loud ringing broke through the quiet air. Her heart jumped, not at the unexpected bell, but at the expected caller. *Adam.* A lifetime of friendship, years of trust, and moments of something special converged on one February morning.

The ringing continued. Britney arranged the words in her mind, but at once her heart tore them apart, preferring to open up and tell the truth. She imagined Adam in his bed, sore and shaken; a terrible nightmare coming through, climbing from his dream into his very bedroom and breaking this already tortured man. The ringing grew louder.

Britney questioned who was in control, as her hand slid along the duvet. She trusted her brain to speak, but the fear grew inside when she thought about what her heart may say. Either way, her fingers slid around the vibrating phone. The noise was becoming unbearable. Britney coughed a little, clearing her throat, but her trembling fingers acted. *Silence.*

Chapter 22

Murray parked at the entrance to Louver Street. He decided to walk to the Fletcher home located at the end of the street. The weather was unusually calm for this time of year, drops of melting snow slid onto the pavement from the mounted piles in the gardens, and even though there were no signs of the first green shoots, Murray smelt the milder weather approaching. No longer was his chest filled with the sharp breeze of winter, instead, a smoothened version sailed into his lungs.

Even without his morning run, Murray felt energised. A case that once seemed dead and buried had come to life. While thanking his new *style* of investigation, Murray realised why some detectives bent the rules, and why all good detectives broke them. Laughing, he remembered how his superior told him to stick to the official route of investigation. Yet, where would he be now had he stuck so rigorously to the rules, Murray pondered. All it took to kick-start the case was a polite word, a few CD's and a young forensic analyst eager to impress. No forged warrant necessary either.

He likened the outcome of this case to the path on Louver Street, straightforward. In a few moments, he thought, Adam Fletcher would give details of the driver of the car. So, the person responsible for the crash will already have clocked up years for dangerous driving, grand theft auto and fleeing the scene of an accident. All of this, including a major fraud charge, *when* the fingerprints confirm the person's identity from the bank. It could not be easier.

He dismissed the phrase, *two birds with the one stone*; the potential existed to be so much greater. When this person is behind bars, there will be a knock-on effect Murray hoped. It seemed very likely to him, that the person has links to some criminal activity. What the detective found out over the years is the upper class of criminal are very adaptive; stolen passports, forged driver licences or a pre-meditated car accident are well within their capabilities. Throwing in $1 million only added spice to the mix.

Passing the second last house on the street, Murray felt a pair of eyes settle on him. A dark curtain shuffled, stopping his enthusiasm in its tracks, he walked slower and steadier. Glancing up at the porch, Murray caught a glimpse of a man inside the front living room. Walking up the Fletcher driveway, Murray kept his eyes on the dark front window. *Do I really stand out that much as a cop?*

Erin opened the door before Murray reached it, greeting him with a smile.

"He is in the living room," she said, motioning for Murray to step inside. The midday sun shone in the front window, filling the living room with a cream glow that splashed over Adam.

"How are you?" Murray asked.

"I'm good, thank you," Adam said, extending his hand. Murray could not help but notice the increased strength in Adam's handshake, such improvement since their first visit. Inside he fought the feelings that threatened to give rise to a sense of pity for this young man. His eyes failed to dismiss the wheelchair-worn track leading into the living room, this man confined to a seat, his opportunity of an enjoyable life being kept out of arms reach.

Murray shook his head, banishing sensitive thoughts from his head. Back on track, he reached for his dictaphone and notepad.

"So, Adam, what can you tell me about the accident?" Murray started, straight to business. Adam fidgeted in his chair.

"I have been having...flashbacks." He was staring at the floor, as if trying to shape the carpet into an image of the accident.

"I can remember being in the back of the car. I know there were others with me, but one face stands out."

Murray jotted down on the notepad. His eyes never left Adam's.

"The man driving the car was Shaun McCoy."

Immediately, the detective's mind went crazy. Memories and memories were searched, looking for something to connect that name with.

"Can you tell me about this man?"

131

"I know very little of him. I don't think we are friends...well, I hope not. Every time I think of him, I feel...anger."

"What else? Where does he live? Who are his friends?"

"He lives in Canal Street I think, Dorchester."

"How do you know this?"

"Facebook!" Adam smiled.

Murray again ran through his internal database, *who is this Shaun McCoy?*

"When I saw him in the Banshee bar, something clicked," Adam said. Murray had dealt with many interviews and statements in his twenty years in the police force, but this was his first full statement with a medically proven amnesia patient.

"His face, I knew I had seen it before. Even though Britney told me he and I were never friends, he knew me, I knew him."

"Who is Britney?"

"She is a friend, my best friend."

Murray interrupted before he fell into an emotional trap, fearful Adam was about to go drastically off topic.

"Tell me more about the other people in the car?"

Adam shifted again.

"I don't know who else was there."

"Adam, I am going to ask you a question. Please, don't be startled by it." Murray was an expert at interpreting body language, he always told himself. He observed Adam's pose before the question.

"Are you, or were you, involved in any activity that may pose a threat to someone or some...gang?"

Murray looked close. No movement, giving nothing away. Adam's confused eyes stayed fixed on the detective. Not even a blink.

"Are you asking if I'm involved in something illegal?"

"No!" Murray replied, meaning *yes.*

"I am just asking, can you remember having any enemies prior to the accident?"

"Detective, I am suffering from lacunar amnesia. Everything I can remember, I am telling you."

Murray sat back, noticing the first hint of anger in the young man's voice. He thought about apologising, but something inside shouted stop. *This man, despite his condition, is the main lead in a serious case.* A dull ring tone emitted from Murray's jacket.

"Detective Murray speaking," he answered. The low voice on the other side spoke quickly and sharply. Murray's response was a solitary, "Thanks!" He turned his attention back to Adam.

"Shall we continue?"

When the meeting concluded, Murray realised he had found out very little. Every piece of information he told was an overlap on previous statements, though there was one strain present throughout, Shaun McCoy was the driver. Murray departed the Fletcher home, armed with information that would lead to Shaun's arrest. Despite the meeting with Adam going well, he felt a slight tint of disappointment as he walked down the driveway. He had hoped to hear the name of some big time criminal, and link the accident to him. But instead, he had some young wannabe. Still, Shaun McCoy may have some hidden connections, and taking him out of the equation would ruffle some feathers in the Boston criminal underworld.

Chapter 23

Shaun tapped his iPhone incessantly, intentionally ignoring the worried looks of his two friends, Jack and Tommy.

"What if he doesn't listen?" they piped up.

Shaun glanced and smiled, then went back to playing with his latest application on the phone.

"Shaun? Seriously man, what ya thinking?" Jack said, leaning forward.

"Firstly," Shaun sighed, "Adam doesn't have the balls to rat on me."

The two men looked at each other, still not comforted by Shaun's words.

"And secondly guys, like Britney said, he doesn't even know you two exist. You have nothing to worry about."

Jack and Tommy nodded an edgy relief. While last night's event went well, Shaun knew they didn't have the guts to do it again, should the need arise.

"So, what d'ya think he told the cop?" Jack asked, his voice breaking with nerves.

"He didn't have to tell the cop anything; he is suffering from amnesia, how many more excuses could he possibly need?"

***

Britney's bedroom resembled a prison cell, even the ceiling descended lower and lower with each second. Her cries did not stir the invisible guards in the damp hallway, they only sent her wails back again, doubled and trebled. Britney longed to end this solitary confinement. Would it be easier to open the gates and spill everything? It would hurt at first she thought, but she may eventually breathe air outside of the concrete walls. Britney slumped to the floor and buried her head in the side of the bed, sending out muffled words.

"I'm sorry for letting you down."

A car door closing outside snapped Britney out of her state. Nervously, she peered over the bed and out the window. Expecting to see Shaun or Detective Murray, she relaxed when the slim figure of Rachael bopped up to the front door.

Drying her eyes, Britney opened the door. Rachael's smiley expression greeted her, momentarily pushing away all the negative feelings dominating Britney that morning.

"Hey!" she quipped, "You okay?"

Britney lied, "Yeah, I'm good." Rachael followed her into the living room.

"You want something to drink?" Britney asked, already reaching into the fridge for a soda. They sat down on the couch, Britney afraid to discuss the topic bursting inside.

Rachael did the honours, "Have you been speaking to Adam?"

"No. But he rang me. I couldn't bring myself to answer."

"I was in Shaun's earlier...the Detective had not called, so I guess that's a good sign!"

Britney paused. A tiny spark of optimism ignited within her. Did Adam decide against revealing Shaun's identity? Was he calling earlier to tell Britney of his decision? Did Murray leave Fletcher's home with no new information? The trickle of hope turned into a surge in Britney's veins. Relieved Adam had bought her more time, her chest heaved easier under her top. Rachael held Britney's hand, while a new found look of compassion swept over her face.

"I can only imagine how trapped you feel. It takes courage to do what you're doing," Rachael said.

Britney feigned a smile. She appreciated the teenager's words, but she knew Rachael only saw the story from one side. She had no idea what Britney felt when Adam was around. Her love for Adam got drowned out by guilt, her hopes for him massacred by lies and his trust poisoned by deceit. And there she sat, strangely feeling more at ease when she thought Adam stayed silent. *There is something wrong with me* she mimed, not spoken, yet her mind screaming it.

Glimpses of her prom night flickered in Britney's thoughts.

"What you smiling about?" Rachael interrupted, questioning Britney's first smile in days.

"Prom night, five years ago, it was magical."

"Yeah!" the teenager jumped, "I had mine last year, we got so drunk-"

Britney shook her head, "No, no. I don't mean drink, drugs, or whatever else."

Britney remembered being in the Fletcher's kitchen. Erin was admiring Britney's black dress as she flicked her curled blonde hair over her shoulder, the faintest of tingles on her breasts reverberated around her body with excitement. A final glance in the vanity mirror, check, everything looked perfect. The sensation in her stomach kept growing as she approached the living room door.

"So?" Rachael asked.

"He looked so amazing," Britney whispered.

The moment she stepped into the living room, Adam jumped up. They stepped closer, every cell in her body wanting to reach out and kiss him. How she hoped he wanted to do the same. No, he never was the most outgoing.

"It sounds so weird to be saying it, but, we danced the whole night together."

Rachael sat upright, "You had nothing that night?"

"A glass of wine at home was all I needed. I was so high on another chemical that alcohol didn't matter."

"Ha, knew it!" Rachael said.

"You silly girl," Britney laughed as she playfully pushed at Rachael's shoulder, "the chemical I'm speaking about is love."

"Oh," was all Rachael muttered.

Chapter 24

After spending twenty minutes at the station, Detective Murray set about driving to Canal Street, Dorchester. Depending on the time of day, the journey could take anything from fifteen minutes to an hour. Despite the heavy traffic as he left the city centre, Murray was relaxed about the journey because according to Adam, Mr. Shaun McCoy had no idea he was coming. Still, he had to ask an officer to accompany him, police force protocol. The Hancock building grew smaller in the rear view mirror as Murray travelled along Dorchester Avenue, glancing up at street signs to confirm his target.

He resisted the temptation to tell the accompanying officer the details of the case on the car journey. Murray had learned from that mistake last year. Working alone was now preferable to the man. Divulging every thought and idea to a work partner was like opening up a book, labelled 'My weaknesses'.

Eighteen months previous, while investigating a number of bank robberies, Murray's trust in his partner nearly got him killed. He *was* the detective the public want to see. Loyal, determined and most of all, he obeyed the rules. His partner helped him along in respect to the latter, he urged Murray to seek warrants, stick to official police procedures and policies. Little did Murray know all the red tape he waded through was only a distraction from the real business going on, his partner was an informant for a gang in Charlestown.

After a failed bank robbery, Murray interviewed witnesses, checked surveillance tapes and did the work the public expected. But, his partner spoke with the bank officials and security teams, gathering information about the specifics of the inside of a bank. An attempt at opening another vault by the thieves again resulted in failure and the loss of two bank officials' lives. Still, Murray occupied himself with the mundane and routine chores.

While out for an after work beer one Friday, Murray aired his thoughts on the two failed robberies. His partner dismissed any similarities between the two and insisted they were the work of separate gangs, stating that Charlestown is the 'home of bank robbers'.

Within two weeks, an early morning bank robbery in the city centre was successfully executed. Armed with weapons and information, the thieves were two-thirds of the way there, all they needed was a diversion to attract police attention elsewhere. While Murray and a large percentage of the police force were being utilised in South Boston, a gang entered the city centre bank shortly before nine. A team of tranquilised security guards and fourteen minutes later, millions of dollars were quietly driven along the I-93 in the rush hour traffic, peacefully and pleasantly. Screeching sirens travelling in the opposite lane towards the city ended up over ten minutes late to even catch a glimpse of the thieves.

After the Police Commissioner and the Mayor got a public roasting, an investigation was launched to ask how Boston police forces were so slow in responding to the bank alarms. The reason they offered: an unusually high number of crimes reported in the South Boston area that morning. The various GPS locations gathered from the calls suggested a large number of individuals were involved. However, when the calls were intensely scrutinised, it revealed they all routed back to one location, Boston police department on Park Street. It was obvious the thieves could not have initiated the calling spree from inside the building, they needed help. It showed Boston that a new breed of criminal had been born; one armed with technology, precision and probably the scariest thought, a gang with help in the police force.

While the city reeled from the raid, another bank was hit. This time, there was no need to divert the police forces attention, it was the fourth of July. The criminals were persistent no doubt, as their target was a bank previously proved unbreakable. The bank had, after the first failed robbery, planned a date for renovation of the CCTV system, advised by a certain detective of the Boston police force, Murray's partner.

The bank manager reopened on the fifth to find the construction crew and security team locked in the vault. The almost fully installed additions to the CCTV system captured enough to tell the story of the successful break-in; every step where they failed previously, the gang found a way around it. From hidden alarms, to infra-red traps, to using micro-sensitive equipment to open the vault, the check list was virtually a match to the report Murray and his partner had submitted in the weeks previous.

One night while he was in the station alone, Murray looked for information to prove all the events were done by one gang. Everyone in the department, including his partner disagreed, stating one gang would not have the ability, technology or information to attempt four bank robberies in under a month. Murray never doubted the ability of the criminals to pull off a successful bank raid, and the question of technology was a no-brainer. It was the source of the information that baffled Murray.

He spent days looking for one link to connect all the robberies, brushing off a thought that trickled into his mind every few hours, his partner was involved. In the dimness of his work station, a light across the hall kept calling to him. The light came from his partner's office, yet Murray resisted the temptation to step towards it. Instead, he went to the local with a few workmates, eager to get the negativity out of his head. He found no respite, only tapping bottles and laughing with the man he secretly felt was responsible for the information leak. Midnight approached, the bar got quieter as the men left to go home to their wives and children, yet Murray and his partner continued drinking alone. Within minutes, the conversation had turned to the bank robberies, and Murray collapsed into a freefall.

Theory after theory was blurted out. His partner re-confirmed his loyalty to Murray by agreeing with him on almost every point. Murray left the bar, intoxicated, but relieved. His partner was firmly on his side. Tomorrow, he thought, the two men would present their ideas to their superior. A sick day the following morning from his partner, while inconvenient, was no major problem for Murray. He held off on submitting his ideas, he wanted to be part of a team, each man backing up the other.

That day never came. Only an early morning wakeup call from his partner, "Get outa bed, I'll be over in five."

While Boston slept, Murray and his partner trawled the Charlestown streets, believing a tip as gospel, a tip that did not exist. The last thing he remembered was looking at his partner's face, the emotionless stare, and someone in the back seat shuffling closer. Then a pang of pain in his side, taking over his whole body until everything went black.

Over the next month, the truth emerged about his partner's betrayal. Afraid that their connections with the police force may expose them, the thieves cut their ties, Murray was the sole survivor. He knew he was lucky to be alive, but he kept damning himself at the realisation he uncovered very little. When Murray eventually left his hospital bed, the criminals, no doubt, had a good suntan in Thailand at that stage.

***

Shaun sat at the kitchen table alone, yet at ease, content that Adam did not speak after the threat. He sent his spy to find out what the latest developments were, and as Rachael had not called in a panic, everything was going okay. The previous night's events were playing over in his head, he relished every repeat of it. Shaun had never felt such power, pushing the gun in Adam's face, watching another man squirm helplessly. The feeling he scared Adam so much to keep him speechless just confirmed Shaun's self-worth.

Loud thuds in the hallway shook that belief. Shaun could tell who was passing the door just from the sound of their footwear. This stomp was new. New was never good. His curiosity lessened when the thud stopped, only to be reignited with a knock on the door. Shaun stood up and walked silently to the front door. Two men were outside, their murmurings brief and sharp. They knocked again. Shaun stood taller, and swung the door open, "Yeah?"

"Shaun McCoy?" The man in the suit asked.

Shaun leaned forward to see a police officer in uniform standing in the hallway.

"Yes?" he replied.

"I am Detective Murray. Would you be able to come to Park Street police station with us? We'd like to ask you a few questions about a car accident that happened September last."

"Yeah, I guess I can," Shaun said, accepting his fate for now. He had seen this day coming for a long time, and he knew exactly how to get out of it.

Chapter 25

Shaun imagined police stations differently. There were
no clusters of cops around the coffee machine, chatting
endlessly about anything but work. No headless running
around, pretending to be working. Shaun was surprised
by the look on everyone's face; they all seemed to have a
purpose, a target.

A police officer led Shaun down the hallway and into
interview room number 2, where his mind pictured a
stereotypical room, similar to one portrayed in movies: A
large table in the centre, a wall with a one-way mirror
and cameras placed in all corners. But no, two small
chairs, directly across from each other and a table were
the only items in the room.

The detective entered and placed a pen and notepad
on the table. Shaun raised his hands to him, hinting to
release the handcuffs. The detective blankly ignored his
request, and instead sat down opposite him. He nodded
to the arresting officer, *thank you.* The officer did not
need any more hints as he quickly stepped outside and
closed the door.

"I assume you know why you're here?"

"Enlighten me!" Shaun started, eager to lay down a marker.

"Okay. It is claimed that you were the driver of an Audi A4, which crashed south of Canton on September 2nd last. How do you know Adam Fletcher?"

"Adam Fletcher? Don't know him!"

"I think you do Mr. McCoy, he knows you."

Shaun had played this situation in his mind over and over. He knew that Adam would crack some day, while he hoped it would be more than five months after the accident, Shaun was prepared.

"I know a lot of people, Adam Fleming isn't one."

"Fletcher!"

"Whatever."

"Ok, just to re-jig your memory. Mr. Fletcher claims you were the driver of the car. A car that was reported stolen hours earlier."

Shaun tried to lean back, but the plastic chair did not budge. He traced a path along the grey walls around the room.

"Can you take these off?" he said, raising the handcuffs towards Murray.

"Furthermore, it is claimed that you deserted the scene of the accident, an accident that you caused by reckless driving," Murray said.

Shaun broke out in a smile, "If I was in a car accident, I think that I'd remember it."

"I have a statement here, claiming that you..."

"You have a statement!" Shaun interrupted, "Is your source reliable Detective?"

A sigh escaped from Murray's lips, Shaun caught it.

"So, your source isn't reliable Detective?"

"I ask the questions here Mr. McCoy...and yes, my source, Mr. Fletcher is reliable."

Shaun knew Murray was stumped. The whole charge lay on the memory of a man who was suffering from amnesia. While Shaun knew this may not be the case forever, he knew it would throw the investigation out for long enough to be forgotten about. He needed to get Murray to admit Adam is suffering from amnesia, without revealing he knows Adam.

"Detective, if Alan is claiming that I was driving a stolen car in which he was a passenger, why is he only coming forward now?"

"Mr. McCoy, I recognise your schoolboy attempts at trying to change the focus of this investigation. Whether you call Mr. Fletcher Alan, Adam, or Alex, you will still be in the same position."

"Yes boss!" Shaun said, winking at the detective. "So, what's the delay all about?"

"As a result of the injuries he received in the accident, he was unable to produce a statement until now."

"Oh! What kind of injuries?"

"Leg and back injuries," Murray answered. "Mr. McCoy, I am interviewing you in relation to a crime, you will not speak unless I ask you a question, or if I ask for your opinion on a matter. Is that understood?"

"Sir, yes Sir," Shaun chuckled. The detective leaned forward onto the table, closed the notepad and crossed his arms.

"Hey, what about you tell me who else was with you in the car, we'll try cut a deal?"

Shaun glanced downwards at the cuffs, throwing the idea that he was contemplating a big decision to Murray.

"What kind of deal?" he murmured, eyes still fixed on his hands.

"Mr. McCoy, if I'm being perfectly honest with you, you could serve some serious time if you make this investigation any harder than it needs to be. With a little cooperation, you may get a lenient sentence," Murray said, sitting back in his chair.

"And all you want to know is who was in the car with me?" Shaun asked.

Murray nodded, "Yes, that will do for now."

"Ok, there was you, and some other officer in the car with me," Shaun said. Murray raised his hands over his head.

"So, you're gonna play it that way?" Murray asked, gnawing his teeth with renewed vigour. Shaun did not budge, only raising his eyes upward to meet the detectives stare.

"Detective," he said condescendingly, "if you have real proof, I'd like to see it. If not, just let me get on with my life."

"Hey kid! I've been dealing with guys a lot tougher than you for years. Remember, you're a small fish in a small bowl," Murray said, standing up and knocking on the door. Shaun lay back in the chair, forcing a smile, as if he had won the battle.

"Mr. McCoy, we have you for the next 23 hours, make yourself comfortable."

***

148

Murray was losing this battle. Rusty from his lack of recent interrogations, he fall into Shaun's hands and was pushed around in the questioning. Shaun McCoy was not a typical criminal, Murray felt, rather he is a criminal with some common sense, a dangerous mix. Studying Shaun's build, Murray tried to fit him in with the man on the bank's CCTV. The man in the bank bore some similarities to Shaun, mainly patience and determination. Yet, Shaun had an eerie stillness about himself, and his hard, brown eyes added to the effect.

Murray thought about telling him where he stood, but decided to let the man sit there for a few hours, let the doubt grow inside. Despite feeling Shaun was guilty, Murray knew *feelings* do not stand up in court. Underneath it all, unless the fingerprints came back with Shaun's name on them, the investigation boiled down to one man's version against another's. The only problem was the word Murray depended on, was the recollections of an amnesiac.

Chapter 26

Adam never saw his mother cry. Not that he would remember anyway, Erin figured. She assumed she possessed an emotionally tough persona in Adam's mind. Should he have seen her falter, the knock on effect could have been detrimental. When Adam arrived home from the hospital, Erin spent the night crying on her husband's stomach, away from her son's gaze. In the morning, she swapped the grieving mother for the more determined, battle hardened mother. Erin had to. Adam needed it, and she needed it.

The accident opened Erin's eyes. While being considerate to those less fortunate than her, she never really understood what real pain could do. The image of Adam in the hospital bed would never be removed from her mind, a constant reminder that life is fragile and flimsy.

Her body shut down in the days following the accident. She used to spend a few moments outside the ward every day before entering, painting a facade of strength and hope to cover her true appearance.

The Fletcher breakfast table caught its first ray of hope in months, a contagious smile worn by Adam caught Erin when her son arrived into the kitchen. Pain endured by the family since September showed signs of the first melt. A tingling sensation grew inside Erin, an immense swelling of pride. She wanted to hug Adam so tightly and never let go. The darkness that flooded the home only a few months previous began to recede, yet while there were still signs of the harder times, the clouds had relented to show a brighter future. Recollections of drenched pillows and sleepless nights began to evaporate from Erin's memories, with the feeling that everything was about to fall into place.

**

"Good morning Adam," Madison said gently, as he walked along the access ramp to the porch.

"Hi Madison."

Madison settled on the top step and faced down the driveway.

"It's nice to see the snow melting eh?" Madison said.

"It's crazy the difference a day can make," Adam started, in pensive mood. "One day I'm bottled up, but the next I'm almost walking outa' this thing."

Madison could not keep his eyes off the wonderful expression on Adam's face. He was like an explorer who stepped onto the shoreline of a new world, gazing inland to the adventures ahead. The men's eyes connected briefly.

"You ever get that feeling?" Adam asked.

That feeling! Madison thought. He struggled to pinpoint the last time he felt pure ecstasy. It felt like another life had been lived in the meantime, one of dedication and devotion. Madison looked up, to see Adam still awaiting an answer.

"Yeah sometimes."

"So, what exactly has you in this good mood?" Madison asked, already knowing the answer. Adam looked out over the neighbourhood.

"I'm gonna sound so philosophical here, but, when you live in a dark, dark world, any light is welcomed. For months now, I believed my life began in September. I knew nothing of the life I supposedly lived before that. However I am seeing more and more."

The irony of the situation did not go unnoticed. Two men sitting on the porch, Adam knew nothing about his own life, yet Madison knew more than he should about the young man's life. A momentary silence developed, yet it was comfortable. Adam looked down the driveway, his blue eyes seemingly buoyed by expectation. Meanwhile, Madison expected the future, waiting for the right moment to open up and reveal what he knows.

Adam spoke softly, "I think that you're a lot like me."

Madison smiled, "Oh yeah, in what way?"

"I'm not sure if it's a good thing or not, but I think we are both prone to bouts of ...day-dreaming ...if that makes sense," Adam laughed.

Madison looked at Adam, "What makes you say that?"

"I may be in a wheelchair, but I'm not blind. You spend more time gazing from the porch than I do. It's all new to me, what's your excuse?"

"A very good question Adam, I'm afraid I can't answer it!"

Nodding his head, Madison laughed on the outside, but in reality he cursed his lack of observation. *Remember the plan* he reminded himself. As he tried to cover his nervous expression, Adam's sudden start alerted Madison.

"You okay?" Adam appeared lost for a moment. Was it another memory coming back to him?

"What's wrong?" Madison asked through the confusion. Shaking his head, Adam muttered randomly in no particular direction, just outwards.

"Whoa," he drew a deep breath, blinking his eyes incessantly, "that was the craziest case of Déjà Vu ever!"

Chapter 27

A gentle wind ruffled Adam's hair, sparking ideas of the adventures ahead when his memory would paint fuller pictures. Water coloured inks would redefine themselves, splitting until the image was crystal clear, reshuffling to leave nothing but wonderful recollections of a young man's life. Adam's smile widened at the thought of Britney. He longed for the day he wakes up, full to the brim with images of the growth of such a beautiful woman. Adam loved what he knew then and the thought that there may be more to Britney felt like heaven.

After lunch, Adam sat alone on the porch. But, unlike other times when the young man sat still while the world revolved without him, Adam felt for the first time, he was moving with it. Such simple words uttered the previous day lifted a weight from him, *Shaun McCoy was the driver.* While Adam cared about who was responsible for the accident, he got more satisfaction in the knowledge his memory was coming back. Although the amnesia was retreating at a slow pace, a new confidence grew within Adam that the curtain would continue dropping, until he could see everything.

***

"I need to get those results now!" Murray pleaded with one of the analysts, standing at the reception to the forensic laboratory, impatiently tapping the counter top. Two levels up, Shaun McCoy neared the end of his 24 hour holding time, after which unless a charge was brought, he would walk out a free man.

Murray threw every piece of evidence against Shaun, only for it to be shielded by very coincidental alibis. For every action there was a reaction. But no reaction confirmed Shaun's presence at the scene. Murray peered in through the glass panels. The young woman who took the prints in the bank stepped out into reception with the fingerprints match, tucked in a large envelope.

"Did you get a match?" he quizzed, as he took the envelope in his hand.

"Yes there was a positive match Sir." The analyst stated, seemingly eager to end the conversation there and then. It was policy that results of DNA, blood or fingerprint tests not be discussed with the laboratory staff, should a suspect be known to them.

The elevator moved slower, as if it wanted Murray to open the contents of the letter there and then. He paced the hallway quickly, nodding at his superior as he passed. Murray decided against hiding the envelope, instead walking with it swinging, as if it were the daily paper. His index finger slid inside the seal, tempting Murray to press on. The contents were almost speaking to him now, but he resisted the urge to open it, instead

155

he imagined the look of Shaun McCoy's face when he realises he is done for.

The shabby door of interview room 2 looked a lot better. Shaun, on the other hand looked anything but. Murray often found that a long night spent in the cold cell snapped most people out of their comfort zone. Many times he had seen so-called tough guys remain intact during the initial interview, and how he relished the following morning. It was as if the damp, cold and loud conditions of the basement cells in the station brought the suspects to a conclusion; co-operate and hope for something better, or be found out and spend years like this. Murray sat down and placed the envelope on the table.

"They my stuff?" Shaun muttered, his eyes red from a lack of sleep. A smile ran onto Murray's face.

"Yeah, I think that they are yours!" he replied, buzzing at the thought of revealing the contents.

"So?" Shaun said.

"So! Before we go any further, is there anything you would like to admit?"

Shaun shook his head. "I thought we'd finished all this questioning? I'm innocent, you were wrong, let me go."

While slightly taken aback, Murray decided to give Shaun one more chance to come clean.

"Kid, this is your last chance to co-operate. Are you going to admit to driving the car in which Adam Fletcher was injured, or are you going to keep up that tough guy image?"

Shaun lowered his head for what seemed an eternity. Murray imagined a trickle of common sense seeping into

156

the young man. He waited for a changed attitude when Shaun raised his head again.

"By my count, unless you charge me, I should be free to go soon," he whispered, showing the tiniest hint of a smile to the detective.

The smile was multiplied on Murray's face, *you asked for it kid.* He dragged the envelope closer to the edge and slid his finger underneath. Shaun's eyes gazed upwards in an attempt to peek at what new weapon Murray had enlisted in an effort to break him. The white sheet of paper, decorated with Boston Police force tags and data, slid out easily. Murray's eyes skipped all of the irrelevant figures, instead zooming in on the results. *Positive match* was the first item that caught the detective's attention. Shaun's eyes were focused on the paper, he leaned closer, silent. A surge of joy rushed through Murray, but the joy was quickly extinguished. Murray glanced up just to check if he had received the right results.

Bank of America, February, Det. Murray, BPF. It was the correct form. How is this result possible Murray thought? Shaun leaned back, gaining confidence with every moment Murray hesitated. His silent smile picked at Murray, it was clear to Shaun, he knew the detective aimed for something huge, and missed.

The video footage from the bank played over and over in Murray's head. Shaun showed such calmness over the last 24 hours to confirm he could have pulled off the bank deposit and withdrawal. Yet, the piece of paper in front of Murray did not agree. Like an experienced poker player, Shaun read the detective's face.

"So, I guess that will be all?" he sniggered, switching glances between the officer at the door and Murray. The

officer awaited a signal from his superior, Murray did
not utter a word, only flicking his hand upwards, *let him go.*

For the next hour, Murray sat alone in the interview
room. He replayed every event culminating in Shaun's
interrogation, asking himself how he could have done
better. Was there any convincing evidence Shaun could
not wrangle out of? Murray knew despite this setback,
he was not finished with Shaun. The question was how
to prove his involvement. He folded the piece of white
paper into his jacket pocket and started all over again.

Chapter 28

The stinging in her feet grew, from uncomfortable to chronic. Hours of wandering Dorchester irritated Britney's feet until she had no choice but to turn for Louver Street. She deliberated all morning about visiting Adam, using the various streets as diversions to making a decision. It had been days since she last spoke to Adam, it was time to make a choice. How she longed for a friend to sit with, and throw the pros and cons of the situation out there and come to a sensible conclusion.

Her tummy stirred uneasily when she analysed the details and conjured a sickening motto, months of lies and deceit. Britney never planned for it to be like this. She pictured the day of the accident again, her mind sick of the guilt swelling inside every time she re-imagined it. Fear overruled every aspect of Britney that day. The caring girl from Quincy momentarily turned into a selfish, ruthless creature. When she decided to go back, she was already locked in chains of silence.

The quiet street seemed shorter today, a sign that a worried mind can let the body wander alone, as Britney struggled to recollect the journey. Approaching the Fletcher home, Britney's decisions were made, as Adam immediately saw her. His smile spread from the porch, lighting the driveway for Britney. How she longed to see him smile like that every day. She hurriedly bounced up the pathway.

"Hey!"

"Hi, great to see you," Adam beamed, "what have you been doing the last few days?"

"Ahh the usual," she smiled, "tell me about you, the Detective came, yeah?"

Adam's smile diminished, "Yeah, but it went well."

"Great! Have you heard anything since?" Britney quizzed, her mind balancing Adam's energy and Shaun's threats.

Adam shook his head, "That could be a good sign?"

"Yeah, definitely," Britney reassured him as she rubbed his leg. "Wanna go inside?"

"Before we do Britney, about what happened between us, I'm sorry about the way I reacted, it was childish of me." Adam said.

"No, no it wasn't. Don't worry about it now," Britney spoke sincerely, leaning in to hug him.

Adam's muffled voice came out, "Thank you Britney."

The pause seemed irrelevant to Adam, yet she asked,

"For what?"

They leaned out, intermittent eye contact reignited a nervous tingle inside Britney.

"For everything."

***

The door of Shaun's apartment shuddered, sending vibrations throughout the hallway, pulling Rachael from her light sleep. Shaun opened the bedroom door and threw an envelope towards the bin.

"Hi babe, I'm back," Shaun smiled.

"I've been waiting for you, I was worried. You shoulda' texted," Rachael said.

"Just as I planned Rach, twenty four hours later I'm free again."

Shaun lay down on the bed as Rachael snuggled up to him.

"What did the police say?"

"Does it matter what they say? They can't prove anything." Rachael leaned up and kissed Shaun's face, it did not register with him.

"What was that letter about, on the door? Is it from the college again?"

"Rach, what's with the questions? Can you let me relax without bugging the hell outa me?" Rachael buried her head under Shaun's arm. His breathing was unusually loud.

"I just wanna help."

"Well don't!" Shaun barked.

Thoughts of leaving ran into Rachael's mind, yet if she left, who would be there for Shaun. His mood would change soon, she reassured herself.

Rumbling in the hallway momentarily reminded Rachael they were not alone, but she knew the man outside was of little comfort to Shaun. As Shaun's neighbour, and then girlfriend, Rachael knew him for years. While his father strived to give his son a decent life, Shaun was malnourished when it came to love and affection. During his teenage years, Shaun transformed from a quiet, shy kid to the *tough guy.* All the while, his father was getting earfuls of advice from his in-laws about how to quell the tide rising in the boy. Shaun knew what he was good at, and he knew what he was poor at. Overheard words from his father spoke about love for his son, but no medium in which to show it, shrugging he is merely a 'provider', and not in the emotional sense.

Lying in bed, buzzed about ruining another man's life was not the way to be, Rachael thought. The mention of such a fact to Shaun would end their relationship on the spot, better get used to it she figured. Where did he go wrong?

Years of being the top student in the class, complete with manners and innocence, were refreshed with manliness and ignorance. The former were weak traits to have, Shaun used to say, seeing the swarms of kids who longed to be the top pupil. Evenings spent playing sports or studying soon lost their appeal as Shaun delved into a darker world, one where he felt the thrill of being alive, the thrill of being *a man.* Instead of playing football, he played the local shopkeepers. Discarding running for the school athletics team, he used his speed for legging it from local gangs. He was earning more money being a lookout for dealers than he was ever going to make working legally.

During his last year in high school, Shaun undertook an intelligence quotient test. College students asked the high school could they conduct an IQ test as part of some PhD research project. Details of the event got messed around in the translation, but Rachael's version said Shaun was the first to complete the test by some distance.

He was not motivated by the challenge to be number one in the class. Shaun's drive consisted of much simpler things - when you finish the test, you are finished for the day. The teacher noted Shaun's eagerness to finish quickly and she assumed he rushed through the test blindly.

The customary shrug from the teacher came as Shaun jogged up the class. He dragged a light school bag over his left shoulder and threw the answer sheet on the desk. The paper touched the wooden table as Shaun closed the door behind him. In boredom, and while waiting for others to finish, the teacher threw a glance over the young man's results. What she and the college found was quite startling.

Here was a man, who attended just enough days of school not to be reported to social services, never attended any extra-curricular activities and slept most of his high school classes away. However, he completed the test in record time, achieving a result university graduate's would be proud of. When the college students submitted the report to their superiors, the administration was immediately drawn to the anomaly.

Over the next few months, Boston Community College contacted Shaun on a weekly basis. Every call went unanswered, every letter helped to heat the living room. After nearly twelve months of hiding the approaches, Shaun's father found out. Enlisting the help of a local welfare officer, he eventually swayed his son into taking up the college's offer of a guided tour.

Shaun's muted reaction to his private tour of the campus slightly diminished the college's eagerness to entice him into a mathematics and statistics programme, their contact slowed from weekly to monthly. Yet, every envelope that came through the door carrying a BCC tag was immediately pinned to Shaun's bedroom door, his father hoping someday his son would open his eyes to the opportunity. He never did.

Regret never manifested itself in Shaun, instead it showed in his part-time working father. He could not ask where his son's money was coming from, that always resulted in a loud, angry confrontation. Even Rachael learned not to ask. Every time she considered breaking up with Shaun, a glance at his face softened the anger and a hug reassured her that he cared.

The hours ticked by as Shaun and Rachael lay on his bed.

"You okay Shaun now?" Rachael whispered.

"Yeah, just thinking!"

"About what?"

Shaun smiled and squeezed Rachael, as if trying to pass the question off.

"About what Shaun?"

"Ending it all."

Rachael sat up and grabbed Shaun's face.

"You mean...hurting yourself?"

Shaun burst into laughter.

"Wow you're a naive little woman Rachael. I'm on about the person responsible for putting us here, putting me and you in this mess, Adam."

Chapter 29

A steady stream of noise from the police station penetrated the windows, filling Murray's office with a constant buzzing. Struggling to concentrate, Murray drew the blinds in an attempt to suppress the unfiltered chattering from coming into the room, from coming into his ears.

He met some tricky cases throughout his career, and while he knew very few were straightforward, there was no way he could have anticipated this one. Murray pictured Shaun McCoy in court. The familiar scent of the courthouse was conjured up in his nostrils. He smelled the rich mahogany odour from the Judge's bench, contrasting with the cold sting in the courthouse cells. Shaun McCoy was nowhere near either at the moment. Murray demanded an answer from himself, how could Shaun not be the man who was in the bank? Everything pointed to it, a simple fingerprint should have confirmed it.

Murray scratched his head constantly, trying to find an answer from somewhere. During previous cases, he met many dead ends, where he worked backwards and started again. This case was different, unique, like a dead end mixed with a crossroad. While there appeared to be avenues to take, each one was guarded with a spike strip, trying to pass would result in the case falling flat. Murray tossed the available options in his head, until one kept repeating. He flicked open a contacts diary on his desk, tossing pages until he reached *Fletcher home, Louver Street, Quincy.* Sighing, Murray dialled.

***

Britney picked the ringing phone up, "Hello?"

She turned to Adam, seeing his inquisitive stare. Trying to conceal her worry, she stuttered, "It's the Detective."

Adam gripped the phone loosely, his fingers trembling when he drew breath to speak.

"Adam here."

Britney stepped back, preferring not to hear the contents of the conversation. Adam had other ideas, he motioned for her to come close, laying the phone on the table and pressing the loudspeaker button. Murray's voice came through loud and scratchy, a constant buzz emitted from the speaker.

"I had to release Mr. McCoy earlier due to the lack of evidence."

Adam rolled the wheelchair closer to the kitchen table and lowered his head to the phone,

"Released?" he shook his head, "But how?"

"At the moment Adam, in reality, it's one man's word against another's."

The detective's voice ceased momentarily, yet the low buzzing continued, as if trying to torment Britney. She leaned closer to Adam and watched him digest his disappointment. One sentence from her mouth could end this mystery, yet her head shouted stop. *Silence.*

"I had hoped to link Mr. McCoy with the bank deposit and withdrawal..."

"And....?" Adam asked.

"The results of the fingerprint testing did not reveal the answer I was looking for," Murray claimed, quite calmly.

Adam pushed his wheelchair away from the table. Silence sailed up from the speaker, maybe Murray wanted more information Britney thought. Was he awaiting a confession? Did he find out anything over the last few days? Was he waiting for Britney to speak up?

Dusk dropped outside, covering the street in a dim haze. As it seeped in through the glass, Britney felt it blackening the investigation, keeping her secrets safe until her heart and conscience relaxed. Adam was too engrossed with deciphering the detective's words to notice the change in Britney, he rubbed his forehead, as if to mix up the sentences and come out with something relevant.

"So, did you find anything at the bank?" he blurted out. Britney immediately realised Adam sounded more like Murray's superior than the victim. Intentionally or not, Murray's long pause unsettled her, sending tons of questions into her worried mind.

"This baffles me," Murray began, surprising Britney with his honesty towards Adam.

"Fingerprint analysis at the bank revealed an identity, but not who I was expecting."

Adam and Britney glanced at each other, neither saying a word. Adam slid his hand along the table and reached out for Britney's. She reluctantly grabbed hold, realising a potential escape would be even more difficult. Adam lowered his ear closer to the speaker, "Tell me who stole my identity!"

"Adam, it's you," Murray croaked into the phone, "the fingerprints are yours."

***

"February 19th; broadcasting transmission 1.4...It is nearly time."

An outline of Madison's face looked back from the monitor. Relieved the darkness prevented a clearer image coming through, he leaned forward onto the desk and ran his hands over his head.

"This is the toughest thing I've ever done," he confessed to the blinking LED's, sick of hearing no reply.

"Creating all of this was nothing," he whispered, throwing his arms out wide. He kicked an empty box that had fallen close by, sending it flying into the pile of rubbish which filled over half of the living room.

"This, this waiting could kill a man."

The computer buzzed, making Madison sit up. *Are they replying?*

The screen flickered into a rainbow of colours, darting and dashing. Madison reached for the headset, "Hello?" Through the interference and buzzing came a noise, a human voice.

"Madison?" someone croaked faintly, "Can you hear me?"

A sense of relief washed over him, "Yes, I can hear you."

The sound of a familiar voice invigorated Madison as he sat upright in his chair and smiled.

"It's been a long time!"

A laugh came through the headset, "No, no it hasn't!"

"Well, it feels long for me, I can assure you." The interference lessened, making Madison sit back in his chair.

"So, what has changed since I've been gone?"

The voice on the other side seemed delayed. A momentary pause due to the distance the signal travelled.

"Not a thing, it's just the way you left it." The voice returned, giggling.

"That is not a good thing!" Madison said, taking the smile from his face.

"Madison," the voice sounded more serious this time, "you have to hold on, you need this."

He closed his eyes, imagining his reasons for being here, re-confirming his motivations to himself.

"Do you think that I am greedy for doing this?"

The pause worried Madison. He awaited an answer to confirm he was doing the right thing.

"Madison, do you remember the day you told me of your plan?"

"Yeah, the reaction nearly put me off."

The voice chuckled, "Nearly! I admit, when I heard the theory of the plan, I was not convinced."

"What changed your mind?" Madison interrupted, eager to learn more about his friend's initial doubts.

"While you tried to convince me your motivations were purely scientific and experimental, I knew otherwise." Madison sat in the darkened room, illuminated only by the flashing LED's and the street lights, yet here was a voice attempting to throw colour onto what drove him.

"Yes?"

"'Love is the emblem of eternity: it confounds all notions of time, eradicates all fear of an end' - sound familiar?"

Madison smiled. He had written that quote down in the days after his wife died. He hoped it would give him comfort in her passing, knowing that in time, they would meet again. Yet, when Madison decided to let go of his faith, the quote still seemed relevant.

"How long have you known about it?"

"I've known for years. I must say I had different motivations, but we had one goal, and we succeeded thus far," the voice replied softly.

Chapter 30

Britney offered to push Adam up the wheelchair ramp outside the police station, but he refused, instead propelling himself up with force. Murray tried to explain about the fingerprints on the phone, but the constant buzzing became too much for Adam.

Following Murray's instructions to find his office, located on the fourth floor of the Park Street building, Adam wheeled himself through the corridors, reminding Britney of times when she had seen such determination in Adam. Soccer was the number one source of this courage, the young man used to do everything in his power to avoid defeat, often running himself into the ground in an effort to drag his team over the line. But, should defeat come his way, Adam was the first to shake hands with the victors.

The pair passed through the station, Britney felt all the eyes set on her. *If they even knew,* she thought, she would be arrested on the spot for what she knew. If a choice existed, she would not have accompanied Adam, for her conscience had taken enough beating for one day.

Murray opened the door of his office and welcomed them in. Two large filing cabinets were situated in each corner of the room, like two sentries, armed with evidence. Murray sat behind his cheap timber desk, which was impeccably kept. A computer graced one side, a diary and a contacts book balanced the desk on the other. In front of the detective lay the fingerprint results.

Britney sat by the window in an effort to stay out of proceedings, until Adam nodded for her to come and sit near him, opposite Murray. The detective's eyes asked Adam to confirm Britney's attendance.

"This is Britney, I want her to be here," Adam muttered, "I trust her." Murray smiled and gave the slightest of nods,

"Okay."

He slid the fingerprint results across the table to Adam, pointing out where his name was typed.

"How is this possible?" Adam asked. His eyes fixed on the black letters claiming he was in the bank in September.

"I double-checked with the hospital; your stay was 2nd September to 17th October."

"I know that!" Adam interjected, pushing the results away, "how can I be in two places at once?"

"It looks like identity theft," Murray spoke, gathering the results and placing them in a filing cabinet.

"Someone stole my identity?"

"Yes, I think it was someone that knows you, otherwise, had they lodged the money to your account, chances are you would have noticed it within the two week timeframe."

Britney, while regretting coming to the station with Adam, was intrigued.

"Why would a lottery winner not just lodge it into their own account?" she asked.

Murray's eyes flicked to the young woman, "There are many reasons, maybe they are receiving some life-long benefit, or they might just want to keep it secret from their families."

"Hmmm," Britney murmured, "seems like an awful lot of trouble to go to, stealing someone's identity just to hide it from your wife." A smile crept up on all the faces, lightening the tone momentarily.

"Indeed! But, the most likely scenario is that your identity was stolen by a person, or persons with criminal connections."

"You mean a form of money laundering?" Britney spoke again, getting more engrossed in the topic with each passing second.

"Yeah, now there is $1 million loose on the streets of Boston, with no record of where it went," Murray said.

A sense of self-worth sweep over Britney with Murray's positive answer. It was new. It was strange. Like a flash of lightening, it came and went so quickly, back to reality, where she continued to lie to her best friend.

"It's ironic," Adam spoke. "Only days after I lose my identity, someone else finds it and uses it, and now they are returning it, broken."

Murray and Britney looked at each other, neither knowing how to react to Adam's sombre statement. Rubbing his back did little to stir Adam out of his condition. He kept staring blankly at the desk.

"Shaun McCoy?"

Murray let out a sigh, "I'm sorry Adam, he could not be charged."

His trembling hands slid off the desk and onto the steel handles that extended from the wheels and he twisted the wheelchair towards the door. Britney immediately stood up and let him out.

"Can I have some time alone, please?" he whispered, as he pushed himself out of the office.

Britney and Murray watched Adam push through the police station until he went out of sight.

"What can we do for him?" Britney asked, blanking her mind from answering itself.

"Go back to the start, and follow a new lead...if it exists," Murray replied.

The detective's bluntness surprised Britney, but it comforted her when she thought the case may be filed away, stored under *incomplete.*

"Oh! It could be over? Just like that!" she returned, careful not to show her relief.

"Britney, you are a grown woman so I am sure you can understand," Murray said, leaning forward in his chair.

"While we may be so sure of some things in life, we cannot prove them. Just because we know Shaun McCoy was driving the car, it doesn't matter, it's not gonna hold up."

Britney let the words float in her mind, rearranging them to make sense.

"So, what you're saying is, Adam's word counts for nothing?"

Murray nodded, "I know McCoy was driving, Adam knows he was driving. The trouble is to convince the judge."

Britney struggled to suppress the ideas which bubbled up inside, to speak or stay silent. Today, although nerve-wrecking, was productive for her. The case hit a dead end, and the likelihood of Murray finding out the truth was slim, considering that interrogating Shaun revealed nothing. The road thus far almost broke Britney. The only question that remained was, to journey onwards, or turn back to the previous junction.

"I guess all we can do is hope?" Britney said.

Chapter 31

Britney trudged up the path to her house. The front door's new form as a barrier never looked so appealing. Britney twisted the door handle, hearing a familiar empty echo reverberate around the dreary house.

What a difference one man made, remembering the light her father used to bring to the home. Any day could be a fun day. No need for a birthday, anniversary or public holiday, he worked from the cuff. That was Britney's favourite trait of her father, his ability to see when she or his wife was down and to turn it all around with a simple gesture.

Britney turned the kettle on and slumped on the living room sofa. She tossed ideas around in her head, searching for an excuse, should the truth come out. A dead father, an alcoholic mother, Britney Davis had suffered. In reality she knew so many others had it worse, yet one thing they managed to hold onto was their honesty.

Honesty, Britney thought, feeling a heavier sensation in her tummy. Earlier, when Adam mentioned he 'trusts' her, it took all her strength not to vomit there and then. She let her best friend down, her father down and most of all, herself. There were two options forming in

Britney's head. One, pick up the already packed suitcase, or two, do what should have been done months ago.

The clock in the hallway chimed. This charade could not be carried for much longer. Her hands got weary, as did her tongue. Trekking up the stairs, she changed her mind with every swing of the pendulum.

There it lay, still packed, under the bed. The black suitcase developed a voice of its own, urging Britney to grab hold and run. The tag from her last trip still dangled from the leather strap, *Buffalo, New York.* She tore the paper tag and threw it into the bin. Imagining her next destination, Britney decided it need not be hot, or scenic, or inexpensive. Only one condition applied, it had to be far away from here.

Luckily for her, in one of the largest countries in the world, distance was not a problem. Travel southwards toward Providence and New York. Trade the ford in for something different, the first step in giving Britney a new life. Find a job, probably working in some bar or restaurant, keep the body and mind active.

Yeah, a fresh start sounded good to Britney. Very little in this town encouraged her to stay. The suitcase squeaked as it was pulled out from under the bed, seemingly eager to start its journey of freedom. Britney's mind was a leaking dam, letting trickling doubts seep through, hoping the flow slowed enough to repair the cracks. A trembling hand lifted the suitcase onto the bed and flicked it open to give one last glance.

***

Adam swatted at the flies gathering around his front porch light. He sighed at his inability to perform the task, cursing silently at the fleeing insects. *What d'ya expect*!

A crescent moon rose overhead, casting its minimal glow over the Atlantic and the north-eastern United States. The small shine tried to compensate for the flickering streetlight at the end of Louver Street, another irritation for Adam to worry about. He imagined a large swatter in his hands, one big enough to quench the faulty light.

He compiled a list of his worst moments. Each memory since September was outdone by another, only reinforcing the negative thoughts inside Adam. From the hospital bed, to the consultant's room, to his failure with the physiotherapist, Adam could not rub all the horror from his memories. An inkling of hope and positivity stirred within him, but it was drowned by a flood of damp and painful flashbacks.

Adam's eyes traced a line down the driveway, along where the melting snow revealed the grass margin and out onto Louver Street. He dreamed of throwing the wheelchair aside and feeling the cool concrete on the soles of his feet, squirming at the tingle of the grass as he swings his legs along the strands of green softness. Such freedoms lay only inches away, yet the wheelchair creaked when Adam shuffled, laughing at him. His hands gripped tighter, eager to push themselves away from the teasing metal frame. Legs fell off the footrests, dangling freely. Sporadically, there was enough strength in the heart, not enough in the supports.

Settling back in the chair, Adam consigned himself to the shackles and chains. The dark sky sampled his life, even the moon took part as its tiny crescent mirrored Adam's hope.

***

An early morning shower turned into a downpour, soaking Britney as she ran to her car, suitcase in hand. Gasping, she slammed the car door and settled into the driver's seat. Her house did not warrant a fleeting glance, she started the car and pulled away. In reality, the building ceased being a home the day her father died. Invisible decorators had come while Britney slept and painted over all the warmth and heat, leaving nothing but a heavy splattering of hurt and despair.

Britney now realised why her mother was so frequently absent from the house, she was surprised for not noticing it before. The home held so many memories for Mrs. Davis, a daily reminder to the widow must have been too torturous to take. Alcohol was much easier to digest.

Red lights stopped Britney in her tracks. The traffic junction, while allowing her body to rest, jump-started her mind into thinking about Adam and what she did. An eternal red light allowed more guilt to seep into her thoughts, diluting the determination that existed minutes earlier. A certainty which was so visible in her sights dissolved. Her forehead relaxed, easing pressure on her eyes. Britney loosened her grip on the steering wheel, reached for knotted hair and tucked it behind her ear. So many excuses for her actions lined up in mid-air, assembling, waiting for her to pick one, Britney swiped her hand through the imaginary list and sighed. She was twenty-five years old, it was time to make her own choices and stand by them.

The lights turned green. Life had a funny way of making it so clear; go left, to the highway and a new life, or right, to Adam and the truth. Britney inhaled and pressed the accelerator.

Chapter 32

Britney stopped the car at the top of the lookout.

It is time.

"Is everything okay Britney? You have been so quiet?" Adam asked, splitting his time between exploring the view and Britney. She knew it was time to reveal all to Adam, yet she struggled to find the words to start it off. Instead, she cheated.

"He wanted to call me Violet," she whispered, looking out over the tree line and towards Boston.

"Wow," Adam turned to her, "that's an awful name. I'm glad that your mother got her way."

A smile escaped Britney's mouth, surprising her with its unfamiliar feeling. She lowered her head and rubbed her father's ring.

"They compromised. Violet is my middle name."

A surge of guilt attacked her, like a spark of electricity on her skin, she tingled all over. Her pulse quickened, she felt Adam's stare fixed on her squirming fingers. Britney tried to arrange words in her head. She wanted to throw it all out to Adam, tell him everything. It was all mumbled inside. Her tense state did little to help the situation, only sending more fuel to the chaos.

"Britney, is everything okay?"

"Yeah!" she lied. "All is good, just memories."

An image of Adam lying in a crashed car struck like an arrow, piercing a hole in her heart. Britney could not take many more hits of that magnitude. Taking a deep breath, she tried again to conjure her manic thoughts into something resembling a sentence.

"I have something to say," Adam spoke, breaking Britney from her trance.

"I do too," she replied, eager to get in there first.

"I just want to say thank you," Adam continued.

"Thank you?" Britney asked, deliberating whether or not she wanted to hear the reason for such a statement.

"Over the last few months, you have been one of the few good things in my life."

Oh no, Britney thought, "No, Adam, stop."

"Please, let me finish," He spoke up, reaching over and holding her hand.

"I want to say thank you for everything-"

"Please stop Adam!" Britney shouted.

Adam sat silently, his crinkled expression awaiting a reason for the outburst.

"Just stop," Britney said. A drop of rain bounced off the windshield. Within seconds, the lone drop was joined by friends, rain bombarded the glass. Words jumped around in Britney's head, she grabbed the most basic and ran with them.

"Adam, I was there."

He smiled, "You were where?"

Pelting rain blurred the windscreen, cutting off the surrounding view from the pair. The splattering was deafening, it was surrounding. Britney struggled to breathe. The elements were against her, or else the guilt had manifested itself in her lungs and it was hell bent on taking her down from the inside.

"No Adam, I was there, when the car crashed."

Still, the words did not register with the young man. His fingers were motionless on Britney's skin.

"I was in the car."

Time paused. Adam jolted backwards until the car door held him. His arms failed, trailing away weakly from Britney's skin. A hand extended in love, withdrew covered in lies and deceit. Lowering his head onto his lap, Adam curled his arms around the back of his neck and closed his eyes tightly. For a moment Britney thought about reaching for him but decided against. The last five months had been easy compared to this.

Britney struggled to hide the trembling in her voice,

"I'm so sorry."

"Don't, don't," was Adam's muffled response.

Tears trickled down her face and jumped like fleeing soldiers onto the safety of her blue jeans. Britney mustered the courage to turn towards Adam.

"Adam, I really am sorry. I tried to tell you."

"You tried to tell me!" Adam said, raising his head from his lap.

"All this time my best friend, my only friend has been lying to me."

Britney's hand crept closer, trying to intertwine with his.

"Don't touch me."

The rain subsided momentarily, allowing a silence to grow in the car. Adam's trembling hand wiped the condensation from the window as teary red eyes looked out through the smeary glass.

"Please, let me explain," Britney said.

"Just take me home....."

***

Britney stopped the car at the top of the lookout.

This is heaven.

Above the dark clouds, there lay a sun. That sun was sitting next to Adam.

"Is everything ok Britney? You have been so quiet?" Adam asked, trying his best to hide his excitement, intentionally gazing out his passenger window over the viewing bay. Britney looked more beautiful each time he saw her. Again, more perfect now than ever, wow.

"He wanted to call me Violet," Britney whispered.

"Wow," Adam turned to her, "that's an awful name. I'm glad that your mother got her way."

Adam caught the smile that came from Britney, yet it seemed suppressed. *Don't mention her father again.* Adam watched her fingers glide over her father's golden ring and tried to imagine what it was like, losing him.

"They compromised. Violet is my middle name."

Adam found himself staring at Britney's fingers as they squirmed in her palm, like she was moulding some invisible dough. He leaned sideways and grasped her hands.

"Britney, is everything ok?"

"Yeah!" she said. "All is good, just memories."

184

Glimpses of the previous five months played in Adam's mind like a silent film. He hid the smile that threatened to envelop his face when he pictured Britney at the hospital, or Britney getting into his bed on New Year's Eve. Recovery would be difficult, Adam knew. However, recovery without Britney would be impossible.

"I have something to say," Adam said.

"I do too," Britney said, trying to jump ahead.

"I just want to say thank you," Adam continued.

"Thank you?" Britney asked.

"Over the last few months, you have been one of the few good things in my life."

"No, Adam, stop."

"Please, let me finish," he grabbed her hand tighter.

"I want to say thank you for everything-"

"Please stop Adam!" Britney shouted.

Ok! What the hell?

"Just stop," Britney said.

A drop of rain bounced off the windshield. Within seconds, the lone drop was joined by friends, rain bombarded the glass. Adam reviewed his words, looking for clues to what may have upset her. Did I mention her father again? Have I relied on her too much?

"Adam, I was there," Britney said.

"You were where?"

For a brief second Adam realised that rain was beating the window, until more important thoughts gained the limelight. Britney jerked, her chest heaved. Tears gave a hint of their developing presence through blinking eyes. Curly blonde hair fell over the side of Britney's face, providing cover from Adam's stare. Her once pale skin seemed energised, or troubled, it filled

185

with a sweaty red. Intermittent breaths reminded Adam that she was alive.

"No Adam, I was there, when the car crashed."

Adam questioned his senses, did he just hear that?

"I was in the car," Britney said.

Adam's body fell limp. He struggled to pull dead arms back, he could not touch her. Adam's brain worked overtime, it searched and searched for a way to prove Britney's words untrue. A smidgen of hope would do now, anything would do. He looked for a tiny grain that would seep into Britney's words, finding cracks and splits and uncovering her statement as a lie.

Britney failed to hide the trembling in her voice, "I'm so sorry."

"Don't, don't."

The truth became obvious. There was a lie to be found. It had been hiding for months in plain view, disguising itself as a best friend. Adam needed to escape but the condensation soaked windows only added to his predicament. Now he could see why Britney took him all the way out here, there was no way for him to escape her confession.

"Adam, I really am sorry. I tried to tell you."

"You tried to tell me!" Adam said. "All this time my best friend, my only friend has been lying to me."

A shudder erupted throughout Adam when Britney touched his skin, his reflexes pulled his arm back quickly and wrapped around his own body. Still, Britney's hand crept closer, trying to intertwine with his. Her fingers rubbed his shoulder, until they were shrugged off with a violent swing of Adam's elbow. He forced his eyes tightly closed, in a futile attempt to suppress the tears.

186

"Don't touch me."

"Please, let me explain," Britney said.

"Just take me home!"

He longed to open his eyes and be at home, away from the woman who was responsible for all of this. Instead, here she was, trying to gain Adam's trust again with fickle touches. Such touches had already broken Adam, shattered him like a vase that had fallen from the mantle. In Adam's eyes, it was impossible to put him back together again.

A long, silent and awkward drive home followed. Adam went through what had happened over and over in his head every inch of the way. Random sniffling was the only noise from Britney, she constantly wiped away tears. *Why is she crying? I am the one who was betrayed and lied to. I am the one who is stuck in this stupid chair.*

Relentless rain welcomed them back to Louver Street as Britney parked as far up the Fletcher driveway as possible. She opened Adam's door and placed the wheelchair next to him.

"I'll do it myself!" he barked. While he struggled to hoist himself from the car to the chair, Adam preferred it rather than to feel Britney's touch.

Minutes disguised as hours passed in Adam's mind. The laptop loaded up with a reminder that sent a dart of pain throughout his fragile body, Britney's smiling face. The picture, once a symbol of hope for Adam, was now the force that shook his entire world. Quick movements of the mouse changed the wallpaper on screen, changing it to a mundane grey. While it accomplished very little for now, Adam knew it would take time to rid his life and mind of Britney Davis.

Britney's best friend left her and yet she could not find words to say. Dots of speech tried to depart her mouth, coming out mumbled and irrelevant. Even one last glance from Adam when he clumsily opened the front door and went inside would have sufficed for Britney, but none came.

Cold rain beat her, turning her skin a paler shade of white. Her once blonde hair seemed darkened as it hung lifeless over her shoulders and chest, soaked through and flattened. Drops of water flowed down her neck and onto her back, making Britney shiver. Yet, still she waited. *He might come back* she told herself. The Fletcher home did not change. An unlit porch still stared at the young woman, the front door handle still dripped from Adam's grasp.

Britney held her stance for over twenty minutes, standing in the downpour for as long as her body would allow, her tears blending in with the rain. Her whole body felt white with cold. Even her underwear was drenched. Britney resigned herself to the fact Adam was not coming back. Numb fingers struggled to open the car door, stinging with pain when she pulled at the handle. Father's gold ring caught Britney's eye as the door popped open. A surge of guilt gushed through her when she imagined how he would feel now. She quickly pulled the ring off and stored it in the glove compartment.

Chapter 33

"I know that look Shaun," Rachael said.

Shaun's ears were fixed to the sounds of the bar and rain muddled together. His eyes, distant, followed the random path of the rainwater on the window as it darted back and forth on its downward journey. Outside, the Avenue was being drenched as the rain dragged pieces of litter to the sewer grates.

"That look?" he smiled, "What is that look?"

Rachael held Shaun's hand, "You okay?"

His eyes stayed focused on the rain splattering on the pavement outside, "Yeah!"

That look still lingered on Shaun's face. Rachael flicked back to when she had seen such determination before, where memories of a violent Shaun emerged. She loved him, but hated what he could become. Shaun turned away from the window and reached for Rachael, pulling her close as he kissed her temple.

"Don't worry....everything will be taken care of."

Rachael wanted to lean away from Shaun, but his arms were locked too tightly around her small body, forcing her to inhale his strong odour. She raised her arms up and wrapped them around Shaun. Rachael relaxed, massaged by the powerful frame that seemed to protect her from the world while also hiding her from the realities of their actions.

Rachael had met Shaun years earlier in the park outside their apartment block. Despite being several years younger, Rachael became infatuated with the rebellious Shaun. There was something in the tough version of the man that attracted the young girl. Secret meetings between the pair turned into a full blown relationship. Unfortunately for Rachael, at times the commitment seemed one-way.

Frequent rumours of cheating percolated through the chitchat and into Rachael's innocent ears. Every time she batted the gossip away, preferring to believe Shaun's decorated words instead.

So many friends had told Rachael to leave Shaun. Like Rachael, they knew he held the keys to her head and heart, controlling her whenever the need arose. What they did not know was she loved it. Thoughts of rebelling crossed Rachael's mind from time to time, but Shaun always found a way to make her feel important. Like on the day of the accident.

"Babe," Shaun let his grip loosen and turned his gaze toward Rachael, "I need you."

A police car stopped outside the Banshee bar. A disinterested Shaun stood away from the window and motioned for a drink. Rachael held her boyfriends hand in an effort to coax more affection from him, but the previous statement exceeded his quota for the day.

A plain clothed man and a police officer stepped through the front door. Too lost in thought, Shaun did not turn around, only shivering as the cold breeze sent a chill up his spine.

"Shaun McCoy," The plain clothes officer began, making Shaun turn around.

"Yes?"

"You are under arrest for motor vehicle theft, inhibiting a police investigation and dangerous driving resulting in grievous bodily harm."

Rachael grabbed the officer's arm, "What is this all about?"

"Excuse me miss," he said, brushing her back. Shaun laughed as he turned back towards the bar, once again motioning for a drink.

"You guys can't be serious! Guess you're gonna do the whole movie cop act, read me my rights."

The police officer grabbed Shaun's arm. He snapped on a handcuff before the young man had time to react.

"No, Mr. McCoy, we are not here to waste our time."

Standing up, Rachael tried again to force the police officer away from her boyfriend, but the plain clothes man stepped in and pushed her out of the way. Shaun resisted the second handcuff being put onto his right wrist, forcing both men to restrain him against the bar counter.

"What lame excuses have you this time?"

"Lame excuses! Don't worry Mr. McCoy, this time it will be worth our while taking you in. We have a witness, a reliable one."

The officers bundled Shaun out the door, leaving a stunned bar and a shaken girlfriend behind.

Adam cursed himself for not cancelling the appointment. The last thing he needed was an eternally pepped up physio throwing out motivational speeches like confetti. Black clothes and graveside prayers danced in Adam's mind, and no amount of brave stories and Buddha inspired words of wisdom would remove them.

An hour of leg massage and motor tests later and Adam still felt dead. His world collapsed on him, and with each passing moment he felt the walls pressing in on him like a boa constrictor. Pain that dwelled in his head doubled and set up in his heart, jumping to all his arteries and spreading like an infectious disease. Michael Lenard's dose of inspirational antibiotics never stood a chance.

"I was planning on putting you through a session of the walking bars, but I'm not so sure now."

"Huh," Adam sighed. "Is it that obvious?"

"You're probably sick of hearing me say it, but."

"I'm sorry," Adam interjected, "I have a lot going on these days. My head is not in it."

"It's not all doom and gloom."

Adam shook his head, such a statement could not go unchallenged he thought.

"It is all doom and gloom. That's all there ever seems to be! I doubt all this happiness that I'm being force fed even exists, because all I've ever known is pain and misery."

Michael's eyes glanced everywhere but into Adam's. No doubt words were arranging themselves in his mind, searching for some reliving quote.

"Adam, I..."

"I just hate my life and everything about it. Even the only bright spot turned out to be false," Adam said.

"In time you will walk again. In time, you will have all your memories back."

"I don't want them back, they're all lies."

Chapter 34

"He did not go into detail Adam, he just told me to get you to the police station as soon as I could," Erin tried to explain as they travelled along the I-93 highway in to Park Street police station.

"There must be new evidence? Hopefully it will be something to link Shaun to the accident," Erin said, glancing at her son in the passenger seat. Adam nodded, eager to comfort his mother, but in reality he did not want to get his own hopes up. He had visited and spoken to Murray enough times to know this case had an unnatural ability to excite and disappoint in equal measure.

"Mother, there is something you should know about Britney," Adam whispered.

"Yes?"

"She knows about the accident," Adam began, immediately realising his words did not convey what was intended.

"I mean, she knows all about the accident. She was there."

Erin slowed the car, taking a moment to digest what Adam said.

"What?"

"She was in the car when it crashed, she knew all along."

"Adam, are you sure about this?"

He motioned for her to pull over, this needed some explaining. The car slowed to a stop on a side lane, Adam spelled it out as clear as he could.

"Britney was in the car the day it crashed and she has kept the secret from me, you, all of us."

Erin frowned, showing a map of lines across her face. The last five months were hard for Adam, they must have been hell for his mother. Her hand shook as it tried to reach her face. Her eyes darted all over, only resting when she closed them tightly. Trembling lips stuttered, "How do you know this?"

"She told me."

Months of memories flashed in his mind. While the sadness he felt for himself was debilitating, the sheer anchor of pain was incomparable to Adam when he saw the tears on his mothers face. How he longed to see her younger form. Even though his memories only stretched back five months, he could see wrinkles which were previously non-existent had hit land, spreading out in all directions from her weary eyes. Trembling lips failed to hide the signs of countless tears dripping over them. A hoarse voice spoke up, yet while it came from this woman, the voice was not that of Adam's mother. It was the voice of a woman who had just cracked, like a porcelain doll dropped while everyone's eyes were looking in the opposite direction.

"Why? Why did she not tell you earlier?"

"I don't know. Afraid I guess," Adam said.

The whizzing cars passing by seemed intent on irritating Erin, she lowered her head to hide her eyes from her son. Trickles of tears broke out onto her face. The aching inside Erin drifted onto the passenger seat and set itself even deeper in Adam.

Perhaps it was some invisible feed from his mother's inquisitive thoughts that kick started his brain into thinking overtime, or possibly it was nature's way of protecting part of a negative mind in an effort to save it, but either way, snippets of what new method Murray had found circled inside Adam.

"Come on, we'll see what Murray has to say," he whispered.

Over three miles later they arrived outside the Park Street police station. A quick glance at his phone still showed no sign of contact from Britney, *good.* As Erin placed the wheelchair next to the passenger door, Adam found new strength in his arms and swung himself from the seat downwards.

"I just need this to end today."

"I hope it will end Adam, I really do." Murray must have gotten Shaun to confess, or else he picked up some substantial evidence to prove Shaun's involvement in the accident, Adam thought. Now, it was time to see what trick Murray had up his sleeve.

Murray shook Adam and Erin's hands as they were lead into his office. Closing the door, Murray's smile grew contagious.

"We have proof Mr. McCoy was the driver of the car Adam," he said, clenching his hands tightly together.

"Furthermore, we can charge him for withholding information from police in an ongoing investigation."

Adam threw his head back and sighed. An invisible weight loosened its grip on his shoulders and floated upwards to the fluorescent lights in Murray's office.

"You can't imagine how good it is to hear that," Erin said.

"How did you get it out of Shaun?" Adam asked. Murray glanced to his right ever so briefly, an involuntary reaction to when a person tries to recall a memory. Adam duly noted this, and double checked it was indeed to Murray's right, as a glance left indicates the person is creating something from nothing, also known as lying. With that Adam cursed his ignorance; Britney had to be doing it for months now. *Love is blind* was his excuse.

"I don't deserve as much credit as you may think. Really, it fell into my lap."

"What? One of Shaun's friends squealed?" Adam asked, failing to hide the joy in his voice.

***

Holding cell 2A had no doubt seen some hard men and women over the years. Late night brawlers, fuelled by cocktails of drink and drugs, all thrown head first into the narrow 12x6 concrete and steel cage. Most people deserved its coldness, and a few deserved worse. If the cell had a memory, it would struggle to remember a time when someone was thrown in there for being honest.

Britney lay sullen-faced against the concrete wall, and while she expected such treatment after the statement to Detective Murray, the irony was evident. Stay silent, yet be free. Speak the truth and be here. Britney's heart shouted at her head. *This is not about you, it's about Adam!*

A swiping noise came from the holding cell entrance, a police officer running his key card through the control panel. Little murmurs spread down the hallway, filling every cell with tiny vibrations. Britney drew a sharp breath. That voice was familiar. Her suspicions were confirmed with the seemingly random creaking from Adam's wheelchair. A whisper from Adam's tongue found Britney's ears, he asked the police officer to be left alone.

Even though Adam was getting closer, Britney could not lift herself off the ground. Her mind manifested the guilt in mid air and turned it into a dead weight. Now, this weight hovered over her.

"Hi."

"Hey."

Britney struggled to turn away from the grey floor, a magnet in her eyes found its opposite in the concrete. Adam had no such problems. Britney shuddered at the thought of looking at him, at his once peaceful blue eyes.

"Can you look at me please?" Adam asked.

Britney climbed to her feet and placed her hands on the bars.

"I now know how you have felt all this time," Britney whispered, sliding her hands along the metal cage that held her in. "This is hell."

"No, no you don't know how I felt. A couple of hours in a cell and you try to compare that to what I have dealt with?"

"I did not mean it...!"

"Just don't! I can't handle listening to you speak, every word that comes from you is poison," Adam claimed loudly, the echo bounced around again and again, the walls drove the words into Britney's psyche. She stepped back into the cell, hiding from the glow of the hallway light, her eyes finding anything but Adam.

"The detective told me I should not come down here, but I had to."

Adam lowered his voice, yet the cold reverberations continued to bounce into the cell, reassuring the beaten woman there was no escape.

"But, I have some things to say...do me a favour and hear me out."

Britney pushed her hair behind her ears and begged her eyes to stay dry. Tears now would only mock Adam. Strangely, he looked more able now than any time since September. Britney thought about bringing pre-crash memories to the fight, but what use would that serve, only more *lies* for Adam, no way of defining the truth. Either way, it was his time for words, true or not.

"I loved you," Adam said. There it was again, the echo, repeating every word to Britney.

"I have been so down since the accident, but every now and again there were glimpses the struggle may be worth it, this life may be worth living."

Britney was not blind, she had seen Adam's bright moments since the accident when she visited. She assumed her modesty stopped her from relating the smiles to her presence.

"You were that glimpse," he said.

"Adam-" Britney began.

"I can only say for sure what I have felt since the accident. I *had* hoped there was something between us before the accident, it sickens me to my core to think I actually wasted my time, effort and life on someone like you."

Dark spots on Britney's jumper appeared below her chin. Moisture soaked through the slim garment and touched her chest. In their trip from her eyes, the tears lost their heat and by the time they penetrated the fabric, they were ice cubes on Britney's chest.

"I don't know what will happen next," Adam whispered, "but if you are set free, please stay away from me."

Britney gasped. It was as if a giant vacuum cleaner sucked every molecule of oxygen from the building and left her speechless. Adam's words morphed from vibrations in her ears to knives in her heart. His actions made Britney fall to her knees. Her eyes could not believe what they were witnessing, Adam turning and making his way to the entrance. The thud of Britney hitting the ground must have chased after Adam, she thought, but he chose to ignore it. It was the least she deserved.

Chapter 35

"Mr. McCoy?" Murray asked, "I understand your son has already contacted you?"

"Ahh yes officer, yes. Please, come in."

Murray stepped inside Shaun McCoy's home, scanning every detail on the dark walls. He reached into his pocket and pulled out a small flashlight, keeping it unlit.

"I appreciate you agreeing to this search Mr. McCoy. It saved a lot of unnecessary paperwork."

Mr. McCoy nodded politely and opened Shaun's room door.

"I assume this is what you came for?"

The officer brushed past Mr. McCoy and stepped into Shaun's room. Murray placed the flashlight back into his pocket and adjusted his eyes to the light. A smell of aftershave filled the room. Murray expected worse, and aside from the messy bed, it was not the typical room of a young man. But, this made the detective even more suspicious.

"I will leave you to it," Mr. McCoy whispered.

The door closed, revealing the presence of a deadbolt on the inside.

"Why would anyone need such security?" Murray whispered to his colleague.

"Abusive father maybe?" the officer replied.

Murray smiled, that suggestion did not warrant a reply he thought. Shaun McCoy was a powerful young man, he towered over his father. Even if the deadbolt was the result of abuse from years previous, Murray struggled to see how Mr. McCoy would have possessed such intentions, judging by his obliging nature. But, the words *book* and *cover* popped into the detective's conscience. He reminded himself he had been wrong before.

"Shaun did not want to keep someone out, he wanted to keep something in here hidden."

With that, Murray dropped to his knees and rubbed his hands along the dark red carpet, looking for openings or lacerations where Shaun may have hidden sensitive information.

"What exactly are we looking for?" the officer asked, upping his search.

"If I'm being perfectly honest, I don't know," Murray said, reaching under the bed. "But something doesn't feel right."

His fingers rubbed the corners of a box hidden beneath the bed, he searched for something to grab. They gripped around a smooth metal handle and pulled.

"What's this?"

Murray threw the box, a suitcase, onto the ruffled bed sheets. The latches clicked, the case popped open. Murray stopped. Although he had not found anything incriminating, something told him to be professional, be sure. He reached into his side pocket and pulled out an unused pair of forensic gloves.

Snapping the latex tightly around his hands, Murray examined layer after layer of irrelevant newspaper cuttings. Sports events, school plays and previous exam papers provided plenty reading material for the police officers. Murray was not here to read. He dug again. His fingers came across something cold, something familiar. They clawed again. Yeah, Murray thought, that shape is unmistakable. His hands threw off the paper as he pulled them out of the suitcase.

"Today is going pretty well!" Murray smiled, thinking of Britney's confession. Her words re-opened the investigation, and her suggestion had just given Murray another piece of evidence against the main suspect, an unlicensed firearm.

***

Two miles south of Dorchester, Madison sat alone in Adam's room. Even though the midday sun was peering in the window, he calmly flicked page after page of an old photo album. A creak in the hallway did little to unsettle the intruder. A magnet on the pages drew his eyes closer with each glance.

"Oh, time is nearly up!" Madison spoke softly, fidgeting with the chunky album before placing it back on its perch, the bedside table.

He stepped out of Adam's room and into the hallway, raising his hand and touching every photograph that hung on the Fletcher's wall. Once outside, Madison pulled the door shut without worrying about noise and pulled a key from his pocket and locked the door. The slightest glance around was followed by Madison bending down, and sliding the key under a dislodged panel on the front decking.

Moments later, Adam arrived home. After basically throwing himself from the car to the wheelchair, his arms worked overtime to propel him up the wheelchair ramp that worked its way up to the front porch.

A sigh accompanied his inquisitive look toward his mother, who was busy trying to carry as many shopping bags as possible from the car.

"There is a key under the decking panel Adam, directly out from the door frame," she whispered in an effort to keep the information from the neighbours.

"Oh?" Adam muttered, leaning down and searching for the dislodged member.

***

The dustbin was strategically placed next to the wheelchair, so when Adam opened the photo album and ripped each photo one by one, the contents fell into the trap. Years of memories shredded in an instant. Even a second glance at some made his stomach react, like turning on a blender inside and at any moment, the contents could spew out. With each sharp sound of tearing paper, Adam ensured there was no power supplied to the blender.

However, the slightest peek at the photos reignited some recent memories and imagined what some older ones might have looked like, whether Adam wanted to remember or not. Glimpses of Britney and Adam sharing birthdays or playing in the front garden seemed to pop up everywhere. His gut spoke ahead, knowing what picture was going to appear next.

Adam's fingers slid under the next page, eager to press on and finish this job. His head shouted for revenge, as did his heart, so what control within him was asking for the next photo to be spared. Either way, if he was going to destroy it, he had to physically see it first. The sound of the crinkling plastic covering paved the way, and there it was with a page to itself, the prom photo.

For the last five months, it appeared so many times, in dreams, in memories. It was a national treasure, like the American Constitution or the Eiffel tower. Was it right to destroy it? Adam flicked the photo from underneath the plastic covering and tore it in two. Within minutes, the photo album was stripped and the contents filled the dustbin on the floor. Clenching his fist, Adam pounded the fragmented photos deep into the bin, knowing he would never have to see them again.

Chapter 36

It had been the longest day of her life, or so it felt. Britney's eyes had seen every part of the grey walls confining her on three sides. Yet, the fourth side was guarded by the ultimate ironic soldier. A soldier that let Britney see freedom, smell it, even touch it. But, it never let its guard down. Constantly alert, he did not do sick days, holidays nor tea breaks. He reached from the floor to the ceiling with arms of iron, far enough apart to reveal everything in the hallway, but close enough to keep Britney confined.

If there was one quality Britney could bestow on this watchman, it would be a sound barrier. Shaun McCoy was two cells up, and called Britney since he arrived.

"I know you're there Brit," were the whispers, "I can hear you breathing, crying."

She raised her hand to her mouth. Bleary eyed she glanced out into the illuminated hallway which showed nothing but a mundane concrete passage. The cell opposite was in total darkness, an iron soldier stood guard.

"Here, here, here, little birdie!" Shaun said.

"What, what do you want?" She replied, so delicate that it struggled to reach Shaun's ears.

"I just wanna talk. It gets boring in here, let's chat."

"I'd rather not," she said, "I have nothing to say to you."

Shaun sniggered, sending a chill through Britney.

"You have nothing to say to me! After all we've been through!"

Britney bit her lips, despite the words wanting to break free. But, it did not deter Shaun from firing again.

"When we get released, how about-"

"Released?" Britney interrupted, "We are not going to be released!"

"What do you think they're gonna keep us here on? Our word against amnesia man! What sane Judge is gonna hear that case?"

"Yeah, Adam is not going to be the most reliable witness, I agree with you."

The darkness seemed to echo Shaun's laugh as it sent it bouncing around the holding cells and into Britney's ears over and over again.

"But, a Judge would listen to the claims of someone who was in the car?" Britney said, listening intently for the laughing to stop. There it was, silence. Seconds seemed like minutes as Shaun deciphered what Britney said, taking it in, and repeating the process again just to make sure he heard right. Judging by the sounds, Shaun stood to his feet and pressed against the iron bars.

"What person in their right mind would do such a thing?" Shaun's rebuttal came, heavy, threatening and dripping with anger. *He cannot touch me*, Britney reassured herself, rubbing the bars, and for the first time, thankful for their presence.

"Shaun, I have confessed already. I'm the reason why you're here this time, and as I have the power to ensure that you stay here, I'm going to do what's right."

"Do what's right? Yeah, tell the detective you made it all up, you'll get a slap on the wrist but that'll be it!" Shaun said. She shook her head, seeing how his words were so changeable, always trying to look out for himself.

"This time I'm doing what's right for Adam. It may be too late for us, but it's the least we can do."

"You will regret this Britney, don't do it," Shaun threatened. "Don't do it."

Britney sat on the ground and leaned against the bars. Moments of peaceful silence were hijacked by Shaun's words.

"It's just that," he spoke softly, "I cannot go to jail."

Yes we can.

"Every week my father has a different letter from the college pinned to my door. If I get locked up, I'm never going to get that chance again."

Cold hard thoughts in Britney's head travelled south and met with the compassionate feelings coming from her heart. Despite what Shaun had done to Adam, despite what she had done, was it right to destroy three lives instead of one? Contrasting feelings took control of the woman's eyes, lips and hands. Flexing and fidgeting, they battled for a decisive answer. The cold thoughts were warmed from underneath by Shaun's careful words and no matter how hard she tried to deny it,

Britney felt the pressure building up inside, causing her once solid stance to melt.

"Is it gonna be five years of prison, or five years of study?"

"But what about Adam?"

"I do feel sorry for him. But, is it not better to save two lives than to ruin two lives, especially when it is unnecessary?"

"Yes, I guess so."

"My father, what will he do without me? And who will look after your mother if you're locked up?"

He was right, Britney knew it. Why ruin three lives, when one will suffice. Inadvertently, Shaun gave Britney an idea, one that would not benefit him. A swiping noise accompanied the opening of the holding cell entrance and in stepped Detective Murray. Britney shivered when the tapping of leather soled shoes came in her direction, slowing as it reached her cell.

"The phone call you requested Miss Davis, do you want to make it now?"

Standing up, she nodded. With that, Murray slid his card key into the electronic panel hanging on the partition wall between cells and the iron soldier retreated.

"This way please," Murray said, pointing up the hallway.

Constant blinking and random swipes at the strands of hair falling over her forehead kept Britney from catching a glimpse of Shaun. Yet, she imagined the burning stare on the back of her head when she passed his cell. The low evening sun peered in Murray's office window and caught Britney in the eyes as she entered the room. The dark cell made her vision sensitive, and now here she was, in a white, sunlit office with no time to acclimatise. With a helping hand from Murray, Britney found her bearings. Sitting in front of the detective's desk, Britney fumbled for the telephone already neatly placed within her reach.

"Can I have a moment?" Britney asked, pulling the telephone closer to the edge. With the slightest nod, Murray stepped outside.

Even though she was alone in the office, Britney shivered at the thought of being watched. Her slender white fingers rubbed the large plastic numbering on the phone as Britney threw names around in her head, she had to call someone. Shaking, she dialled, swallowing hard as the phone rang. But before anyone could answer, Britney pulled the line from the back of the telephone with the niftiest flick of her thumb and middle finger. The ringing buzz turned silent.

"Hey, it's Britney," she said into the dead line.
Over three minutes of fake call later, Britney pressed the phone line into its slot again and lowered the telephone.

"Thank you Detective," Britney whispered as Murray stepped back into the office.

Chapter 37

The sobbing reflection in the mirror added to Rachael's tears. She wiped her eyes roughly with some tissue and reached for the mascara again. The previous coat had come off with the tears. Pulling the door closed, Rachael threw her robe to the floor and stepped into the shower. The cold water did not bother her.

Why did she have such problems? She should be worrying about what dress to wear at the weekend, or what make-up was less obvious to the teachers in school. But Rachael had to deal with significantly bigger fish.

Her boyfriend, if he should be called that, had just been arrested. *Scratch that, Shaun does not deserve the title.* Her insides shook with embarrassment every time she dipped into her memories and dug out images of Shaun and her. Questions bobbed around in Rachael's head for hours, but when the tips of answers peeked above the surface, they were slapped away with disgust. Age was an excuse she felt. But, for how long can it be an acceptable one?

Eighteen year old girls in school were still fighting a battle every morning with their mothers, in an effort to use the latest product from Maybelline, or pull their skirt one inch higher, just to prove that they have kneecaps. The same story was alien to Rachael. It took until now to register, Rachael had grown up too quick.

Following Shaun was not something she planned. *Shaun just happened!* He was like the sweetest drug to teenage girls, he had everything they wanted. Girls craved him, guys were afraid of him. From the first time Shaun convinced Rachael to sneak out of her bedroom window, until today, she was under his spell.

Rachael stepped from the shower and grabbed a towel. The wood was cold, tingles in her legs made her toes squint. Creaks reverberated around the house when she stood up and walked to the window. The time for following passed, no longer would she be a part of Shaun's life.

Rachael remembered Louver Street differently. No longer was she the passenger in a car filled with dark motives, only there to sneak and investigate. Shaun's words faded, but they were still lingering traces in the back of her mind. She shivered at the thought of Shaun patrolling the street every week. It only became apparent now how wrong that was, Shaun had a purpose for everything, and even the surveillance of a wheelchair-bound amnesiac had its reasons. There were few things more terrifying to Rachael than a Shaun McCoy outburst.

Fear was like a disease, spreading with each word that came from Shaun's mouth. It set itself firmly into Britney Davis as well, Rachael knew. Constant surveillance was a reminder to Britney that, unless she kept up her end of the bargain, Adam would be the one to suffer. Shaun did not have to utter a word about his twice-weekly visits down Louver Street, like any good virus, it reached Britney within hours.

A warm breeze encouraged Rachael that she was doing the right thing as her shoes clapped on the concrete sidewalk, like a drum beat leading to the grand finale. So much more was visible when one walked down the tree-lined street. Home after home of middle-class families resided there, a natural haven dropped into the south side of the Greater Boston area. Through the windows, Quincy families prepared their dinner as mothers called from the front door to the children. Faint groans travelled up the neighbourhood as the kids plodded their way home, not understanding tomorrow is another day to play.

Tomorrow! Rachael thought. What could it possibly bring that would make her smile a little more? In Rachael's eyes, tomorrow was a black canvas. Flicking the pages over to reveal the days after showed no respite. Black, black and more black. Visiting Adam may relieve her guilt momentarily, but Rachael knew once she stepped out of the Fletcher house, the pain and embarrassment would catch her on the way down the steps. That is the reality of it she told herself, knowing it would be almost unimaginable to live with. Rachael reached the Fletcher home, a last chance to turn back.

"I have to," she muttered, stepping up onto the front decking and pressing the door bell.

***

The words came so easily to Adam as he scribbled furiously on the notepad. With each beat his heart sent streams of despair to his brain, which translated the feelings into words on the page. Britney was the subject and the intended recipient. She was everything, and now she was nothing. One last rant to rid his heart of her being and put the last words between them on paper, ensuring he will never have to see her again.

Erin tapped on the bedroom door, "You have a visitor," she said.

Is it Britney?

"Tell her to go away."

A faint conversation outside the bedroom door drew Adam away from his letter. He waited for the noise to pass, to let him be alone again. It did not go away. It only grew in the form of the handle twisting and the door popping open.

"Hi Adam," came the sound before the sight. The voice unsettled him, confirming it was not the drone he was writing about.

"I'm sorry, I had to come in," The girl said.

"Oh!" Adam said, "I wasn't expecting anyone."

"I'm Rachael Anderson, I'm Shaun's girlfriend. I was."

Adam did not remember the nervous eyes, or the young face of his guest, yet her voice burrowed its way into his brain and touched on a memory.

"Your voice... we have met before?"

"Yeah, I was in the car when it crashed."

What! How many were in the car?

The fidgeting young girl stood in Adam's room, yet he just observed. Uncomfortable eyes had not found a

214

place to rest, her slim frame swayed and words got caught in her throat. Adam motioned for her to sit down, an attempt to stop her discussing Britney.

"I have to tell you something," she coughed, "I think you need to hear it."

"Let me guess, another confession? I think I'll survive without it, thanks anyway."

Rachael's swaying grew into a full-blown shaking.

"No Adam, you have to hear this," she said, clutching her own hands and making Adam sit up a little more in the bed.

"It's about the day of the accident."

Adam inhaled deeply and sharply. For months he longed to know what happened on that day in September, at times he would have given anything to hear a recount of the day. But a lot has come to the surface recently Adam figured, he wondered how his heart would react to such news. The half-written notepad lay on his lap. Glimpses of words conceived with such pain and anger only warned him of future worry. Did he really need to find out about another level of Britney's devious facade? Would his heart recover from another body blow? Or was it all a failsafe for Shaun, should he be arrested? With his eyes still burning the notepad, Adam questioned his guest.

"Why are you here?"

Rachael swallowed hard.

"Amm?" she stuttered.

"I'm just asking, why do you suddenly want to help me?"

Facing towards Rachael, Adam's stare penetrated her doubting brown eyes. His chest expanded as he drew breath, unintentionally stirring the girl into a response.

"I want to help myself," Rachael said, "I feel so guilty like you wouldn't believe." A smile crept out onto Adam's face, melting the stare.

"I admire your honesty," he said, deciding to ignore the obvious irony.

Rachael took that as the sign to begin. As she uttered her first words, images that seemed like recollections of dreams flooded back into Adam's mind. They turned into what Adam assumed were memories, playing out like a movie that was hidden behind his eyes. Memories of the day his life changed forever.

Chapter 38

The summer heat was fading as Adam walked down
Dorchester Avenue with Britney. Despite being
surrounded with concrete on every side, there were
moments when a leaf with the slightest shade of brown
would dance across the pathway and get caught on the
garden walls lining the avenue. September had arrived,
and with it the last of the warm sunny days, one last
outing for the flowery sleeveless top on Britney.

In the stream of afternoon traffic along the avenue, a
car stopped ahead of Adam and Britney. Approaching it,
Shaun McCoy stepped out of the black dodge charger.

"Britney, what's up?"

"Hey Shaun!" she replied, "Nice car."

Adam's eyes were drawn to the car like a moth to a
light, he gasped at Shaun's new purchase. While they
had met previously, they were not close. Yet, the
common interest of a new car brought them together
momentarily.

"Is it fast?" Adam asked, running his hand over the
black exterior.

"Yeah, it's sick!" he said, throwing a reply in Adam's direction before concentrating on Britney.

"Wanna go for a ride?"

Adam stooped to see the car already full, with Rachael in the front, and two guys in the back.

"Maybe another time!" Britney said.

"Ahh come on Brit! Just a quick spin!" Rachael said, poking her head out the window.

"You can even bring your boyfriend!"

Adam shuffled, "We're not..."

"It doesn't matter man!" Rachael interrupted. "Just get in!"

"I think you've only room for one," Adam said.

A brief connection, Adam looked at Britney until she brushed her curly blonde hair away from her face. A smile came to her face, as if she did not want to show Adam every emotion that lay inside.

"It's okay, I'll pass," Britney said. Shaun fidgeted and began looking around.

"Just get in Britney, bring him as well so!" he relented, slamming the driver door shut and telling the two guys in the back to make space.

"I'm ok Britney, give me a call when you get back?"

Britney bit her lip, her gaze fell to the concrete sidewalk. Her right hand reached for Adam's side and gently tugged at his grey t-shirt.

"I'd really like it if you came too," she said.

The scent from Britney made Adam linger for longer than he meant to. Arms grew a voice, demanding they be wrapped around her perfect body. For now, he knew, they had no right to do such a thing. A muffled shout

218

from the car snapped the couple out of their developing trance.

"Okay," Adam said.

Back in his wheelchair-bound reality, Adam lay in bed, carefully listening to Rachael's description of how he got into the car.

"Yeah, it's coming back to me," he said.

"Maybe this is what you needed all along?" Rachael replied.

Adam nodded, careful not to show Rachael too much thanks. Anyway, he had found out very little so far he figured.

"We all drove out to Canton, Shaun was eager to show off....." Rachael continued.

The packed car turned off the I-93 highway and onto the slip road for Canton village. The black dodge shook with the music that blared from the speakers, almost deafening the occupants until Britney reached through the front seats and relieved them.

"So, Shaun, how the hell can you afford something like this?" Britney asked, causing Rachael to snigger.

Through the smiles, Shaun answered, "Let's just say, I acquired it! Oh yeah, wipe any prints you have left and put these on!"

Rachael handed white latex gloves to everyone in the car and wiped the dashboard and the door handle. Britney lay back again and sat on Adam's lap, who was squashed into the rear left seat of the Dodge. *Oh great,* she shrugged.

The car gained speed as it rushed through the twisting roads of Canton. Wooded roadsides echoed the roar of the engine and sent it back double to Adam's ears, etching an obvious sign of worry on his face.

"You ok Adam?" Britney asked, turning back to look at him. Adam nodded, lying. But years of friendship told her better.

"Here, let me help you."

Leaning closer to Adam without uttering a word, Britney's gentle hands reached over his left shoulder and onto his back. The smell of her hair was intoxicating as it touched Adam's nose. He breathed it in and in, his hands wrapped around her midriff. Pushing back to reveal her beaming smile, Britney pulled the seat belt free and clicked it into place.

"There you go," she whispered, without taking her eyes off Adam.

A pang of excitement coursed throughout his body whenever her soft blue eyes made contact with his. Every cell in his body wanted to reach forward and kiss those red lips. Swishing from outside caught their attention and pulled them from the developing moment, Adam cursed it silently. The trees passed so fast they turned into one blur, causing Adam to get dizzy.

"Shaun, slow down!" Britney urged.

"This is not dangerous! I'm able to handle this speed," He retorted, sending the two guys in the back seat into raptures, singing Shaun's praises.

"Wait, wait, wait!" Adam interrupted Rachael, "You want me to forgive Britney because she put my seat belt on?"

"No that is not what I'm telling you. That's your decision, I'm here to tell you what I know."

Each word coming from Rachael's mouth reignited an old memory within Adam, until it played in his mind like a news reel.

***

"I'll never forget the accident...."

Until that day, Rachael never heard such a variety of sounds in such a short time period. From the roar of the engine, to the shiver-inducing squeal of the tires on the road, to the sickening thud of a sudden stop. It took the occupants a few moments to fully realise what had happened. Shaun staggered out first, trying to get his balance on the tarmac road. As his vision stabilised, he saw the devastation. He had underestimated the severity of the right hand turn in the road and slid sideways into the remains of an old wall. Jumping back into the car, he helped Rachael crawl out the driver side door and lay her down on the road. Tommy and Jack lent Britney a helping hand to get out of the back seat.

"Thank God it's so quiet," Shaun muttered to a barely conscious Britney.

"What, what do you mean?" she replied.

Shaun did not answer as he led the occupants across the valley road and up a small incline where they were hidden by the trees. Britney's head throbbed with pain, she lay on the forest floor.

"You ok Adam?"

No reply came, only a nervous silence. Standing at the edge of the forest, the trees ruffled with the breeze. They only sent it back again and again. Rachael turned her gaze to Shaun. *What now?*

221

He was eerily calm. Rachael crouched down, holding her head while Shaun stared into the forest. Tommy and Jack switched their focus from the car down on the road, to their leader, like twitching idiots awaiting instructions.

"Adam?" Britney asked.

Rachael held Britney's head and pulled it close, the only way she knew how to avoid the question. It did not work. Despite Rachael holding Britney's head tight to her stomach, a muffled question escaped again.

"Is Adam ok?"

Letting her arms loosen, Rachael lowered Britney's head just enough to see her face.

"He is still in the car," she whispered.

Nodding, the severity of the statement passed Britney by.

"Ok. Tell him I wanna to speak to him."

Rachael swallowed hard. A fake smile covered her face, giving Britney temporary respite. Blood on her jacket startled her, making her search her torso for an injury. But, as Britney lay back down, the source of the blood became apparent.

"Britney, your head is bleeding."

Britney slapped the top of her own head, disinterested. Even the sight of her blood-smeared hand did little to unnerve her. Her eyes, though weary, had to find Adam. She struggled to get on her feet, swaying like Rachael's classmates after too many shots.

"Where is he?" Britney said, stepping closer to the edge of the bank.

"He is there," Shaun answered, pointing the way down the small slope and across the road.

Tracing the path, Britney aimed for the car. Shaking legs carried her down the bank and onto the tarmac. The evening sun setting behind the trees threw figures onto the high old wall, were the car came to rest. Through the open rear door, Britney saw Adam in the car, motionless.

"Adam!" she stuttered as her throat dried up with shock. Her shivering body fell towards the car and into the back seat.

"Adam, wake up."
Britney pulled at his arm, quickly tracing a path to his hands.

"Please, wake up." She crawled backwards out of the car and looked at the men on the bank. Only Rachael moved from her perch.

"It's no use Britney," Shaun shouted.

"What do you mean? Has anyone called an ambulance yet?"

Shaking his head, Shaun remained steady. "We cannot save him now, we can only save ourselves."

"Are you messing with me?" Britney asked, her voice gaining strength in line with her body. Britney searched frantically, Rachael realised it was for her phone.

"We need to call Adam an ambulance, please guys!"

Something dawned on Britney. She dived back into the car and dug into Adam's pockets. Every avenue of hope was quickly closing it seemed. Looking at Adam again, she held his head tightly. His limp body scared her, it scared Rachael. Yet Britney pulled him closer. Tears started to flow from her weary eyes and down onto his cheek. The forest grew higher, covering the sun's heat. It sent shivers through Rachael's body time and time again. Seeing Britney's delicate hands rubbing

Adam's torso and legs caused a crack in her mind. Shaun covered it up each time.

"We will all be in trouble if we're seen here. No witnesses, no proof." On the bank, Shaun had enough. He ran down the slope and across to the car.

"It's time to go!"

"No, I'm not leaving him here."

"Britney, be realistic, look at his legs."

She shook her head, afraid to see the truth. She clung even tighter and buried his head in her chest.

"Look at his legs you fool!"

"NO!"

"He will not survive, but you can," Shaun mellowed slightly.

A trail of blood flowed down the left side of Adam's face and dripped onto his neck. Britney's glove covered thumb failed to stop the bleeding, it seeped out and trickled down the same path.

"I'm staying," she whispered into Adam's ear.

Shaun looked at Rachael, they knew how lucky they had been so far. Firstly, not to get killed in the crash, and now the fact no car arrived in over ten minutes. His fingers twitched, he motioned to Tommy and Jack to come down. Rachael rubbed Britney, an attempt to break her away from the car. Unfortunately for Adam, what Shaun perceived as common sense, prevailed. Without warning, he reached into the car and dragged Britney out.

"What the hell are you doing?" Britney shouted.

"Getting us out of here," Shaun said, "no-one can know it was us."

Britney tried to stay, but even with one arm, Shaun dragged her across the road and up the embankment with ease.

"You can go, let me stay!" she pleaded.

"I'm afraid I can't let you stay, it would raise too many questions."

Britney slumped to the ground in an attempt to make it difficult for Shaun. Like a sit-in protest, she hoped this would change his mind, she looked Shaun dead in the eyes.

"One of you is going to call an ambulance, you can all then run away, but I am going back down there and staying with Adam."

Shaun knelt down in front of Britney. He took a deep breath, just another small way to intimidate her, Rachael figured.

"This is how it's gonna work. Firstly, we are all leaving here together. No arguments, no discussions. Secondly, we are going to get alibi's to cover ourselves in case this mess leads back to us."

"How can you be so cold? Rachael, tell him how sick this is!" Britney cried. Rachael did not dare to look at Shaun, she reluctantly shrugged and walked on.

"I'm sorry Britney, it's for the best."

Shaun did not even acknowledge the question and continued on with the plan he had forged.

"Then, we will never, ever speak about this accident to anyone other than the five people that are standing here today. Understood?" Rachael, Tommy and Jack all nodded. Shaun turned his attention back to Britney, awaiting an answer.

"I understand, but I'm not agreeing. How can you even contemplate leaving Adam here?"

"Listen to me Britney. If we stay here, all of us will be sent to prison. I'm not exaggerating just to freak you out, that is cold, hard, fact baby."

"You will be sent to prison, we won't," Britney retorted.

"You took part in the theft of that car if I remember correctly? You were responsible for the accident also? Ask any of the occupants, they will tell you!"

Britney looked at Tommy and Jack's smiling faces, it was obvious they were going to do anything for their leader.

"You're just as guilty as the rest of us," Shaun said.

The wind blew through the forest, pushing the leaves downward towards Britney as she sat on the damp ground. All eyes were on her.

"I'm not guilty yet, but if I leave, I will be."

"Britney, stop acting like you have a choice!" Shaun said.

"Adam!" she screamed, facing the car, until Shaun's mud-stained hands reached over her mouth and cancelled out the noise. Adam lay still on his bed, his eyes closed, trying to picture every scene Rachael painted.

"I can hear her scream my name, I think it is real...I can't be sure."

"She cried your name all the way back to town. Shaun arranged for a friend to collect us on the other side of Canton hill, and during the drive back to Quincy, he devised excuses for all of us, including Britney. I was there when your parents rang to tell her the news... she was trembling before they called...I assumed you were dead."

Rachael stared at her fingers. The guilt was too great to look anywhere else she felt, as if it would cause offense to gaze upon Adam.

"The only piece of good news that day was when your mother told Britney you would survive. She cried even more after that, with happiness."

"It would have been easier for everyone if I had died." Adam said. Rachael chose to ignore that, instead continuing on with her plan.

"Shaun made me stay with Britney that evening...."

An eerie darkness occupied Britney's home, did it know what we'd done, Rachael wondered. Britney trudged in the back door. She did not reach for the light, she seemed more comfortable in the dark. Luckily for Rachael, the pace was comfortable.

"We have to get you into the shower, you're wrecked."

Like a funeral procession, the women mournfully climbed the stairs, silent and solemn. Rachael turned on the shower and went to get towels for Britney in the upstairs closet. When she returned, Britney was already in the shower, fully clothed. She acted like Rachael was invisible, never acknowledging her presence. Britney let the warm water run over her hair and clothes, gently massaging the blood from her head. The shower floor quickly became a mash of blood and mud, yet it bothered Britney little. Rachael knew time would heal, but Britney had a hospital visit to prepare for, and soon.

"A few minutes later Shaun arrived at her house," Rachael told Adam.

"What did he want?"

"Two things. Firstly to see how well we were keeping the secret. Secondly, he wanted to ensure the secret stayed intact."

"Why didn't Britney tell me sooner?" Adam asked.

"When the news came through you were going to survive, Shaun had to find another way to keep Britney quiet. He knew there were few things valuable enough to her to threaten her with, but he managed to find one."

Time seemed to slow down, making Rachael appear to take an eternity to speak.

"What was it?"

"It was you," Rachael said.

The answer did not seem to fit the question, Rachael felt. Adam shook his head, as if trying to sort out the words and make sense of them. Rachael reiterated.

"Shaun threatened Britney, using you. Should she speak out, Shaun promised her it would be you who would suffer."

Silence enveloped the room momentarily as Adam tried to come to terms with Rachael's words. Through the quietness, any sigh that escaped Adam appeared amplified.

"He did not let up, she had weekly reminders."

The neighbour's rooftop appeared as a dark silhouette when Rachael looked out Adam's bedroom window. She had to look somewhere she felt, after a conversation comprised of her staring at her hands and the floor. Darkness crept in unknown to her, with it an excuse to leave. She had said what she came here to say, it was all up to Adam now.

"I'll leave you in peace," Rachael said, pushing the chair back against the wall and reaching for the door.

"Rachael, you didn't have to come here and tell me this, but I'm really glad that you did," Adam said.

"It is tough to live with a secret Adam... I didn't want the responsibility anymore."

Rachael closed the door, leaving Adam alone to stew the contents of the conversation in silence. The long walk home gave her time to remember the good deed she had done, bringing with it memories of the wheelchair, and memories of her guilt. *I helped cause this.*

Chapter 39

"She has been in there for quite a while," Madison said, sending words throughout the darkness of his living room. Green flashing lights were the thing he could interact with, unable to reconnect with his friend from earlier. Like a kid who tasted fizzy cola, he wanted more. Reverting to the original one-way transmissions drained Madison and despite confirmation his messages were making it back to base, loneliness did not subside.

"Part of me wants to go into the Fletcher home and tell her it's gonna be ok. Tell her there is no need to worry anymore. But, I know I'd be lying."

Madison's reflection gained years over the last six months, making the fifty-two year old man appear to be upwards of sixty. Madison pressed the monitor to reveal an internet web page, taking his daunting image with it. In the stillness of a late spring evening, the sound of Fletcher's door closing snapped through the air and into Madison's living room.

"Rachael is leaving," he whispered, sliding his hand over the power button, leaving him in total darkness.

The street lights threw an orange haze on Rachael as she darted down the Fletcher driveway and onto the sidewalk. The large window of Madison's living room was like a TV, documenting the movements and motions of the woman. When she went out of view, Madison stood up and walked out onto the front porch. His legs shuffled, unconsciously, wanting to follow Rachael. Madison knew better. He had been the epitome of patience for the last six months, it would be a shame to break now, he considered.

Madison spent the following hour sitting on a kitchen chair which he had dragged out onto the porch. A bottle of Irish whiskey sat next to him and with a glass in his hand, Madison took small, timed sips. Uncorking the bottle, he poured another shot. Toasting to an invisible body, Madison raised his glass.

"If patience is worth anything, it must endure to the end of time."

What started off a sigh grew into a giggle, Madison sipping the whiskey again until a familiar sound repeated, the Fletcher front door opening. From his vantage point, Madison saw Adam struggling to keep the door open and push through at the same time. Despite his nature yelling for him to run over and help, Madison stayed sitting, stayed sipping. *The time will come when I have to act.*

Oblivious there were eyes fixed on his every move, Adam pushed through the front door and down the driveway. His breath was like a trail of smoke as he propelled himself along the sidewalk and down Louver

Street. Seeing Rachael dart out of view was tempting, but with Adam, there was no question, Madison could not fight the temptation any longer, he had to follow. The analytical part of his brain shouted stop, now was not the time. Madison had a plan, and while the plan did not involve following Adam at this moment, he felt like it had to be done. Leaving the bottle uncorked, Madison walked down the timber steps and onto the concrete walkway that led to the street.

***

The streetlights cast shadows on Adam as he passed under the glowing columns along Quincy's neighbourhoods. Looking up at the street sign hanging overhead, he could not help but smile, *Adams Street.* Turning right, he travelled for a short distance along Beale Street and then took a left for Harvard Street. For once, Adam thanked Facebook. It was there he obtained Rachael's address, she, like most young users, provided great detail when signing on to the website.

A deadening pain grew in Adam's arms, he had pushed the wheelchair for close to forty minutes before arriving at Rachael's home. He waited outside in order to compose himself. While he was never friends with Rachael, some part of him demanded he thank her properly. Speaking out must not have been easy he figured, and judging by the apparent weight of depression she held when leaving, it could affect her for some time to come.

Adam heard many people encourage and give him hope since the accident, and while most of those words went unnoticed, he still understood people react

232

differently. So, in his mind, a *thank you* to Rachael may be enough to snap her out of her guilt-ridden state.

It soon became apparent to Adam that no matter how long he waited on the sidewalk, mulling words and thoughts over in his head, a long, epic essay would never compose itself in his mind. Despite the uncertainty residing inside, his hands kick-started the wheelchair, moving Adam up towards the front door of the large Anderson home. Shaking fingers pressed the doorbell and pricked ears awaited confirmation. Words Adam arranged in his head mattered little when Rachael's mother opened the door.

"Ahh!" stuttered Adam, desperately trying to find a suitable greeting.

"Hi Mrs. Anderson!" he assumed. "Is Rachael in?"

Mrs. Anderson's look was like a laser, piercing and precise. Her eyes studied Adam's face at first and then set upon the wheelchair.

"You're the Fletcher boy I suppose?" was her preferred greeting, heavy with the arrogance of someone who rated themselves highly.

"Ahem, yes I am," Adam replied, eager to show respect. He sensed Mrs. Anderson had slammed many a door on people whom she had no interest in.

"My daughter has been distraught all day. She's had enough stress for now, what with the police interview and all."

"I understand Mrs. Anderson, but please, I'll only keep her one minute," Adam argued, joining his hands as if in prayer.

"You're the reason why she is so upset! Why couldn't you leave well enough alone?" she retorted, her rose tinted glasses working just fine. Adam took a sharp breath. Finding words was no problem now, so many gathered in his throat, waiting to be spat out. His hands slipped apart, each gripping a side of the wheelchair.

Looking at Mrs. Anderson's greying hair, she seemed more like Rachael's grandmother than her mother. Her self-obsessed views could force a Buddhist monk to turn violent, and Adam was about to snap. *One more try*! Ignoring the obvious irony of Mrs. Anderson's argument, Adam forced one last polite request out of his mouth.

"Please, all I want to do is thank her."

There it was again, the look of utter disgust on her face. Adam imagined the door being slammed shut, any second now. The queue of words in his throat built up, each knowing there may be only one chance to get even. Fortunately for Mrs. Anderson' ears, she relented.

"Wait here."

Mrs. Anderson left the door open and climbed the stairs. The anger within Adam receded, he got back to his original plan of sorting out the words to thank Rachael with. He never got to use those words. Mrs. Anderson screamed so sharply, it shook the walls holding the home together and sent chills through every cell in Adam's body. Yet, she did not stop. The scream emanated from the upstairs bedroom, continuing, turning into a wailing cry. Paralysed with shock, Adam did not dare move from the front door. It was not until Mrs. Anderson's muttered cries to her husband had reached Adam he realised the horror. Rachael was dead. Her darkest thoughts must have overpowered her, turning the day into a permanent night.

234

Turning his wheelchair around, weak hands struggled to push Adam away from the house. Even so soon, he knew why Rachael did it. There was no need to perform a post mortem, the killer was obvious. In time, there would be some source of healing for her parents, the knowledge the killer was dead. And there it was, precisely the reason why Rachael committed such an act. Daggers of guilt which penetrated her since the accident grew larger and sharper. Adam could see she did not throw in the towel so easily, he assumed speaking to him was her last hope for survival. However it did not work.

Like an immune system, Rachael tried to fight off the infection. But, guilt lived for thousands of years, it had many forms. Unfortunately for Rachael, she could not keep it at bay. Adam imagined life through her eyes, there was only one cure. *Kill the host, it will kill the virus feeding off the host.*

Its simplicity in young eyes must have been clear. Eyes that never lost a loved one, nor seen dark days in their short time. Rachael's life poured onto the carpet and the last of her killer seeped out. It should have died there on the young girl's floor, but it sensed another victim. Adam pushed himself away from the Anderson home, not daring to look at Rachael's window, fearing the guilt would see him. *Too late!* In his mind it floated toward the window and stared down its next prey, prey that was already shaken, physically and mentally.

The wheelchair moved slowly on the sidewalk, trickling along like a wounded animal. Sharp breaths tried to keep Adam from crying, it was no use. Acidic tears poured from his eyes, blurring his path. While his guard was down, the virus got sucked into Adam's body and started to reproduce. It turned anger, fear, love and hate into a perfect version of itself. Nothing could stop it.

Chapter 40

On the other side of Harvard Street, guilt found yet another victim. Madison stood behind a large oak tree, careful to hide himself from Adam. He heard the scream, he knew what happened. He tried to fight the oncoming guilt, but images of Rachael passing his door only hours earlier kept replaying in his mind.

"I should have spoken to her!" he muttered, burying his head in his hands.

Memories of his wife mixed with present day emotions, blurring both considerably. While the pain of losing his wife never left, Madison found another way to deal with it. He turned it into another form, one more physical and real. Madison had no way to hide this new form, it was etched on his once-youthful face, like a disease had pulled a facade over the man.

***

Adam heard the church bell ring on his way home. Arms powered by a weak mind made the journey seem even longer than the previous trek. Squeaking wheels reminded him of the chains he carried, yet the knowledge of Rachael's passing turned them from iron to lead, intensifying gravities effect. The route home was strangely quiet, like Quincy was already in mourning. The random passing cars moved quickly out of sight and out of mind. Squeaky wheels gave away Adam's position when he pushed himself along the hallway and into the kitchen.

"You've been out quite a while?" Erin said.

Adam shrugged, moved towards the kettle and flicked it on.

"I went to see Rachael Anderson," he said.

"Oh!" Erin exclaimed. "That was really nice of her to visit earlier, I hope she helped you?"Adam struggled to rest, *is this real?* Fidgety hands searched aimlessly for something to grab.

"Is everything ok?" Erin asked.

"No, nothing is ok," Adam replied, lowering his head into his lap.

"Rachael is dead."

"Adam?"

"She has committed suicide. I was there when her mother found her."

Erin's hands rushed to her mouth as her eyes widened. She shook her head, there was no way to undo what she heard.

The girl that stood in the kitchen hours previously was dead. Adam tried in vain to erase the information from his mind, yet the portrait of Rachael's face kept forming in mid air. It floated toward him, touching him, until a dull sound from the front door made the figure evaporate.

There it was again, the loud and dull knock on the Fletcher's door. Adam's heart jumped when his paranoia uttered who it might be. He could not face anyone now, least of all Mrs. Anderson, who no doubt blamed him for Rachael's guilt.

"I can't answer the door," he whispered.

Again, the knocking sent waves into the kitchen. Erin finally stood up and walked to the door.

"Hello Mrs. Fletcher," the voice began. "Is Adam here?"

Who is that?

Erin took a moment to reply, adding to Adam's worry.

"Yes, he is...Mr. Clancy is it?"

"Please, Madison!" Adam heard.

"Madison, yes he is. It's pretty late. Maybe tomorrow would be better?" Erin replied.

"I understand, but I was at home and I saw Adam passing a few moments ago, he looked pretty down," Madison said, "Is there anything I can do to help, maybe speak to him for a few moments?"

"Ahh..." Erin said, shuffling her feet on the tiles. "I suppose it can't do any harm Madison."

The kettle finished boiling, yet Adam still stared at the vapour escaping from the top. He placed his hand over the steam, within seconds he retracted it sharply. The feeling in his legs may be poor, but his hands were still perfect.

"Hey Adam, how're you?"

Turning around, Adam's face tried to show the surprise.

"Madison, what are you doing here?"

"I saw you passing, I decided to call in, see if everything was ok?"

"Yeah, everything is ok," Adam said, trying his best to hide the lie.

Erin stepped into the kitchen for a moment, just to close the door, leaving the men in peace. Madison reached for a cup and placed it near the kettle.

"Will I make you a cup?"

"Sure."

Madison navigated around the kitchen with ease. From locating the tea bags and the sugar, to the cutlery drawer, it seemed like Madison knew exactly where everything was. It struck Adam, he realised Madison's home, being on the estate, could be designed to the same specifications.

"How are you coming along with your rehab?" Madison asked, motioning to Adam's legs.

Shrugging, he rubbed his hands along the dark blue jeans.

"Ok, I guess. I have had other things on my mind over the last couple of days!"

"Yeah...like what?" Madison asked.

Adam paused for a moment, not to arrange the answer, but to ponder should he give an answer. Here was Madison, a neighbour whom he knew very little about, asking about very intimate details of Adam's life. Madison would have to understand if he declined to answer Adam felt, but on the other hand, what harm would telling another pair of ears do.

"You remember Britney?"

"Yes, of course."

"She admitted she was involved in the accident." Adam said, lowering his tone, it hurt him to hear those words again. Madison sat at the table.

"I'm sorry to hear that."

The sympathy in Madison's voice was obvious. Placing his cup on the table, Adam continued with a recount of the last few days.

"I visited her in the police station earlier, which was torture as well."

"What did she have to say for herself? How on earth could she pass the blame on in these circumstances?" Madison asked.

"She didn't try to pass the blame on," Adam said, with more than a hint of defiance. Madison had kick started a train of thought within him, he had no need to ask another question about Britney, the momentum of Adam's last statement propelled the conversation along.

"Britney handed herself in, and in the process, got Shaun McCoy arrested."

"Shaun McCoy?"

"He was the driver of the car when it crashed. It was Shaun that threatened Britney to stay quiet," Adam replied.

"How do you know all of this?" Madison asked, "Did Shaun admit to it all?" Shaking his head, Adam responded in a slow, thoughtful tone.

"No, Britney did not tell me why she kept the secret. Maybe it was because she did not want to make me feel guilty, whatever! But, Rachael, another occupant in the car came here earlier and told me the full story."

"Rachael? I saw her leave a few hours ago?" Madison quizzed.

"Yes, she was Rachael," Adam said, the guilt inside woke from its momentary slumber, dragging and pulling his head and neck down.

"You mean *is* Rachael!"

Adam shook his head and rubbed his hands over his face, stuttering words that tore at his ear drums.

"No, she was Rachael, she is gone."

"Gone?"

"She killed herself," Adam whispered bluntly.

"What? Why?"

"I guess she couldn't face the prospect of prison. I bet you weren't expecting to hear that when you came over eh?"

Madison shook his head. Adam noticed his beaten face, he wasn't the only one struggling.

"Maybe it was something else!" Madison said.

"No, it was my actions that lead her to fear going to prison."

"It was the driver's actions that have led to this. Rachael stayed silent at first, but in the end she did what was right. Not for you, not for him, but for herself."

"What are you trying to say?" Adam interrupted. His ears not deciphering the messages Madison was sending out.

"Maybe," Madison paused, trying to emphasise the word, "Rachael felt her last hope was to save you and Britney?"

"Why would she want to save us?"

"Perhaps she felt responsible for what happened to you two? Her last chance was to reveal the true story and hope it would bring her peace."

Adam stared at the still full cup of tea. He lost his urge to drink, now that Rachael was the subject of the conversation.

"But it did not bring her peace," he whispered. "And now she is gone."

"I do not mean to be insensitive, but maybe one life is worth sacrificing in order to save two?" Madison said.
Tossing off notions of martyrdom, Adam shook his head at Madison.

"I would rather to have given my life than for Rachael to take hers, at least she had something to live for. Me, I will be chained to this collection of metal, plastic and cloth for the rest of my days."

"Ok," Madison started, "What about Britney then? Where would she be without you?"

Adam smiled for the first time in days, not a genuine smile born out of happiness. It formed from the ironic words which travelled the space between Madison and Adam and tickled his thoughts.

"She does not depend on me, and as far as I can remember, she may never have depended on me."

"Adam," Madison said, leaning in closer, "you and I are very alike, we don't know as much as we think we do." With that, Madison stood up and patted Adam on the back. Spilling the contents of his cup into the sink, he walked towards the kitchen door.

"Madison," Adam said, "if you don't mind me asking, how did you learn to live with the loss of your wife?"

"I didn't."

Madison gently reached for the kitchen door,

"Goodnight Adam," he whispered.

Chapter 41

The night brought no respite for Britney. Shaun continued to speak in her direction even when a man, who had been dragged in during the night, threatened him. Pleading and seemingly caring words travelled on the air and into Britney's ears. In such a small time, so many sides to Shaun McCoy came and went, changing facades to suit the situation. By now however, Britney was too versed in Shaun's deceptiveness to fall for it. It had taken her long enough to see his true nature, she was determined not to slip backwards again.

Early the following morning, Britney heard Shaun speaking to detective Murray. No insults thrown back, no cheeky outbursts, had Shaun broken? Within moments of Murray leaving, the sound of clicking high heels entered the holding cell hallway. Britney struggled to make out what was whispered through the bars to a silent Shaun, a random sound of an angry spit travelling with the words was all she deciphered.

When a key card swipe signalled the woman's exit, Britney braced herself for the continued onslaught from Shaun. It never came. In a way, the silence was nearly as upsetting. Britney leaned closer to the bars, placing her fingers onto the cold iron. Every ounce of curiosity in her wanted to ask what happened, it fought with the negative side of drawing Shaun McCoy on her again.

Over an hour later, a police officer escorted Britney to Murray's office. Prying eyes followed her every step through the police station. Sitting her down, Murray waved at the officer to give them some privacy. He grasped her hands and released the cuffs.

"Thank you," she said, rubbing her wrists. Murray sat down opposite Britney and leaned back in his chair.

"I must admit Miss Davis I'm not used to these situations," Murray began, smiling across the table.

"These situations?" Britney asked.

"Yes, the one where someone just turns themselves in. It doesn't happen too often in my line of business."

"Is that your way of saying thank you?"

"I guess it is!" Murray relented. "That is also why you are being treated a little differently Miss Davis, we value co-operation around here."

Britney shrugged, unsure of how to act.

"While I appreciate what you have done, I will be honest with you."

"Please," Britney whispered, imagining the dreaded words, yet needing to hear them.

"A date has been set for this case to be heard in court... I know that you were not the main perpetrator, yet it is likely you will spend some time in prison."

A wave of shock swept over Britney. Seeing it coming was difficult, hearing it confirmed went off the chart. She raised her hands up to her eyes and dragged them down her face in disbelief.

"Detective," she started, clearing her throat, "how much time?"

"It's difficult to say, while it won't be severe, like the charges facing Mr. McCoy, they are serious nonetheless."

"A few months, a year, more?" she asked, her eyes searching for anything but the look from Murray.

"I would say the latter."

Britney knew she would be punished, she accepted and deserved it. Yet, it only hit home now that the next number of years of her life would be spent behind bars. Britney cared little for what the neighbours would say, she cared little for what her mother would say. The image of her father came to mind, Britney struggled to wipe the guilty stains from her skin, like permanent ink had spilled on her porous exterior and etched itself firmly on her life. Her mind attempted to go one further and imagine Adam's reaction, but somehow she pushed the thought away, *enough embarrassment for one day.*

"I understand this may be difficult for you Miss Davis, but can I still depend on you to testify against Mr. McCoy?" Murray asked, breaking up the depressing film playing in Britney's head."

"Yes detective. You can."

Murray stood up and opened his door to the waiting officer. He motioned *no cuffs* as the officer stepped in and placed his hand on Britney's shoulder. As she was being led away, Britney turned to Murray.

"Detective, can I ask you a question."

"Yes."

"What did that woman say to Shaun?"

Hesitating, Murray glanced at the accompanying officer.

"Please?" she begged, not out of nosiness, but out of concern.

"That woman was Rachael Anderson's mother, Rachael committed suicide last night," he said.

"I'm sorry for your loss," Murray said to a frozen Britney.

***

Regaining the strength and movement in his legs had become a side issue over the previous weeks, pushed to the corners of Adam's mind, something Michael Lenard would soon change, he guessed. Adam adapted to the wheelchair, and while it was not very accommodating, its squeaky grasp lessened over the previous week. Many other forms of torture stepped into the void, eager to take over the role of *up-setter*.

Adam sat in Michael Lenard's waiting room, changing his focus momentarily. Preceding weeks showed improvement, minimal feelings in his legs grew in sensitivity to a point where Adam felt they were attached to his body. Daily sessions with the masseuse turned into tri-weekly visits since the beginning of January, a sign Adam was going in the right direction, even if it took months at a time. He realised how easy it was to forget about his physical progress when matters of the head and heart were concerned, each fighting for the limelight.

Michael Lenard and his force-feeding of positive thinking lined the menu again, Adam thought, pushing himself into the physiotherapist's treatment room. Today was not the day for invisible encouragement, physical proof would be required. Michael could not perform miracles, and Adam knew this well, it was up to him. He planned ways to keep his frustrations under wraps, picturing Michael Lenard picking and picking until he revealed something. The problem being, Michael may not like what he finds.

"Hello Adam, how are you today?"

Don't get me started, Adam thought, "I'm ok Michael."

"You're making good progress I hear," Michael began, gently closing the door behind Adam.

"Yeah, I guess."

Little had changed except for the curtains, from a dark brown to a light cream. Adam thought about asking Michael the reason for the change, but something inside shouted it was best to let it be, do not give Michael a reason to burst out into a nostalgic story of survival.

After helping Adam up onto the treatment table, Michael set about massaging his two legs. He rolled up his long grey sleeves and started to dig into the deep muscle fibres in Adam's legs. Keeping his eyes on the ceiling, Adam avoided every hint from Michael to tell an *inspiring story.* From tensed forearms, to past patients, to modern treatments, Adam avoided them all.

"You are really quiet today, is everything ok?" Michael mused.

"Yeah," Adam stuttered as he lied, "I'm good. Just a little fed up."

Ahh! He said silently to himself, recognising the opportunity he just handed the physio.

248

"I understand how you feel, it's a long road and I won't lie to you about that. But, we are making good progress."

Biting his tongue, Adam nodded at Michael. The frustration inside was growing, like a volcano dormant for millennia, it had to blow some day. Nerves sent signals up Adam's legs and spine and then onto his brain, causing pangs of pain to dart throughout his body.

"See, that's progress!" Michael said, labelling the pain as something positive. There it was once more, like knives being pushed into his femur bone, the stinging sent shock waves around the young man's body again and again and again. Sweat crept, dripping into Adam's eyes and mouth, sending him into a coma of sheer aching. Michael's hands worked the same routine over and over, each press of his fingers sent waves of numbing pain through Adam.

"Stop, too much!" Adam said.

Michael smiled, he pressed on. "You need this Adam! Do you remember when you left the hospital last October?"

"Yeah?" Adam said, unable to see what exactly Michael was getting at.

"Can you remember what your legs felt like?" Michael said, his hands seemed to press harder with each syllable that left his mouth.

"No, there was nothing?"

"Exactly Adam, no feeling, no hope... this is progress."

Michael let up. Adam squirmed on the treatment table, his body turning the pain into a tingling memory of touch, his skin buzzed.

"Determination and time Adam, and you have plenty of both."

In Adam's mind he surpassed a checkpoint, a barrier where pain ceased to be classified as *pain*, where his body froze in an effort to survive. When Michael let up, he freed Adam's body from the most intense pain it had ever experienced.

"That's your break over," Michael said.

Forty-five minutes of hell later, Michael relented. Adam leaned up on the treatment table to see his two quadriceps red raw.

"That's a good sign, red shows there is blood flow," Michael said, wiping his hands on a towel.

"Let's go onto the bars Adam?" he suggested, pulling the wheelchair towards the treatment table. A trail of sweat dripped on Adam's back and down along his spine. His once light blue shorts were dyed dark blue, wet with moisture.

After helping Adam into the wheelchair, Michael positioned him in front of the parallel bars. The three feet high wooden bars seemed worse than ever, were they still the same ones, Adam wondered. Such small supports dangling over a no-go area, the thought of falling to the floor sent a shudder throughout his aching body.

He lifted his arms, feeling cold beads of sweat trickle down his triceps and into his armpit. Failing to hide his sigh, Adam reluctantly gripped the bars. Such effort just

250

to reach the starting position, Adam thought. Yet, he still had to stand in order to reach the true starting position.

"Let's go!" Michael said, in his most encouraging tone. He stood in front of Adam's chair and placed his arms around his stomach and lifted Adam up. Trembling arms helped provide some assistance to Michael as Adam stood upright. Looking along the length of the bars, Adam noted his impossible goal. He had fallen before, and the thought of hitting the floor again made his body curl inward. Sweat formed rivers and ran down his shaking body. Gasping for breath, Adam fell backwards into the strangely comforting wheelchair.

"I can't do it."

Chapter 42

Murray remembered his last view of the Fletcher driveway as a white one. A snow-filled path led to the front door that time, but now the ice had melted and revealed the underlying concrete.

Through the open curtain, Murray saw Adam in the living room. While he regretted not calling ahead, he assumed Adam did not fear him as much anymore. Murray kept his eyes on the young man as he rang the doorbell, yet the sudden noise did little to unsettle him. His mind raced, wondering about what could possibly be going on in the young man's head, until the opening door snapped him back to reality. It mattered little, for he knew the chance to see what lies inside Adam would soon present itself.

"Hello Mrs. Fletcher," Murray said.

Erin disguised her surprise with a smile, motioning Murray into the hallway.

"How are you today?" Murray continued, closing the door.

"I'm good detective, what can I help you with?" Erin responded, Murray immediately noticed the hint of impatience in her voice.

"I was hoping to speak to Adam, is he here?" Murray asked.

"Yes, he is in the living room."

"How is he?"

"See for yourself," Erin said, stepping aside.

Two tall lamps in the far side of the living room cast a dark orange glow onto Adam's back. The quiet television whispered in the corner, Murray doubted any information leaving the set reached the young man's eyes or ears.

"Detective!"

"Hello Adam!" Murray responded, changing his tone and vocabulary to suit the situation.

Murray gently stepped around the wheelchair and sat on the sofa.

"I know you've had a tough few days."

"Ha," Adam sniffed, "months."

Murray knew his limits, he knew his skills. Sensitive psychiatrist was not one of them. Still, he felt he had to try. All the muscle and brawn in the world cannot help one to comprehend what happens inside the human mind.

"There is hope for you at the end of this," he began, picking the lightest words from the air. "A date has been set for the court case, and after that, there will be nothing more to bother you."

Biting his bottom lip, Adam shook his head.

"I don't mean to be disrespectful, but I can see no end to this."

Murray stepped back sharply, eager to suppress any growing worries within Adam.

"McCoy will be in prison soon, along with everyone else responsible. Miss Davis identified the others earlier."

Murray was too late, the worries had grown to maturity.

"Yet, I'll still be here with crippled limbs and blood-stained hands," Adam said.

Murray was thankful that Adam's eyes did not meet his. He knew he could not hide the expression that won over his face. Playing with his chunky fingers, Murray tried to arrange a counter argument in his head, however he failed miserably.

"It was my actions that drove Rachael to her death... and I must live with that," Adam said.

Murray leaned towards Adam and placed his hand on his knee.

"You have to realise you're the victim here. You have to realise these people did you wrong."

"All of them?" Adam asked.

"Yes, all of them, and when this case is closed, you can return to living a normal life," Murray said, breathing sharply to continue, just in case Adam interjected with another dose of depression talk.

"I have decided to treat the bank lodgements and withdrawals separately from this case."

"What is going to happen with them?" Adam asked.

Sighing, Murray struggled to find a meaningful answer.

"I suppose the case will remain open, and should any new information come to light, we will investigate further."

"A nice way to say that you're gonna do nothing!" Adam said, his gaze drawn to the living room window.

"We can do nothing for now, it's a dead end," Murray admitted. What a change, Murray thought. Months ago, a shy Adam was a suspect. Now, a more outgoing, opinionated Adam was the victim. Murray rubbed his hand lightly over Adam's shoulder.

"I'll be in contact Adam, should anything come up."

Chapter 43

No matter how hard Adam tried, his senses found information. First, there were the muffled cries as soon as the car door opened. Then, despite his eyes being locked to the ground, he still saw the mourners passing him by and stepping into the cemetery. One sense disabled, another took its place and painted the scene for Adam.

A wave of paranoia seeped through Adam's veins when the congregation passed him by, in his mind, each one threw a disgusted glance, realising he was the man who caused all of this. Reassuring pats on his shoulder from his father did little to change the feeling, which grew bigger with each mourner. The midday sun seemed to add to his woes, moistening his suit from the inside.

His heart thumped a little harder every time he imagined how Mrs. Anderson would react should she see his face. He considered the possibility she may actually drag him out of the wheelchair, or slap him in the face. There was a reasonable chance of something happening Adam felt, but the real pain would not be physical.

Adam shuddered when he saw Mrs. Anderson's lonely eyes. A picture replaced the thousand words. Dead eyes surrounded by a cloak of black, multiplying the aching ten-fold and sending it straight to Adam's conscience. Tears on her face glistened in the sun, making her pain even more visible. Guilt surfaced once more, rising in his throat, threatening to spill out. The mother of a dead daughter could possess the power to make guilt seep from every pore Adam thought, he sighed at what lay ahead in the next twenty minutes.

When the main procession passed through the gateway, the Fletcher family followed. Erin momentarily took the pressure off her son as she pushed the wheelchair under the large iron arch and up the concrete walkway that spread out in all directions. Passing each headstone threw up so many comparisons in Adam's mind; almost all of the engravings showed long lives, some told of little more than thirty years on this planet. None were like Rachael. The walkway grew narrower as the procession went further in to the cemetery, pushing each headstone closer and closer to Adam.

When they arrived at the plot where Rachael was to be buried, six men carrying the coffin placed it over the open grave. Through the crowd, Adam saw Mrs. Anderson standing next to the grave, tears jumping from her face and onto the wooden coffin. Murmurs from the priest became diluted as they reached Adam's ears, yet it did not worry him. Instead, it was the woman who was making her way to him. Erin's gentle touch seemed to warn Adam of the oncoming danger, but there was no need, he could see it.

"Hi Adam," Britney whispered, stepping out from the main congregation and placing herself directly in front of the young man.

"I know that you don't want to speak to me, but please take this."

Her long black coat extended below her knee where tights continued the colour co-ordination down to the ground. Reaching into her right pocket, Britney took out an envelope and gently placed it on Adam's lap. The Fletcher's eyes remained fixed on Britney. The quickest of glances at Adam's parents, sprinkled with the tiniest helping of *sorry* on her face had to suffice. The envelope slipped into Adam's grip and rested on his hands. The sun splashed on the white paper, sending a brighter form of itself into Adam's eyes. Shuffling his hands, he questioned whether to tighten his fingers, or let it slide to the ground. In the time it took him to decide, Britney had stepped out of Adam's view again. For a moment he traded places with Mrs. Anderson, for that split second he realised he was indeed a victim in this tragedy. But, the congregation were in on the act it seemed. Random sways let Adam's eyes lock on Mrs. Anderson through the crowd. Her face, distorted from an unimaginable aching. Adam gasped for air. A tightening in his chest amplified the feeling further, as he lowered his head in a futile attempt to relieve the terror.

"I can't stay," he murmured to his mother, reaching downwards and placing his hands on the wheels.

The envelope spent the next two hours serving as a placemat under Adam's numerous cups of coffee. Stains developed on the white paper, painting the exterior with a distinctly old look. He imagined the contents to be used and pitiful words. Words thrown together to form what she considered an adequate apology or words strategically placed in order to divert the blame to someone else.

An already long day turned into an even longer night as Adam spent hours flicking the letter in his hands. Once the seal was broken, he had to read the words that were inside. There was the problem. Words read could not be un-read. There was no way to undo the knowledge he would gain from letting his eyes fall upon Britney's scribbles.

Dismayed, he drew breath and reached for the letter. His eyes burned with a curiosity that attracted them like a magnet to the white paper, yet his hands ruled. Tossing the letter onto the counter top, Adam turned away and pushed himself into the living room. He needed to get Britney out of his head, and he hoped some spring TV series would come to his rescue.

***

"My last night," whispered Shaun in the darkness of his holding cell. Britney successfully applied for bail earlier that day, and while the idea of leaving then entered his thoughts, he figured it easier to wait another 24 hours. The small matter of attending Rachael's funeral would be gone in the morning, leaving Shaun with only one objective.

He experienced some cold nights in the holding cell, but tonight was different. Shaun shed his tears for Rachael. He smiled at the film reel of good memories drifting through his mind, he shook with the pain. When Rachael took to her final resting place, the mourning ended. No longer was the teenage girl the focus of Shaun's thoughts, no longer was her skinny frame the shape that developed in his mind. Where there once was sorrow, there was now anger, rage, resentment. It was all aimed at one man, and tomorrow night that man would be punished.

***

Like a tiny insect, thoughts of Britney's letter dug its way into Adam's brain, pulling and scratching for attention. The attraction of night time television was no match for the curiosity generated by the envelope, as Adam faltered and pushed himself back into the kitchen. There it was, untouched. Split in half, both sides of the young man fought, open it or keep it closed. His mind jumped back to the previous week, to words uttered in a science fiction film that caught his eye. At times his life felt like fiction, how could he be cursed with so much pain, so much misfortune. Words from the male character in the movie started to replay in his ears, a random film portraying itself as meaningful.

"Fifty years from now, when you're looking back on your life, don't you wanna be able to say that you had the guts."

Adam sniggered at his seemingly childish comparison, yet, somewhere deep in the recesses of his mind, it made sense to him. This was not fantasy. His life was not a scene, rehearsed over and over again. He searched for another word, other than curiosity, to define the power that made him slip his finger under the sticky seal and pull out the white sheets of paper. He called it courage. Seven minutes and two re-reads later, Adam leaned back in his wheelchair and gasped. The letter answered questions, and it threw up a new obstacle. Like the black ink on the white paper, the choice could not have been spelt any clearer, "Shit."

Chapter 44

Murray folded his umbrella and hung it from the staff hangers located inside reception. Due to the unseasonal heavy rain, he had been unable to run his usual trek along the Charles River before work. Any thoughts of having an easy morning to compensate were quickly dashed when Murray met Adam at his office door.

"Is something wrong?" Murray began, leaning forward and motioning Adam inside.

"I have a request."

"Official or unofficial?" smiled Murray, bordering on sarcastic. But, the humour passed Adam by.

"It's an official request, it is about Shaun McCoy."

"Oh?"

"I believe Britney applied for, and got bail yesterday?" Adam asked. Murray sat down at his desk, pushing away documents that were placed for his attention.

"Yes, she did. Is there a problem with that?"

Shaking his head, Adam jumped in, "No, not with that. My worry is Mr. McCoy will try to do the same today."

"It is possible. But, he would have to surrender his passport, as well as pay for his bail."

While not admitting it, Murray was on Adams side. Nonetheless, he could do little to prevent Shaun from being released on bail until the trial, should the District Judge decide otherwise.

"I understand how it works," Adam said, "and I know money will not be a problem for Mr. McCoy."

"What exactly are you asking Adam?"

"I wanna speak with Shaun, without the bars, without the cuffs. Alone!"

Was this young man serious, Murray figured? Partially paralysed, sitting opposite his enemy, alone in a room, with no protection?

"Can I ask why you want this?"

"I just want to. I need to."

Murray had seen this before, where a victim builds up enough anger inside and lets it off in one explosion. All of the previous cases called it courage, a fight back. He knew differently. No matter how much the victims wanted to call it bravery, it was merely frustration that had morphed into something else. Regardless of what they called it, Murray knew retaining such emotion was not healthy.

"Ok, let's do it."

"Have you read Shaun his rights?"

"Yes, when we brought him here. Why do you ask?" Murray questioned.

"No reason."

Shaun counted the minutes until seven am, when the morning supervisor started his shift. He knew applying for bail before then was pointless, the night supervisor was basically a babysitter. Once they crossed the threshold in the morning light, the concerns of some imprisoned man bothered them little. The police officer who checked the holding cells shortly after seven was called by an impatient Shaun. He had the task of handing a copy of Shaun's bail request to the District Judge's office, the front reception and to the arresting officer, Murray.

Shortly after nine, Detective Murray walked into the holding cell, accompanied by a police officer.

"About time guys!" Shaun said.

"Oh, I'm sorry to keep you waiting sir!" Murray sneered, placing a set of handcuffs through the bars and into Shaun's hands.

"Why do I have to put these on? I should be free to go!"

"You have an interview to attend, so put them on and come with me."

Shaun hurriedly snapped the handcuffs into place and planned for the judge. The three men walked silently along the holding cell's corridor, up the elevator and towards Murray's office.

Through the glass panels on the office door, Shaun saw the back of Adam's head. Reaching for his hands, Murray unlocked the cuffs and motioned for Shaun to enter the office. Shaun stalled. He looked down at his hands again just to confirm to himself the cuffs were gone. *What is going on here?* Murray leaned forward and opened the door, pushing Shaun through. The noise jolted Adam, who had been playing with his cell phone. Immediately, he placed it down on the table, yet did not turn to look at Shaun.

"Adam, if you need anything...." Murray said, closing the door.

A gentle nod by Adam was the reply, he remained where he was, staring straight at Murray's seat. Shaun stood behind Adam for a few moments, mulling over in his head what to do. When the bail request came through, he figured, that yes, he would pay Adam a visit. Adam visiting him was not in his plans.

Shaun's height advantage over the wheelchair bound man instilled him with an even greater sense of power.

"What do you want?" he whispered, eager to send chills through Adam.

"I just wanna talk," Adam replied calmly. "Please sit."

Shaun continued his slow walk around the desk and sat in Murray's chair. Through the glass in the door, he could see Murray and the police officer had left. He assumed they were close by.

"Rachael died," Adam said, showing his aces first.

Faking a smile, Shaun showed no ill effects, "I know that. How are you living with it?"

"Living with it?"

"Yeah," Shaun smiled, "It was your acts that drove her to do it. It was your confession that turned her."

Adam failed to hide his gasp. Shaun leaned forward in his chair and folded his arms on the desk. Adam leaned back slightly.

"You genuinely think this was not your fault? You dragged this young girl, among others, into a pit of lies and deceit. Now, you expect to throw the blame onto someone else? You are a coward!" Adam said.

"I disagree! I think you're just pissed off that you're stuck in that, and I'm free," Shaun retorted, unable to contain his smile.

"Stuck in that? What the hell is that supposed to mean?" Adam replied, staring into Shaun's eyes.

"What do you think it means, cripple?"

Adam rubbed his forehead, letting his hands trawl down his face until they joined prayer-like below his chin.

"Yes, I may be stuck in this for now. But, at least you're stuck in here."

"You are hilarious," sniggered Shaun, "you are not really up to date are you? Earlier this morning, I applied for bail. And this is Murray's one last trick to tempt me."

"Tempt you? Into what?" Adam asked.

"Put the *criminal* in a room with the handicapped accuser, and watch him fuck himself up. Don't think so!" Backtracking, Adam picked out Shaun's phrase, "You claim that you are free? Enlighten me!"

"I don't have to say anything to you!" Shaun laughed, glancing around Murray's office.

"Yet, you think you will soon be set free? Where do you get this nonsense from?" Adam asked. Shaun unfolded his arms and ran his fingers along his short hair.

"I will get bail within an hour or so, and while you sit in that chair, I'll be walking outa here."

Shaun intentionally hid his smile and replaced it with piercing eyes and gritted teeth. Leaning closer to Adam, Shaun lowered his voice to a whisper.

"And this time, you won't have your little friend to protect you!"

"Britney?"

Shaun nodded, his eyes never losing Adam's.

"She begged and begged to protect you before, but she is not staying around this town. Who knows where she is already!"

Adam gulped again, adding to Shaun's sense of power. Nervous glances by Adam at his hands, the door, the window, all confirmed to Shaun who was in charge.

"I thought I dreamt it, but you actually broke into my house that night didn't you?"

Shaun looked at the office door, still no trace of Murray or the police officer.

"So what if I did, it's your word against mine. And soon enough, you won't have a word."

"What do you mean?" Adam replied, his lips trembled when the sounds came out.

"This will end soon. Well," Shaun laughed, "for you that is!"

"You're pretty stupid if you think you'll get away with that," Adam said.

"I may be a lot of things. Stupid? Cripple? I ain't them. You can't run away from me, hell, you can't even walk away!"

"You're not gonna touch me," Adam said.

"I'm not gonna touch you, but I will hurt you."

"I'm hurt enough. You can't possibly do anymore to me."

Shaun laughed, "Oh, I can do more. You're alive aren't you? Well, for now."

Adam pushed his wheelchair back from the table and tapped loudly on the office door.

"It was nice chatting to you," Shaun stood up and walked to the door.

"Is everything ok?" Murray asked.

"Yes detective, we're just finished!" Shaun said, unable to hide the joy bubbling inside. Murray motioned for the police officer to handcuff Shaun.

"What about my bail?" Shaun laughed, fidgeting with the handcuffs. Murray stepped over to his desk and picked up some documents. Turning to Adam he said.

"This is McCoy's application for bail, it looks like he is going to make it, I'm sorry."

Adam lowered his head. With each breath, more and more escaped until his entire body was shaking with delight. Shaun felt the police officer's grip tightening on his arms, what was happening?

"Adam? What is going on?" Murray asked, as confusion ran across his forehead. This was Adam's request, Shaun thought.

Shaun could not help but notice the new ray of blue that came alive in Adam's eyes. His smile almost touched each ear as he nodded down to his cell phone, which he had left on the desk the entire time.

"Check the last recording before you grant him bail," Adam said.

Chapter 45

The deep sense of loss in his stomach still lingered. Pushing himself to the exit of Park Street police station, Adam wondered why he was still so down. After all, he now had evidence Shaun McCoy broke into his house weeks previously, and that he intended to do the same should the application for bail be granted. Adam searched again for the expected thrill of accomplishment, it did not exist.

Rain overflowing from the blocked gutters made the downpour form a curtain across the front door, forcing Adam to wait in the porch. Reaching into his pocket, he pulled out Britney's letter. He was never going to let it out of his sight, even though the words were sometimes difficult to take in. Fidgeting in his chair, Adam wished there was someone with whom he could talk to, someone to give him their interpretation of the letter. The only person in mind was the author.

A blonde woman ran up to the front of the station, covering her face with an edition of *The Metro*. A spark ignited in Adam's stomach, causing him to momentarily sit up in the wheel chair. However, as the woman stepped inside, she lowered the paper to reveal an unknown face. The image of a rain-soaked Britney standing at the end of his driveway on the day she told him about the accident, popped into his head. Adam rested, back into the most uncomfortable seat, one of uncertainty.

Through the screen of falling rain, Adam saw his mother in the disabled parking zone. Playing with the letter, he asked himself could he show her. After all, as far as he could remember, she was always right. What she said appeared to make sense. The almost deafening splatter of the rain on the pavement seemed to scramble that notion though, and if needing confirmation, she revealed a wearied face through the wall of dripping rain.

Stray thoughts entered Adam's mind, telling him to remember he was the victim. Bombs met those notions, reminders of someone else who was worse off. Yes, he was partially paralysed. Yes, he was suffering from amnesia. Thinking about what his mother felt was beyond his comprehension.

Giving birth to a son, watching him grow, seeing what he became, only to see him knocked to the ground and be dragged for miles and miles. All the while, she remained helpless, like she was trapped behind a wall of glass, airtight, silent. She could only give little expressions to guide her now broken son along a treacherous path. *Did she need to see the contents of Britney's letter?* The expression, *a problem shared is a problem halved* appeared, yet Adam decided that his mother could do without her half.

Murray trotted from his office to the holding cell, replaying the recording on Adam's phone all the way. He was surprised when Adam pointed to the phone, he did not even wait for confirmation, knowing Shaun's bail application would immediately be denied. Or maybe Adam had something more important on his mind.

Murray could have relayed the information on through any number of officers, and even though he could not take credit for the breakthrough, he looked forward to seeing Shaun's face when he played the recording. Tapping the bars in anticipation, Shaun bobbed in the cell like an eager dog, waiting to be let loose. All this added to Murray's developing sense of excitement as he stared into the 8 x 12 room.

"So?"

Murray smiled a greeting. There was no need for words, he figured, he pressed play on the only recording on Adam's phone. An energetic Shaun soon lost his spark as the conversation with Adam played out into the cell, echoing Shaun's mistakes back into his ears two and threefold. Sound transformed him. Every syllable found Shaun's ears, shrinking him more and more, until all that remained was a silenced, frail specimen of a man.

"Mr. McCoy, I'm afraid to say your application for bail is refused," Murray laughed out loud, intentionally prolonging his chuckle.

Stepping back into the darkness of the cell, Shaun's eyes searched for words to say, words to fight back with. All he found was a dry well. Empty, desolate, leaving Murray stunned.

271

"I am now going to add breaking and entering, as well as threatening and abusive behaviour to your charges. Oh, and we won't forget the pre-mediated attack which you intended to carry out!"

***

Madison fell. He screamed, it did not help, he screamed louder. The ground, so far away, was blurry. He stretched his arms wide, hoping to catch something, anything. Fear of the impending thud grew in his body, he scrunched up tight. The ground was getting closer, it was becoming clearer. A surge of electricity erupted, sending a jolt reverberating through every atom in his body.

Snapping out of the dream, Madison awoke on the floor. Panting and sweat covered, he adjusted to the bright green light coming from the super computer and reached for the overturned chair. A different dream he noted, it made a change, though not necessarily a good one. She was always in his dreams. Even when those dreams turned to nightmares, she was ever present. No matter what demons entered his night-times, regardless of what monster he created in his mind, she always saved him.

In the months after she died, friends told Madison to move on. They tried to force ideas into his head there was another *perfect* woman out there somewhere, waiting for him to find her. In time it became obvious to all of his friends, Madison did not want to be found. Fate aligned itself along a new path, one where Madison would trudge through this life, destined to be alone forever. Each day brought memories of his past love, his only love. In his eyes, it was all or nothing.

Chapter 46

Tormenting voices crawled in, begging Adam to open Britney's coffee stained letter once more. Little urges like flies danced in his mind, yet he was unable to swat them away. With each visit, they grew more plentiful and stronger.

Adam grabbed the envelope from his bedside locker, unfolded it quickly and drew breath. *This is the last time, make a decision then Adam!* He knew the contents of the letter, still it was so difficult to re-read. Each word scribbled down by Britney ignited an emotion, one Adam was afraid to admit to. His heart spoke up as he read the words, adding her voice to each sentence.

Adam,

I honestly don't know where to begin, so I'll just say it all out.

Firstly, and I know you're gonna tut when you hear this, but my heart is broken with the pain I feel. Not for me, but for what I've done to you.

I know you don't remember, but we have spent our lives together. And yes, in time those memories may come back to you, ones that we created together. All my life, any happy memories involved you, and I'm not just saying that because of what has happened here.

The night of our prom, I wanted to kiss you so much Adam. If I had my way, we would have stayed on your couch that night. I wish that we could have laid there.

But I don't seem to get my own way, maybe I deserve it. After all, you were the one who saved me when my father died. Without you, I would have given up. Just dropped dead! You urged me to survive. You dragged me onwards. When the news about my father came through, I was in the hospital corridor. I will never forget the feeling of numbness that came over me when I heard the nurses' words. I will also never forget the warmth of your arms as you stopped me from falling to the floor.

And, to think that I've done this to you, Adam, you can't imagine how guilty I feel. I am not expecting you to forgive me, but please, please realise that I never set out to hurt you.

Had I spoken up at the beginning, Rachael would still be alive, Shaun would be in prison, and maybe we'd still be friends.

You were my best friend. If I had your heart, we'd still be best friends.

Your brain may not remember, but your heart still does. It knows that I'm only here because of you, and while I know I cannot save your life, I think that I may be able to make it easier.

Adam, I have wronged you. So, the least that I can do is get out of your life, let you start again, free from me and my frailties.

By the time you read this, I'll be south of Boston. Tomorrow night I'll be booked into the Carlton motel in

Turnpike Street, Stoughton. And from there, to anywhere!

I, Britney Davis did not deserve a friend like you. Maybe, in another life I will.

Love you always,

Britney x x x

Spark after spark of internal fireworks coloured old images and sounds. The prom night came through stronger than before, even the quietest giggle became audible.

Old memories, which had been cut off from conscious recollection flickered into view for an instant, like a shooting star living and dying. Adam sat back in amazement at every hint of a past life with Britney. Tingling fingers came alive with the thought of her skin as it glided over his, two charged particles about to go off. So many variations of her soft voice reverberated in his ear, some with her giggle and some with her full blown laugh.

The elation of the letter died, replacing the joy with Britney's cries. All at once, a convoy of images rushed into Adam's mind; her father, the hospital, the graveside, each one hurting more and more.

Adam forced the cries away and replaced them with sounds of her laughter. Something started inside, the imagined scent of her hair wafted into his nostrils, like each time she leaned close. *The day of the accident!* Her smell was there too. He pictured Britney leaning over to secure his seatbelt, and the peace he felt as her curly blonde hair fell onto his face. *Heaven and maybe hell!* Sitting in his wheelchair, all alone in his bedroom, Adam took one last look at Britney's letter. The words near the end rang out like an invitation, one he could not afford to ignore.

"Carlton Motel, Turnpike Street, Stoughton?" He whispered, folding the letter and stuffing it into the bedside drawer.

The full moon sprayed its light through the glass on the front door, throwing a distorted glow along the hallway. Adam rolled towards the front door, ears perked for his parents. Wrapped in a large jacket, Adam reached up to where the car keys hung and slipped the key ring over the hook. Chiming keys in hand, Adam reminded himself, *now is the time to turn back.* Ignoring his own thoughts, he unlocked the front door. Pausing for a moment, an idea popped into his head. Propelling himself backwards down the hallway, Adam opened the tall cupboard just outside the kitchen door. A moment later, he pulled out two grey crutches and folded them across his lap. Despite only hearing of his father's sprained ankle in the last couple of months, Adam wiped the cobwebs from the metal supports, figuring it must have happened years ago.

The ding-dong of the clock in the hallway rang out, startling Adam. Maybe it was the moon, maybe it was just that hour of the night, but Adam struggled to find something to explain his act of lunacy. His mind searched for an answer, but it closed its mouth before uttering a word. Pulling the front door open, the glow of the moon bounced off the car and into Adam's eyes.

He approached the car, gripping the crutches across his lap. Shaking the keys in his hand, he pressed the unlock button. Worried eyes tried hard to dispel the belief, *he had to do this.* The other force, which Adam was refusing to define, urged him to at least try. He opened the driver's door and looked upwards into the seat. Part one of his journey, climb the mountain.

The outstretched car door became the guide for Adam. Positioning the wheelchair close to the car, he threw the crutches into the passenger seat. With the concentration of a surgeon, he tightened his grip on the steering wheel with his right hand. His left arm reached the top of the door frame as Adam took a deep breath. Tensing his fingers and arms, Adam ignored all doubts about the task ahead.

"One, two....three!"

Every morsel of power in his body channelled into his arms, pulling Adam out of the wheelchair and up into the car. He reached back and pulled his semi-lifeless legs in. Pain grew in his legs, but if there ever was a nice pain, this was it. However, Adam snapped out of his moment and realised he still had more work to do. Part two, learn from watching.

Since the accident and maybe longer, Adam had been chauffeured by his mother. Tiny grains of confidence rooted deep within him started to appear when the prospect of driving arose, yet he had no memory of ever doing such a thing. First things first Adam told himself, he reached for one of the crutches. He placed one near his right leg and pressed.

"Brake and accelerator!" he said, testing each.

One last look up at the house before Adam slid the keys into the ignition and turned. Thankful for the gentle hum from the engine, he reached his right arm up and took hold of the gear stick. Adam released the brake slightly, allowing the SUV to roll forwards down the driveway.

The overhead streetlight played down on the motionless car, as if examining its next move. Adam looked down Louver Street, the easiest part of the journey. Calming his breathing, he pressed back against the seat in an effort to relax. It did not work. Dancing fingers seemed to lead the rebellion, urging the rest of Adam's body to drive the car up towards the house again. He knew there would be no shame in failing. How he wished he had Britney's letter in his hand. The force seeped from Adam's veins, the obvious difficulty of the task puncturing a hole in his motivations.

Sitting, waiting, Adam needed to find the spark again. The hum of the engine was growing louder, it dared to wake his parents should he not decide soon. He glanced up at the front decking of his home, and immediately a smile came to his face. The image of the night out came to mind. Britney had ran inside and brought out a blanket, wrapping it around Adam as they tapped another bottle together and drank. A darker side to that occasion tried to enter Adam's thoughts, but, he built up a wall. Repelling every negative emotion, he inhaled the moment for what it was worth. There it was, he could see it, his fuel. Louver Street no longer seemed so daunting, the trip southwards to Stoughton turned into a Sunday drive. With a determined tug, Adam pulled the gear stick into drive and pressed down on the accelerator.

The town of Stoughton appeared quiet as Adam entered from the North. Travelling, he scanned every sign post, every street name. At the V-shaped junction of Notlama Street and Turnpike Street, Adam took a hard left turn. Britney was moments away he told himself and it was time to sort out what words he was going to throw her way.

While Adam would not provide himself with reason, he knew anger or revenge did not force him to drive to Stoughton. However, regardless of what Britney would say, he was not going to forgive and forget tonight. There was only one thing worse than having a deceitful Britney in his life, and that was not having Britney in his life.

Chapter 47

The flickering lights of the Carlton Motel caught Adam's attention. Coasting into the parking area, he edged the car as close as possible to the receptionist's office. The clock in the car flashed 01:00 when Adam switched the engine off. A light sneaking out from the drawn blinds showed that life existed inside. Flinging open the car door, Adam gave a fleeting look at the six feet of concrete that lay between him and the office door.

"It's only six feet!" Adam said as he placed the two crutches outside. In the car door, Adam's father's wallet came into view. Planning ahead, he slipped two notes from it and held them tightly in his hand. The sting he experienced earlier rose again when Adam lifted his legs and let them hang over the edge of the seat. Gripping the two crutches, he shuffled himself from the car seat and into a standing position.

Pain darted through Adam's legs like knives, causing him to moan deeply. Looking down, he saw the crutches shaking, and his feet flat on the ground. Adam pushed himself upright and started to move on his *four legs*. Six feet became, four, two, zero. Knocking on the office door, Adam glanced back at the car, admiring his achievement.

"Yeah?" mumbled a young man, opening the door. His face fitted perfectly with his demeanour, rough and scraggy.

"I am looking for a guest, Britney Davis. Could you tell me if she is here?" Adam said, fighting the stinging in his legs.

The man stared Adam blankly in the eyes.

"No, can't tell you!"

"You can't tell me, or you won't tell me?" Adam replied.

"Both!"

Maybe it was the job he was in, or maybe this guy just enjoyed ruining everybody's day, but Adam knew this twenty-something man-child held what he needed. Opening his hand, Adam shuffled a note from his grasp and offered.

"Britney Davis, please?"

The man took the money and walked away. Moments later, he returned, emotionless.

"No Britney Davis here tonight dude!" he said.

Dismayed, Adam nodded and turned to leave, "Thank you anyway."

Staggering from the doorway, Adam looked at all the rooms in the motel complex. The two tier building was old and shabby, but judging by the amount of cars in the parking lot, this place did well. How he longed to see Britney's white ford, he would take the odds of having to look through every one of the 27 rooms there.

The trek was there again, six feet to the car. It seemed so much longer this time. Adam's mind searched for something, anything to take his mind off the disappointment. The black painted barriers formed a pathway in front of the ground floor rooms, cheap brown curtains draped over 27 dirty windows, each with their own story to tell. Random lights in almost every room, despite the time, flicked on and off. Garden pots were placed in stages along the exteriors of the rooms, filled with traces of flowers which had died over the winter. So many pieces, all singing to the same tune of despair, even the man at reception was in on it.

Hang on! Adam thought, turning to see dead remains in a flower pot. Closer inspection revealed the name of the flowers that had been planted the previous year. Adam thanked the laziness of the gardener, who had left the paper tag on the plants. Raising his head, he turned back to the receptionist.

"Can you check for Violet Davis?"

His hand was already on the door, about to close it in Adam's face. The request made him sigh, yet the guy's eyes still found Adam's hand.

"That will be another... y'know," he said. Adam opened his hand to give him the last note.

"She is in room 26. It's just around the corner."

A light from room 26 was like a magnet, attracting him toward Britney's room. He expected to hear the hum of a TV or radio as he approached the door, yet no sound found Adam's ears. Walking was not the difficulty for Adam, the crutches taking the majority of the weight. His problems were two fold; the pressure of holding most of his body on shaking arms, and despite having four points of contact with the ground, balancing.

Struggling closer to room 26, Adam searched for words to blurt out to Britney. Emotions battled inside, questions and answers fought for supremacy, each one stating their case to the master and each one being pulled on their shortcomings.

Anger and rage had their moment in the sun, Adam thought, and while they may be deserving of another appearance, maybe now was not the time. Question after question stood in line, awaiting Adam's choice. *How could you have done this to me? Why have you hinted for me to come here? What now?*

Yes, Adam told himself, they all had a strong reason for inclusion. The temptation of hearing the answers only sweetened the deal.

Before Adam came to a decision, the door knob twisted right and left and Britney opened the door. A light from a bedside table seemed to form a shiny trace around Britney's blonde hair. With no time to decide, Adam fell into default mode. He could not help letting emotions pour out. Yet, it was neither anger nor rage. Britney's shaken face made his heart thump in his chest, causing the pain in Adam's arms to fade into the background.

"I promised myself I wouldn't cry, but I," she stuttered, lowering her head into her hands. Between her soaked fingers, Adam saw a trail of mascara running down Britney's face. Constant wiping made her nose red, irritated skin showed hours of crying, and a wrinkled white blouse hung damply over blue jeans.

Exhausted muscles caved under the pressure, making Adam fall in the doorway of the motel room. Britney tried to grab Adam as he fell, but it was no use. He reached down to his legs and dragged them inside the threshold. A motionless Britney looked on, twitching hands looking for a way to help. She closed the door, switching her stare to Adam's face.

"I didn't think you'd come," Britney whispered, kneeling down in front of Adam.

"I'm not here to forgive you," Adam started, scanning her face as the words came out.

"I know. I'm not expecting you to Adam. I just want to see you one last time..."

"Stop," Adam interrupted, "don't say you are going to leave, that is not the answer." Britney lowered her head like a child that had just been scolded, drawing her hands closer together in an attempt to wipe the shame from her mind.

"Rachael told me what you did for me, she told me about Shaun."

Pulling her hair back from her face, Britney forced a smile. Even though it did not seem natural to him, he still found warmth in seeing Britney at ease. But, the fleeting moment of respite was soon hidden.

"I meant everything I said in the letter Adam, I could spend the rest of my life saying sorry and it still would not be enough."

Britney shuffled closer to Adam, cautiously sliding her left hand onto his leg. Even though the smallest tingle darted throughout his legs, Adam kept his gaze locked on her face. Blue eyes did not sit still, trembling white skin marked with two rivers down her face as her chest heaved with deep breaths. Sliding his hand down to hers, Adam sighed with contentment when his fingers touched her soft, delicate skin.

Battles were fought in Adam's head, each side claiming they knew best. The side that had disguised itself as common sense lay its artillery bare, trying to prove fighting is futile, just accept it. It was hard to deny its argument, as Adam thought back to all the chances Britney had to come clean. Understandably, she may have been in shock at the beginning, but how long does that excuse last? She covered for Shaun all along.

It was not a one-sided war, the other side armed up and paraded a convoy of conflicting thoughts. Digging furiously for hints of old memories, it showed replay after replay of Adam and Britney's life together. Rachael's words, recorded in his mind, confirmed the suspicion that Britney had little choice in the aftermath of the accident. She admitted to the crash, she handed herself in, she had kick-started Shaun's arrest. *Is that letter truthful? Are those tears real?*

Adam struggled to find fault with the questions, yet he found it even harder to answer *no.*

"This may sound crazy... thank you for saving me."

"It was me that put you there in the first place, but thank you Adam," she replied. "I would have understood if you had not come here. I'm so happy you did."

"I literally have thought about nothing else the last few days, and I think that if I was in your position, I may have done the same," Adam replied.

Shaking her head, Britney looked Adam dead in the eyes.

"You have more courage than me, I have been weak," she said.

"Don't say that Britney, you did try to make it right in the end," Adam whispered, holding her hand a little tighter.

"There is one last act for me, for the coward."

"What are you saying?"

"Adam, I cannot stay here. I will have to go to prison," Britney replied, sliding her hand along Adam's arms as if trying to distract him from what she has just said.

"No you don't! You can explain the situation to the detective, I will help you," Adam said, leaning forward.

"I know we are not going to be totally okay from the off, what we need is time, time together as friends, as lifelong friends."

"I don't think that will be possible if I stay here Adam," Britney stuttered, standing up and taking a step back.

"Britney, please! There is no need to leave here, or me."

"I have to! You don't understand how hard it is to wake up every morning, knowing that today you'll have to lie again, again, and again. I lied to save you, yet I made things worse than I could have imagined."

"You saved me," Adam said.

"No, I didn't. I was greedy."

Britney sat on the bed and sniffled, her red lips caught tears running down her face.

"I must leave here, not for me, for you. Every time I look in the mirror I'm reminded of the coward who messed up your life. I will survive in this world with the guilt I ruined my life, but the knowledge that I have ruined yours will take me to the brink. Such a reminder, you need to live without. You don't need me here, reigniting that pain every day."

Adam sat on the floor, left reeling with the out pouring of pain from Britney's tongue. She paced the room, hiding her face in her hair.

"Britney," he exclaimed, "look at me."

Composing herself, she laid her eyes on Adam.

"How can you leave me? Look, I'm broken here," he said.

"Your body will recover, your mind will recover, but only if I'm not here," Britney replied. She stepped towards the en-suite and dragged her packed suitcase from behind the door.

"Britney, what are you doing? It's the middle of the night, you can't leave!"

Britney dried her face one last time with a towel, unresponsive to Adam's words. He gazed up at her from the floor, longing for the power to stand up and keep her here. Each time Adam tried to summon the energy to stand, his body reminded him of the reality.

"You get me to come all the way out here just to leave me?" Adam said.

"For our sake, we needed to see each other one last time. I needed to tell you how sorry I am that I betrayed you."

"I thought you loved me?" Adam whispered, his last effort to stop Britney leaving.

"It is because I love you that I can't stay."

Kneeling down, Britney leaned forward and gave Adam a lingering kiss on the cheek.

"I will always love you Adam," she whispered.

In the motel room, Adam remained motionless against the wall. Getting up was impossible, the ceiling had lowered itself and was now resting on Adam's chest. The contagious disease, crying, failed to catch Adam, his body too distraught to cry. The crutches sat at his feet, tormenting him. He had conquered them once before, however, this time they were renewed by his fragile figure. Outside the door, the rain hammered the ground over and over again, forming a barrier between Adam and his drive home. There was no need for it to be so tough, the fight had come and gone.

Chapter 48

Hours turned into days, days into weeks and still Adam struggled to function. He sat in the court room, yet his mind was absent. Even as Shaun was lead in from the cell, Adam's expression did not change. One last act of fighting from Shaun mattered little, aggressive stares neutralised by pain dwelling inside. Taking to the stand, Adam uttered the minimum that one can say, however due to the recording from the police station, coupled with finding the gun, the result was never in doubt.

The jury returned with their verdict, saying words that should have energised Adam like a shot of adrenalin. Yet, the words failed to change the lines that had developed on his face. Tiny movement in his lips, from a frown to the slightest smile, the total of his efforts. Reassuring hands from his mother, when the judge read out the sentence mattered little to Adam, Shaun's life from now on was not one of his priorities.

Reaching the family SUV in the car lot, Erin turned to Adam.

"Are you okay?"

Nodding, Adam positioned himself closer to the car and reached upwards. Hoisting his body up, he sighed,

"I suppose I don't have a choice, do I?"

"This is the beginning of the rest of your life Adam, from today onwards, you can start over."

His mind shouted a reply, yet Adam kept the signal from reaching his mouth. He knew his parents would take time to get over Britney's apparent betrayal, but he would take time to get over Britney's absence.

Sitting in the SUV, Adam ran his hands along his legs. He noted how they used to be thinner. He tried to dig up some motivation from the fact he could now feel muscle along the once bony structures. Silent words screamed, he was entitled to be greedy for once. When he let his mind go free, urging it to be selfish, it always returned with one wish. A wish that was miles away in distance, yet there was no limit on when they would meet. Each time she drifted into his mind, her image reminded Adam of the reality, he may never see her again.

Arriving home, Adam pushed himself up the driveway, intentionally staying back from his parents. Glances down Louver Street were fruitless, each one returning a blank picture. The white ford appeared in thin air, his mind conjured up the image of a slender blonde young woman walking along the pavement, eager to hug Adam's aching body once more. No matter how hard he wished, no image became reality.

"Do you want to have dinner soon?" Erin asked from the porch.

"I don't feel like eating right now," Adam replied, never allowing his eyes stray from the street.

The spring air was losing it sting, replaced with a hint of summer warmth. Trees bloomed again, eager to impress after their season of hibernation, breaking free from the buds. From the end of the street came the sound of kid's chuckling as they kicked a football against their neighbour's car. Yet, despite the growth along Louver Street, Adam's eyes viewed it as if the trees were stretching over the road, seemingly planning to block him here forever. Madison walked across the garden, swishing grass giving away his position.

"How did today go?" he asked.

"It was good, as expected."

Madison took off his jacket and placed it on the ground. Pieces of paper were folded into one of the inner pockets.

"I see you miss her!" Madison said.

"What?" Adam replied, acting as if no-one could see him waiting at the bottom of his driveway for her.

"You have been sitting here for weeks Adam, she is not coming back," Madison said.

Adam could not bring himself to look at Madison's face, he just stuttered in disbelief.

"How can you even say such a thing?"

"Because I know more than you think!"

Madison stood up and walked in front of Adam. The two men stared at each other.

"Adam, this is reality now, you need to wake up."

"You don't know how I feel Madison, you don't know how much I love her," Adam said with gritted teeth.

"Actually, I do," Madison replied.

"You may claim you know, but the only person who truly knows is me. So, unless you have been in my exact position, leave me alone."

Madison turned down Louver Street and smiled. *Is he mocking me?*

"I have been in your position Adam."

"You lost your wife! And while I'm sorry for your loss, at least you had her, I've never been able to call Britney my own," Adam replied, shaking his head at the seemingly trivial comparison.

"Adam, I have been in that chair, I have lived your life," Madison blurted out.

Adam gritted his teeth, "Madison, seriously, stop annoying me. I'm sorry your wife died, I'm sure you loved her, I have my own problems to deal with."

Madison faced Adam again, the smile disappeared from his face. Like an instant transformation, Madison aged ten years when he frowned, crow's feet stretched from his eyes and his stare glazed over.

"Adam, I am you," he whispered.

"I don't know what you're on, but just keep away from me," Adam said, hastily turning his wheelchair away and pushing himself up the driveway.

"Adam, ask me anything, I will be able to answer."

Is this a joke? Why is everybody intent on messing with me? Adam tugged harder, propelling the wheelchair up the ramp and onto the security of his front porch. A quick glance confirmed Madison remained at the end of the driveway, seemingly intent on pleading his case from there.

"I know about the letter, I know about the motel!" Madison shouted.

"All that proves is that you're a stalker, and a pretty good one!"

Adam opened the door, pushed his wheelchair along the hallway and into the security of the bedroom. Adam picked up the photo album and bounced it in his hands. The massacre left no survivor. Sliding plastic coverings aside, Adam searched for a remaining piece of Britney. Glancing at the dustbin, he silently cursed his own rashness. It was strange for him to comprehend how his emotions could change so easily, weeks ago he did not want to see her again. Now, he would give anything. Adam wondered was that a sign of love, or a sign of impending madness. Either way, weary eyes conjured up the prom photo, revelling in every inch of Britney's beautiful white face, her body lovingly adorned with that black dress, contrasting with blonde curls. Adam came back to reality with a start, she is gone. In the void, Madison's words became visible. *Adam, I have sat in that chair, I have lived your life.* What did it all mean? How could Madison have lived *my* life? *Adam, I am you.* Madison had been the epitome of a well-grounded man, until now. Shaking his head, he cursed Madison's insensitivity. Adam tried to forget about the man's words, he tried to go back to thinking about Britney, and Britney alone.

Each passing minute pushed Britney into the background and pulled Madison's uttering's back into focus. *What if he is the key to all of this?*

"No, no he isn't!" Adam muttered, eager to suppress any ideas that Madison is more than what he has portrayed.

"Impossible!" Adam said, in a delicate whisper.

***

"I've messed up!" Madison cried at the monitor, safe for now in the relative darkness of his living room. Even though the image was faint, he could not bear to look at the black, reflecting screen that sat upright before him. Green flashing lights reminded him whatever words left his mouth would be transmitted to the other side, where they would be recorded for eternity. His failure would be recorded for eternity. The ramblings of a man would be the reason why this plan would never be attempted again. Cries of a lost battle would be the stumbling block for generations.

"All this time, and I throw it out as if it meant nothing! I should have known how he would react."

Madison lay his head down on the desktop, a brief respite from spilling his guts to the other side. Within minutes, a sharp knock on the door snapped him out of his self-induced state of pity. Again, the front door vibrated with the impact of something crashing against it. Stepping out into the hallway, Madison reached for the front door. The evening light momentarily blinded him, forcing his eyes to adjust. Seconds later, they felt relived at what they saw. Adam sat in his wheelchair on the grass and two garden gnomes lay smashed on the front steps.

"We need to talk," Adam said, turning towards his home.

***

Britney scribbled over another date in the cheap calendar, shaking her head in disbelief, only a month since she had left Adam. Nights were spent berating herself over decisions made and a lost friend. Sleep provided no reprieve, only reinforcing the hole in her life. Britney spoke to her mother once since she left, just to release basic information, letting her know her daughter was alive. The idea of ringing Adam crossed her mind daily, but what would do for Adam she pondered.

Is he thinking of me? Will I ever see him again? Question after question came, each recycled without an answer. Britney continued to reinforce the reality of her life; you have made your mistakes, now live with them.

"The pain will subside in time." were the words she cried every night when she lay down to sleep. She joined her hands to pray, not for herself, but for Adam, asking her father to look after him, to return the favour. Turning the light off after another day of regret and sorrow, Britney wondered how many more she could take.

Chapter 49

Madison closed the door to Adam's bedroom, separating them from the outside world for now. Adam positioned himself near his bed and folded his arms.

"This is your time, explain what you were on about earlier," Adam said.

Madison shuffled a little, years of planning, he found his moment. Realising his body language was not helpful to a wheelchair-bound man, he sat down against the wall. Taking a deep breath, Madison began.

"This may sound crazy at first, but please, let me explain myself. It will all make sense in the end. I told you my wife died years back, do you remember?"

"Yeah," Adam answered.

"I'm here because I lost her, we lost her."

"Madison, you claim to be me? I don't know why I'm entertaining that idea, but the last few months have been so messed up, y'know what, crazy doesn't seem to have the same ring anymore."

"I can prove I'm you."

Madison searched through his catalogue of memories, finding many from his life, yet few to prove his connection with Adam.

"I was there when Rachael died, I knew she was going to do it, because I went there as you before."

"What? You knew she was going to kill herself and you stood by? What is wrong with you?" Adam said.

"I had to, believe me. I couldn't change it, we could lose her if I did."

"Her? We lost Rachael, her family lost her."

"I know, but there is a bigger picture."

"You have proved nothing," Adam said.

Madison stared at the floor, replaying the words he practised years earlier. In the corner of his eye, he noticed Adam remaining motionless. He just stared at Madison's face, waiting for a signal to prove this story to be lies.

"Britney was my wife, and in time, she will be your wife," Madison said. He closed his eyes and found it, memories to convince Adam.

"The smell of her hair, makes you want to hold her close forever," Madison said, keeping his eyes fixed on Adam, no change.

"She put the seatbelt on you in the car, the kiss on that bed, the letter."

"The letter? What do you know about that?" Adam asked.

"Everything, I read it when I was in your position."

"That's not possible..."

"Her father wanted to call her Violet..." he spoke again.

Adam gasped, Madison's plan finally looked like taking shape.

"Afraid to tell your mother what you're really feeling, because you know it will break her. You're sick of Michael Lenard's speeches, who cares about his old injuries?" Madison said. He stood up and sat on the bed, tracing his hands over the bed sheets.

"Nights spent dreaming of Britney."

"But how...how are you here?" Adam said.

"Years of hell made me fight to get her back. My battle was with nature, physics."

Adam shook his head, "Time travel is not possible?"

"Losing her made it possible."

Adam's wheelchair creaked, filling the void in the room. Madison fired his last bullet, hoping it would convince Adam.

"The prom photo, the first memory, she looked perfect, didn't she?"

Adam nodded, "What are you saving her from?"

"It's not what, but who. Shaun," Madison said.

"What?" Adam said, "Shaun is in prison."

"Adam, in five years and nine months from now, we lose her."

"Shaun gets released?"

Madison stood up and ran his fingers over books on Adam's shelf.

"He was coming for you. Britney happened to be at home, he needed to get revenge."

"How do you know it was him?" Adam asked, "Was he arrested?"

Memories played again in Madison's head, ones that drove him to break the laws of physics in an attempt to remove them.

"He came to her funeral and told me, I was helpless." Adam appeared to speak, words caught up in his mouth, releasing only a stutter. Madison saw sweat form on Adam's forehead, he looked at the youthful version of his blue eyes.

"Britney saved you. Yes, you got in the car together, but in the aftermath she saved you from Shaun. And since, she has been that little ray of hope every day when you wake up. I remember feeling every day was pointless unless I had a glimpse of her. Only we know how that feels," Madison said.

"No matter how much I want to believe, I need you to be able to prove it, give me something concrete," Adam said, focusing on Madison once again.

"Ok, come to my house. I have close to one million dollars in boxes there, I knew...."

"The lottery?" Adam interrupted, "It was you?"

"Yeah, how did you know it was the lottery?" Madison asked.

"The deposit and the withdrawal, the fingerprints, it all adds up now," Adam said, his hands connecting dots in mid-air. That was you in the bank? You didn't pretend to be me, you were me?" Adam asked.

Silence enveloped the room, protecting two versions of the same man from the outside. Each dealt with the same problem, yet from opposite sides. Aching had dwelt for years inside Madison, urging him to do whatever it takes to change what has happened, eager to plant a seed that will save the love of his life.

"How did she die?" Adam whispered.

"Shaun held her until she couldn't breathe anymore," Madison answered, "so, I wasted the next few years of my life feeling sorry for myself," he added.

"Until it hit me one day, I had to try to go back, over twenty years to get here."

"But why come back to now? Why did you not go to the time of the accident and stop it?"

"Just like you cannot remember everything before the accident, I cannot either," Madison said.

"Oh," Adam said, "my memory won't come back?"

His words dripped with sorrow, Madison realised he must keep the young man's spirit up if his plan is to succeed.

"You will make better memories, trust me."

"So, you are back to save her?" Adam asked.

"Not exactly, I'm back for you to save her."

"Me? But you know what is going to happen, why can't you just do it? After all, you are in love with her, the future version."

Madison stood up and shook his head.

"I cannot force the future to change, well, not by physical means. For example, if I go out and kill Shaun, in the future it would remove my need to come back in the first place."

"Paradoxes?" Adam asked.

"Exactly. As far as I understand, physical objects can travel between different time periods, but as soon as they interact in a way that is significant to change the course of history, they create a paradox, which literally stops that action from taking place. But, information is the one thing that appears to be able to transcend all boundaries

302

of time." Madison paced back and forth, using his hands to draw imaginary lines in the air.

"The winning lottery numbers are the prime example," Madison said, becoming more animated as he spoke.

"That is information passing through time and not affecting anyone or thing physically. Yes, the other six winners originally won $1.16 million each, but the difference mattered so little it did nothing to create a paradox. You understand?"

Adam's eyes focused.

"So, why do you need me?" he asked, getting back to the original question.

"I physically can't do anything, I can only pass information onto you in order for you to save her," Madison responded with joined hands, as if praying for Adam to say yes.

"That is ironic! So," Adam said, "when the time comes, I must ensure Britney is close to me and save her?"

Madison stepped closer to Adam, seeing the reflection of his younger self.

"Adam, this will all end soon. As soon as I give you the when, and where to be, in theory, I should vanish into non-existence."

Adam sat back abruptly, "Vanish into non-existence? You may have to explain that one Madison."

"When the information hits your ears, that will alter history, you will know when to save Britney. Therefore, it removes the need for me to travel back in time, which will erase me from existence in this time. I know, it sounds crazy."

"Crazy, yes, but I think I understand.... So, this is the last time that I'll see you?"

"Yes it is," Madison answered, switching from his original excited tone to a more sombre one. The two men nod at each other, both reluctant to say goodbye.

"Before you go, can you tell me what it was like, the time spent with her?"

Smiling, Madison cast his mind back.

"It made me travel back in time, is that an indicator?"

"You broke the laws of physics just to be her saviour," Adam said. Madison thought about Adam's statement for a moment as he stood in what was once his bedroom.

"Being a saviour does not always mean saving the world or someone you care about, maybe, if you save yourself you are a saviour. She is impossible to live without." With that, Madison stepped forward and shook Adam's hand.

"You will get out of this Adam if you keep strong – I did it, and we're the same person. Promise me, that when you get her, you won't let her go."

"I promise," Adam said.

Reaching into his pocket, Madison pulled out a piece of white paper.

"Read this, it will save her, it will save you."

Adam cupped the paper in both hands and laid it down on his lap. Both men looked at each other for the last time, silent and awed. When the door closed gently, Adam unfolded the paper and read the details. As each morsel of information entered Adam's mind, Madison felt his body getting lighter, *this is it.*

Chapter 50

Standing in the home where he grew up, where he felt such mixed emotions, Madison awaited the inevitable. The theory, discussed with his friend in the future was moments away. When Adam's eyes read the information on the paper, Madison should disappear. He felt lighter as he walked along the wooden hallway, but he still existed. He asked himself, what has he done wrong? Adam knows the date of the event, which should lead to him saving Britney, and no need for Madison to travel back. *Why am I still here?*

A horrible thought crossed his mind. Had he changed the future for the worst by giving Adam information? In the future, he had carefully considered the right time to tell Adam the truth. Analysis showed it would work better when Britney had gone, when the feeling of loneliness was greatest. Madison shuddered, did he go too far? Was Adam going to give up on Britney?

Gently opening the bedroom door, Madison saw Adam sitting in the same position. He longed to see what was inside those lost eyes. While he remembered

305

everything up until today as he had experienced it himself, from the moment Madison opened his mouth to Adam earlier, the future he knew changed.

When Madison sat in that same chair, he never had to deal with a future version of himself trying to steer him in the right direction. He had Britney in his life, just like Adam. He lost her, just like Adam. Yet Madison found her again. Considering the change in circumstances, Madison wondered would Adam find her.

Through the slightly opened door, Madison whispered to Adam, startling him.

"Do you still want her?"

"I want her more than anything."

A relieved smile came to Madison's face. He pushed the door open and stepped back in.

"Not meaning to be rude, but why are you still existing?" Adam said, looking up at his older self.

"I do not know."

"How long did you have to wait until you got her back?"

"Close to a year from now Adam," Madison admitted. Adam gasped. Madison knew the previous month tested Adam and the thought of another eleven struck him like a bus.

"She used to email me, after six months or so. I think she felt guilty up until the day she died, even though I told her every day what she meant to me," Madison said.

"A year? That sickens me!" Adam whispered.

Madison closed the door and leaned against the bedroom wall. He failed to hide his expression from Adam, yet both men were a mirror image of each other.

Desolate and down, they sat in their silence for what seemed like an eternity.

"What can we do now?" Adam muttered.

"We can wait. That's all we can do."

Shaking his head, Adam pushed himself out of his room and towards the front door. Dusk fell when the young man positioned himself on the front porch.

"I can't wait that long Madison," Adam said.

Madison followed Adam onto the porch, remembering for a moment how it felt to be trapped in the wheelchair, days spent looking at kids playing on Louver Street, longing to be free. Turning to Madison, Adam smiled.

"Where did Britney go to for the year you were apart?"

The energy on Adam's face disappeared when the answer etched itself on Madison's body, a desolate shrug confirming it.

"When we met, we promised to leave everything from the accident behind. It was the only way we could survive. I never asked her where she had been."

Adam slouched back into his chair again and stared down Louver Street.

"Is she even in this state!" he exclaimed, out into the empty street. Madison shook his head and sat down on the step.

"I don't even know where to begin Adam, she could be anywhere."

"I guess two heads are not better than one, when they're the same head?" Adam shrugged.

"She probably packed her bags and went as far away as possible!" Madison said.

He looked upwards from the steps to see Adam lost in thought, yet he realised the young man's mind had cast a net, and it was close to revealing its catch.

"Madison, I think I know where she might be."

Chapter 51

The town bell rang for midday, pulling Britney from her sleep. The mirror caught her red eyed and ragged state when she stumbled out of bed and into the cold shower. Late night work had become a sleeping pill, draining every ounce of energy from the woman's body as she lay down to rest. Britney needed something to take her mind off Adam. Sideway glances at men in the bar stirred up reminders of the man she left behind, the man she credited with saving her life.

Spring had hit the town, yet a dark cloud floated over Britney's head daily. Jokes from the younger staff played on her mind, they urged her not to take work so seriously, not knowing what anchor was attached to Britney.

A month! Britney told herself, one month into the rest of her life. She shuddered at the thought of a seemingly endless repeat of the last four weeks. Stirring her coffee, her dreary eyes gazed out into the street. With every passing second, couples walked by, smiling, joking, sharing. Memories danced in her mind, back to times when she and Adam were best friends.

The hint of romance had been there for years, yet neither acted on it. Each would tell the other about romantic adventures with other boys and girls. Britney failed to see what Adam felt for her, she only knew how she felt when he mentioned another girl's name. At first, it did not bother her, but in time, she felt her insides burning with each name mentioned.

The idea she was in love with her life-long friend seemed crazy to Britney, *we tell each other everything!* Adam asked her to the prom, more out of convenience it seemed. Disloyal girls had shaken his confidence, and the young man was slow to open up again. Asking Britney appeared to be the safest option, or so she thought. That is until the night arrived.

There was no pressure to impress her date, Britney told herself when she got ready. *It's only Adam!* Arriving at the Fletcher home, the sight of Adam ignited a tingling deep inside her. Assuming it was the cheap wine she drank, Britney initially passed it off. However, there was something different. He changed, no longer the shy best friend, no longer the shoulder to cry on, something more. Unnoticed to Britney, he had matured into a man, he become what she wanted.

In the weeks following the prom, Britney admitted she had feelings for Adam. Speaking the truth in her mind was the limit to Britney's confession, deciding to keep her secret safe. She paid the price in the years since, becoming the first port of call for Adam whenever a new romance came around. Faking smiles and giving advice against her innermost wishes became the norm for Britney, yet she stayed silent.

Silent! Britney noticed the irony. Her silence hurt her for so many years, hiding her feelings from Adam, and her silence continued to ruin her life.

***

"Are you sure about this Adam?" Madison asked, watching him grab the keys from inside the front door.

"Yeah, I can't wait a year," he shouted, pushing himself out the door and onto the front porch. The glow from the streetlights travelled halfway up the Fletchers driveway, spraying the back of the SUV in an orange tint. Madison threw a glance back at the house as the two men crept down the ramp and towards the car.

"I have some bad news Adam," Madison whispered, "You will have to drive."

"What?"

"If I drive, it will only create paradoxes. I can provide you with information, but I'm afraid you'll have to physically do it yourself."

Sitting face to face with the SUV, Adam remembered the pain he went through only weeks earlier to see Britney. Adam's brain conjured up repeats of the agony that travelled along each nerve in his body, sending him to his limits. But, a part of his brain fed the doubting man with the feelings of ecstasy that flowed in his blood in Stoughton, it will be worth it.

"I'll need the crutches," Adam said.

Navigating the Quincy streets was the hard part, but when the Fletcher SUV reached the I-93, Adam relaxed. Operating the accelerator pedal with a crutch, Adam drove westwards from Boston City as the sun sunk beneath the horizon.

"What is it like, the future?" Adam asked, breaking the tedious repeat of passing cars.

"Unbearable," Madison started, "but when you get there, you'll see it in a different light."

A passing car threw its glare onto Adam's face, sparking an idea that seemed so obvious, yet it had not crossed his mind until now.

"Why didn't you go public? Save the world from some future catastrophe?"

Madison stared forward as the SUV travelled along the highway.

"Maybe I was greedy," he whispered, as if trying to hide his guilt.

"If you get there without her, I guarantee you will do the same to get her back. In the future, everyone seems to have everything, except us. It took me years to find a way back, it will be worth it. We were the unlucky one, yet soon, we will have everything we need."

It was clear to Adam now. He had been down, depressed since the accident. The older version of himself sat in the passenger seat, revealing a life which gets so much worse without Britney, showing Adam what hell looks like.

"You changed history for her?" Adam asked, dumbfounded by the epiphany dawning on him.

"We changed history for her! Every day you create your own piece of history, yet how many people get the chance to erase the bad parts, and then become the history maker?"

312

Chapter 52

The blinding sun burnt like acid on Adam's weary eyes, helping him wake up and realise the stinging in his legs. In the passenger seat, Madison slept, motionless. A sense of calm poured over the man's face, taking him into a comfortable sleep, no doubt relived from being released from the confinement of his secret. Stretching his neck and back, Adam tried to snap out of his trance. A small vibration grew in from his pocket, until he could hear his cell phone beep loudly. A few clicks later and Adam rested again, safe in the knowledge that his parents knew he was okay.

Opening his eyes, Madison smiled at their location.

"We visited here many times. While we did not save him, at least we got the chance to save her."

The clock tower rang loudly, sending an echo throughout the town.

"I guess all we can do is wait," Adam suggested, shifting in the seat again. Hours were spent reminiscing, informing and talking about the past and present. While telling Adam most memories would not return, Madison gave him a helping hand, filling the voids with what he had learned from Britney. They agreed to keep the future out of the conversation; Adam was free to make his own, with one exception. That exception trudged towards the cemetery gates as the town bell rang for six. Adam and Madison held their breath when Britney walked near the SUV and turned left into the cemetery.

"You will do anything for her, I can see that already," Madison whispered.

"We already did," Adam replied, reaching between the two front seats and forcing the folded wheelchair through. Reaching for the crutches, Adam used them to unfold the wheelchair as it lay on the sidewalk.

"I guess I'm on my own from here eh?" Adam asked, turning back to Madison.

***

A silent, solemn glance at each other sufficed, as Adam lowered himself into the wheelchair. He gently closed the door, and propelled himself towards the cemetery gates. Watching his younger version go through the gates, a sense of euphoria flushed throughout Madison's body. Adam was getting closer to the love of their lives. One last glance in the mirror at the worn, beaten edition of Adam Fletcher, one last time he would see tears. Madison wiped his eyes and reached forward onto the dashboard, writing with the fluid on his fingertips. On the dark panel, he wrote a shortened version of his name, one his few friends in the future called him when he revealed his plan, *Mada.* Alongside the faint version of his name, Madison painted who he really is, his name in reverse, *Adam.* Closing his eyes, he wore a smile, one that remained on his face until he ceased to exist.

Sitting on the grass, speaking to her father's grave was the only source of comfort for Britney for over a month now. Even when she spoke of her mistakes, she found peace in the fact she did not hide anything from her father. The brief respite was enough to keep her coming every day, a bubble in which the fragile woman could be herself without fear of retribution.

Britney was not delusional, she knew she was alone. Despite the ease of opening up at her father's graveside, this was not the way to be. With each passing minute of every day, Adam flashed in her mind. Customers in the bar sent reminders of Adam through their speech and actions. Wiping the image of Adam from her thoughts turned out to be impossible to Britney, so she embraced them instead. She would spend hours on Facebook, staring at pictures of Adam from years gone by, longing to be back in the moment when they were taken. Wishes and prayers were placed on the green grass in the cemetery, her yearnings floated from her mouth and into the air, each time relaying another hint of her pain. At night, Britney's dreams would play games on her, revisiting past memories and dressing them up as the present. Mornings only came bearing the truth, sending another crack through the woman.

Yet again, another mirage Britney assumed, her eyes showing the image of a wheel-chair bound Adam coming towards her.

"Why do you torture me?" she muttered under her breath at the demonic imagination dwelling inside. Britney shook her head, trying to remove the false image created in her mind, yet it remained. Trembling lips were afraid to venture into the trap, should they call out? Should they whisper? It looked so real, *it was never this vivid before.*

"Adam?" she called out, "Is that really you?"

Nodding, Adam pushed himself towards Britney, her doubting mind started to believe. She stood up and blinked her eyes with determination, eager to find out the truth before she falls again. Brushing her hair back around her ear, Britney stepped towards Adam.

"Britney!" he exclaimed, sending a tingle throughout her body.

It really is him!

Trying to quell the tears, Britney walked towards Adam. He never let his eyes leave her as she approached.

"How did you find me?" She asked, feeling a surge of excitement build inside.

"Airline tags on my suitcase, Buffalo New York," Adam smiled.

"I have been so lonely without you Adam," Britney blurted out, kneeling down in front of him and hugging him so tightly, "I am so sorry."

"I know I cannot live without you Britney," Adam whispered, as she leaned back to look at him.

"You really mean that? After all I've done?" Britney asked.

"I have seen a future without you Britney, and to me it's not worth living. I want to spend the rest of my life being your saviour, if you will let me?"

Tears found a way out, streaming down Britney's face and onto her lips, the warmest tears she could ever remember, cried without a darkening pain. Nodding her head, Britney stuttered, "Oh my God, yes, yes."

Wrapping her hands around Adam again, they hugged intensely, an intensity she wished would last forever. In an instant, all the negative memories which flooded their lives fell into the background, to be replaced with the hint of a life together.

Chapter 53

Five years and nine months later

Adam clicked *calendar* on his iPhone, yes, today was the day. Memories of Madison's warnings played in his mind for close to six years, it would all be in vain should Adam not heed them. He traced his finger around the gold ring on his left hand, a ring that had seen so much love and hate in its life. Two years previously on the altar, Adam considered telling her the truth, *Madison was me*. How would Britney have taken it he wondered? Would she leave Adam, fearing he suffered a breakdown? Lost his mind?

Adam decided that day. Seeing Britney walking down the aisle did it. His love grew with each day, making Adam understand how Madison felt when she was taken from him. Madison broke the laws of physics to save Britney, it was now Adam's job to make it worthwhile. So many options bounced in Adam's head since Madison vanished, tell Britney, leave here, tell the police. Only one seemed right.

Shaun McCoy had ruined so many lives. He would ruin theirs, should he be given the chance, Adam thought. If Madison's words were true, Shaun McCoy would leave prison and within four hours, kill Britney Fletcher. Adam remembered the wheelchair parked in the tool shed, the shiny steel failed to diminish over time, a sparkling reminder of a horrible struggle. The time for hell had gone, Adam chose to see his wife Britney later at dinner, kiss her on the front porch that evening, like his previous version was never able to do.

A sharp siren erupted once, gaining Adam's attention. Across the street, a large grey door opened and a prison officer appeared. Seconds later, a stocky man stepped out. Adam checked twice, three times, yes it was him. Shaun McCoy threw a backpack over his shoulder and started walking, smiling at the breeze and his first hint of freedom in years. Adam started the car when Shaun turned the corner. The hum of the engine silenced the banging of the handgun against the glove compartment plastic as Adam pulled the weapon closer. Flicking it open, Adam adjusted the single bullet in the gun.

The End

Coming in 2013

The Angel of Death

Emily's little feet splashed in the dirty puddles. Tears were the only source of warmth on her body. A dangling teddy bear, held on by a string of nylon, swung wildly from her hip as she ran, like an unwilling passenger eager to get off the ride. Pulling the soaked hair from in front of her face, Emily glanced back down the dark country road to see if her tormentors had given up.

Slowing, her breath caught up.

Emily searched in the darkness for another hint, another sign of the creatures, her tormentors. The gravelly road to her grandmothers had been torn apart by the recent floods, causing Emily to slip on the uneven surface. The easing rain barely registered inside, the wind was still there. Emily knew what wind meant.

"Stay away from me," she whispered into the howling breeze. In her mind, the wind ruffled the spirits, sending them into a rage. Then, no brick walls or layers of bed sheets could keep the creatures at bay. Solace only existed in one place, but that place was three miles away. There was no other option but run through the stormy night alone to reach her safe-house.

Emily's trembling fingers clutched at the teddy bear as she focused on the road ahead. The tree line appeared, marking the half-way stage of her journey, one she had undertaken many times before. She remembered begging her parents earlier that night,

"Please let me stay with Gran."

"No! You will stay here, with us," were the words that came her way as she faced the stairs.

"We will be so close, pet."

Yet, Emily did not call for her parents' help when the shadows manifested into creatures. Sitting upright in her bed, clutching the white sheets up to her face, the frail girl stared into the darkness, waiting. She had tried to ignore the darkness before, *it does not work.* When the wind arose outside and gusted off the country home, they came.

She knew their scent. Before her eyes were subjected to the horror, her nose was bombarded with the whiff of burn. When the scent forced its way into her lungs, the shadows grew legs, arms, a body. From the darkness, flailing limbs appeared, trying to pull the body into being. Creaking floorboards reverberated in Emily's ears. From thin air, it grew mass and pressed down. Legs of some sort tapped the floor, taking steps, stabilising itself. The shadowy creature snorted, taking in gulps of earthly oxygen. Every time was like the first time as Emily's body was electrocuted with horror.

Snapping back to the road, Emily shook her head, trying to rid her mind of such thoughts. Pine trees shuffled in the wind, waving back and forth like a plea for her to stop. Familiarity did not sprout peace in the young girl. It only added to the discomfort, it only asked questions inside, *Will I be like this forever, Will they ever leave me alone?*

Drips of water slid off her hair and onto her back, sending chills up Emily's spine, causing her to run again. The wind direction changed so much, swirling around her. Emily asked herself if the wind was part of the creature's plot? Pushing on through it, the raggedy roadway felt soft under her feet, taking more energy out of her with every step. Emily's breathing grew louder and louder, until it seemed that someone, or something, was breathing right behind her. Her nostrils, furiously sucking in oxygen, found discomfort in the air. *The burning!*

"Who is there? I command you to answer me!" she shouted, without even looking back.

Aching legs pushed harder than before, aided by an eruption of fear in the pit of her stomach. Cold fingers let the teddy bear dangle and then clenched tighter than ever before. Using the shock inside as fuel, Emily drove out the pain in her legs and ran. With each step, her hair bounced on her back, every tap feeling like creepy, slender fingers trying to grab her.

At first, the tree line that ran parallel to the road brought comfort to Emily. Letting her mind drift back to the bedroom, she remembered how the creature would use the furniture in her room to sneak up on her.

Dangling limbs cowered down as it slid along near the small chest of drawers, almost under the cover of darkness, almost. Watery eyes followed its advance along the perimeter, the random scratching of hard skin against the wall confirming its position. Until it reached the tall wardrobe that stood next to Emily's bed. The creature could open its lungs; no longer did it cower as it stretched to its full height next to the wardrobe, bending its head down from the ceiling. The burning smell was so close, it tingled in her nostrils. Her hand jerked, gliding along the bed, reaching for the side light. Little fingers held the switch, yet her mind could not face the light. Darkness may be torture, but a revealing glow may be worse she figured.

Emily only noticed now, after many times running this route, that the line of parallel trees bore an uncanny similarity to a line of wardrobes. *Tall, slender and dark!* She tried to keep her eyes fixed on the road, but, it was to no avail. On her left side, a black object, hunched over yet twice her size ran with her. Where Emily was struggling, the object seemed at ease, long limbs taking one step for the girl's six.

She willed her legs to go faster, they rebelled. A stinging sensation like knives grew in her muscles, sending them into cramps, dragging Emily down. She could not stop her body falling to the ground as her face landed on the grainy surface. Spitting out some gravel, Emily's eyes danced wildly, searching, scanning. There she lay for a few moments, until the throbbing pain in her legs eased enough for her to stand up.

"You, you only come when my Gran isn't here!" Emily said.

She wiped the dirt from her face, and intentionally slowed her breathing.

"Coward!" she shouted, into the swaying pine trees. The wind picked up, swirling the ends of her pyjamas and touching her already cold skin. Immediately, she regretted uttering those words. A surge of fear erupted inside again, sending Emily up the road faster than ever.

After what seemed like an eternity of running, Emily slammed the door of her Grandmother's home. Through the stained glass, the hallway light was on, like a faint calling. The young girl gripped the door handle and leaned downwards, begging and hoping. It opened. Time moved slower than ever as Emily closed the door. Above her, the hallway light sprayed down on her. It would not protect her for long she knew. Leaving her dirtied shoes at the bottom, Emily placed her feet on the carpeted step and climbed the stairs.

"Gran, I need you."

***

Kathleen Dunhurst lay in her bed, sliding her fingers along a rosary bead, whispering in the dimly lit room. Despite her son's plea for her to use the bedside lamps,

Kathleen much preferred to use two roman candles. Electricity, in her eyes, was unnatural.

As a child, she assumed she was cursed. Angelic or demonic creatures ventured into her room and into her mind. The early decades of the twentieth century were unkind to *disturbed* children. But, where most people saw a lost cause, Kathleen found strength in her dreams. She learned to keep her apparitions to herself, acting as if they all went away. They never went away. They became clearer, stronger, and more real.

Each new creature that appeared to her was a blessing to Kathleen. While not all of them were easy to look upon, she felt a certain privilege when souls from other worlds manifested themselves for her viewing, like the spirits were on show for her and no-one else. Years passed by and the visions kept coming, but Kathleen's life meandered on without significance. Could her gift just be a freak accident? Did it mean anything?

The wind gusted outside in time with Kathleen's heaving chest as she quenched the candles on each side. Darkness enveloped the room. Closing her eyes, she felt the last bead slip between her fingers as her whispering stopped. A sloshing sound from outside caught her ears, making Kathleen turn towards the window, yet its unfamiliarity made her heart beat faster. Many times she had heard the stomping of other worldly creatures as they crossed the divide between the celestial planes, but this was different. This was human. A faint voice echoed from downstairs. In an instant, Kathleen recognised the delicate cry, "Emily?"

<u>End of Preview</u>

For more, including short stories and novelettes check out:

www.eamonnhickson.com

www.facebook.com/authoreamonnhickson

Made in the USA
Charleston, SC
18 January 2013